# LITTLE WHITE LIES

**Carol Burns**

To all the newspaper men and women who strive
for the perfect scoop

# ABOUT THE AUTHOR

Carol Burns grew up in the Midlands and trained in regional newspapers before going freelance and undertaking a second degree and MA in Fine Art. She now lives in Cornwall with her husband and son. She is editor of *Cornwall Life* magazine.

# LITTLE

# WHITE

# LIES

# CHAPTER 1

I checked the recording equipment attached to the phone again and wondered - not for the first time - if I was having my chain pulled. Mr Smith had promised to call again at nine and I still had twenty minutes to wait. My eyes rested on the packet of cigarettes next to the phone on my desk and I considered nipping up to the canteen for a quick fag.

The office of the *Leicestershire Post* had become a no-smoking zone several months earlier, not long after I had started as a junior reporter. I looked up and saw plumes of smoke drifting above the head of an old hack with no home to go to, but decided against joining in. Having lied my way onto the paper with yarns of exclusive stories broken in unheard of parts of the country whilst on my journalism course, I was trying to avoid getting myself into any scrapes that would encourage anyone to look further at my CV. After just four months, the editor's file of my fuck-ups was only marginally thinner than my folder of cuttings.

But this story was going to make me. I just knew it. I just had to get a few details like who, what, where, when, why and who knows? Maybe they would make a film about it – Woodward and Bernstein, eat your heart out.

Twenty minutes and two cigarettes later, it became obvious that Mr exclusive-front-page-come-syndicated-story-of-world-importance wasn't going to happen tonight. Unplugging the recording equipment attached to my phone, I carefully replaced it in the bottom draw of the Politics Editor's desk.

I was just switching off my computer when my phone rang.

"Caitlin?" Not Mr Smith but Helen, my neighbour who worked in the police call- handlers' centre. Before I moved to Leicester, I had heard that people in cities never got to know their neighbours. But then most of them didn't set fire to the communal hall carpet with hot rocks and set off the smoke alarm, as Helen had.

Drug abuse notwithstanding, Helen was a good neighbour who could always be persuaded to part with the details of any interesting 999 calls that came in, in return for free tickets for gigs at local venues. At the *Post*, the country's biggest daily newspaper from outside London, most staff seemed to be over 40 so there were always more than enough freebies to go around as long as you weren't into the Rolling Stones, the Bee Gees or Neil Young.

"Can't talk. I'm at work. We've had three calls in about a man armed with a shotgun over at St Joseph's. Escaped during a drugs raid," she whispered into the phone.

"Thanks Hel. Usual arrangements." Two free tickets, unmarked envelope, shoved under her flat door. No questions asked.

She put the phone down.

I glanced over to see if the Crime Correspondent was at her desk, but she had long since gone home – or, more likely in her case, to the pub. Rachel Drake was in her 40s and hadn't spoken to me since I had started working at the paper as a trainee. I only knew two things about her: she had a police contacts' book thicker than a Chinese phone directory, and she was known to store an emergency bottle of gin in the cistern of the disabled toilet cubicle on the second floor. Everyone knew about the gin, but she was never challenged on it for the simple reason she was very good at her job.

One of first things I had learned at the *Post* was that newspaper journalism was the last hiding place for the functioning alcoholic. If she ever dried out she would probably end up working in public relations, as so many had before her.

A surge of adrenaline coursed through my veins as I realised I would have to go out and cover the story. It was moments like this that made the garden fêtes, school fundraisers and Golden Wedding Anniversary stories worthwhile.

Nodding to the remaining reporter, *A to Z* in hand, I made for the lift.

The grand old red brick Victorian building which had housed the *Post* for most of its 105-year history was in the centre of Leicester, close to all the public amenities that generated the news. Across the road up the High Street was the city's Town Hall, where politicians argued out the finer points of everything from traffic calming to closing local schools and pigeon culls. Next door to that, the old Crown Court came complete with a courtyard for the gallows, offering past *Post* reporters a good seat for a hanging. Around the corner, the old central police station had long since been downsized and a new bigger and better headquarters erected on the edge of the suburbs, far away from crime and criminals. King Street Police Station now housed a CID division and a couple of cells which were occasionally used for fundraising events where volunteers from local rotary clubs and round tables were locked up and only released once their friends had coughed up a ransom paid out to their favourite charity.

Leicester's fire station had also moved to a new base, on an industrial estate on the ring road. At the old station next door, *Post* reporters of old had been saved a seat on the fire engines every time they went out – the newsroom still had an old bell which had rung out at the same time as the one at the fire station.

The old station had been converted into the very latest in city centre living space - eighteen flats the size of rabbit hutches complete with a wine bar and a gym where the old water tower used to be.

The *Post*'s office was now close to other kinds of amenities just as important to most of the editorial staff – pubs, and plenty of them. I had arrived in Leicester in the middle of a bar boom that was showing no signs of slowing down, with a new place opening every weekend. The city centre high street was now practically one long bar, broken up by a couple of banks with cash points to ensure you could always pay your tab. There was even one bar called Hacks. Unfortunately it was far too upmarket for most of the scruffy reporters at the *Post*. The owner would have done better keeping it dingy and serving cheap pints and curling salmonella-loaded sandwiches.

St Joseph's council estate was a ten-minute drive from the *Post*'s office and, like many city centre housing estates, it featured a range of high-rise concrete blocks in varying states of decay, with a smattering of town houses growing around its feet. In recent years the city council had made attempts to brighten the place up – adding some public art murals on the walls, which had been enhanced by local youngsters armed with neon spray paint and equally colourful language. What it really needed was a full facelift using large quantities of dynamite and a handful of JCBs.

Within a few minutes of driving around, I spotted an armed police response unit waiting for instruction. The attention seemed to be focused on a small two-storey grey pebble-dashed house squeezed into the middle of a row. Although only built in the 80s, half the houses were derelict and boarded up, metal grates at the windows framed by the scorch marks of the fires which regularly swept through these homes like the world's slowest Mexican wave.

Swallowing my apprehension, I walked up to the van and tapped on the window. A torch light shone in my face, blinding me as I scrabbled in my bag for my press card. The window edged down enough for someone to grab it before winding back up. I stood waiting for a response, wondering if I would get one. The door eventually opened and someone told me to get in.

I found a space to crouch and waited for my eyes to acclimatise to the dark - God forbid I trip over someone's gun by accident. Slowly, I looked around. There were five men. All wore black — from their baseball caps and heavy canvas combat trousers, to their bulletproof vests and ear pieces. The only colour was the word *'POLICE'* written in white on their hats and vests. Out of the corner of my eye I saw the glint of metal from guns housed in leather holsters on their right hips where their truncheons should have been. The guns were smaller than the hand cannons I was used to seeing on American cop shows, but that didn't matter. If these guys came bursting into my house I would die on the spot.

The driver in the front seat turned around to me and smiled. "What can we do for you... Caitlin?" he asked, looking at my press card for the name.

"What's going on? We had a couple of calls at the office saying there were armed police all over the estate," I exaggerated in true reporter's style, reaching for my pen and notepad.

"Okay. Off the record, first."

I put down my pen — wouldn't be able to write in the dark anyway.

"Drug bust at lunchtime today — hauled in a lot of drugs — about £500,000-worth, cocaine mostly. This was the main man and he got away. His missus says he has a shotgun. We're here for that."

The guy turned back to the front as a crackle came over the radio. It sounded like a foreign language to me, but he seemed to understand. He turned to me with a "Stay here," and gestured the age-old 'let's go' to the rest, who slid soundlessly out of the van.

I crouched down and peered out of the window into the darkness, holding my breath. If anything happened I was going to pee myself, never mind worrying about getting it down on paper. The armed officers silently disappeared into the dark night and I was left half expecting an armed drug dealer to get into the van and kidnap me. Maybe my mother had been right. I should have been a primary school teacher. Nothing bad ever happened to them; well, apart from the kids' weak bladders, snotty noses and gooey mouths. I gave a shudder, suddenly reassured by my career choice. At least in this job I only had to worry about my own bladder control.

I crouched long enough to get a cramp in my right calf before deciding to get out and have a look at what was going on. What harm could it do?

Very few of the streetlights were working. The area was not so much red-light as lights-off – the darkness presumably provided a perfect cover to the local prostitutes and drug dealers doing their thing. In Leicester, it didn't take long to figure out that St Joseph's was the place to go to get laid or get high.

I quietly slid the van door open and peered out. I couldn't see anything. I began to step out as a shot rang through the air. I jumped at the sound. I lost my footing and slid to the ground, exfoliating the right side of my face on the tarmac as I went down. Lying there, I heard shouts and a muffled cry of pain.

I felt blood trickle from my cheekbone and gave it a wipe with my sleeve, feeling shards of glass rip further into my skin. At least now I knew what had happened to all the streetlights.

I stood up and made my way back into the van, picking at my face on the way. A police car sped past me and pulled up outside the house. In the beam of its headlights I saw a man being bundled into the back and the armed response team come out of the house, the driver casually carrying a shotgun under his arm.

The van door opened and he poked his head in. "You can come out now. He's been arrested. Tried to shoot his way out with only one cartridge," he snorted contemptuously and threw the shotgun into a large polythene bag before helping me out of the van.

"He'll probably be charged with dealing and possession of an illegal weapon in the morning, but you'll have to check with the press office." He stopped as he noticed my face, "Need any help? There's an ambulance on standby somewhere – the paramedic could give you a few stitches?" Thankfully he didn't ask what had happened.

I shook my head and felt the blood trickle to my chin. I dabbed at it with the end of my scarf and watched as the rest of the men piled into the back of the van before it screeched off down the street and into the darkness.

The story took twenty minutes to write up when I got back to the office. Adding a note to the News Editor that the gunman would probably be charged in the morning, I went home to dress my wounds.

My flat was cold and dark, but nonetheless welcoming as it had been a good twelve hours since I'd last seen it. I noticed the answer machine was flashing as I entered my small hallway, but bypassed it in favour of a hot bath and the two strawberry Pop Tarts I knew were lurking in the back of my kitchen cupboard.

An hour later, my short blonde hair was newly washed and wrapped in a towel, my contact lenses safely nestling in their individual compartments on the bathroom shelf, and the Pop Tarts well on their way to my stomach.

Despite having only been in the city for four months, my little flat had become my sanctuary. Having grown up in a picturesque but dull Nottinghamshire village, I had become a city girl with all the fervour of a Catholic convert. My flat took up half the ground floor of a slightly shabby three-storey red brick Victorian townhouse which must have once housed a well-off family made rich on Leicester's industrial past of coal mining, textiles and slave trading. A couple of hosiery factories producing cheap sports socks were now all that remained of the buildings of industry which were instead being revived as living space. The house had long since been sold off and split into flats like mine.

From the outside, the building had that unloved look of all rented properties. Peeling red paint on the front door gave way to a scruffy communal hall lit by a single bare bulb hanging from the ceiling. An ornate tiled floor was covered in dust and scattered with junk mail, which no one bothered to collect. An even more ornate staircase led off upstairs to Helen's flat above mine, and two others which were rented by students. The basement, which would have once housed the servants, was now home to a couple I had never met, but who proved their existence by noisy amorous encounters which floated up through my floor from time to time. Across the hall lived Ian, a twenty-something singleton, rumoured to be a tax inspector.

The rent was fixed just below extortionate because of its proximity to both a medium security mental hospital – where there had only been a couple of escapes in recent years - and a triple carriageway which became a motorway half a mile down the road, leading straight to London. The city was just an hour away - according to the landlord, who had bought the place in the hope of fleecing rich yuppies interested in commuting. Instead he got me, Helen, a couple of students, a pair of enigmatic shaggers and a civil servant.

My small hallway had doors opening into the kitchen, bathroom, bedroom and the lounge, which housed a huge bay window where I whiled away the hours on days off, watching people argue over precious car parking spaces. The street was one of the closest to the city centre yet to have a residents' parking permit scheme, which made it popular with cheapskate commuters who used it as a free car park.

Across from us was a row of grand Georgian townhouses that had been converted into solicitors' and accountants' offices. Their view of our dilapidated side of the street was partially obscured by a row of poplar trees, which gave the street its name.

The inside of my flat was currently painted a nasty nicotine-tinted magnolia popular with landlords the world over but I had big plans, as the hall wall testified. It looked like an overgrown Dulux colour chart, with more than a dozen splats taken from my ever-growing collection of paint testers. In contrast, the carpet was a cheap grey cord which no amount of skilfully placed rugs or, in my case, dust could hide.

I suddenly remembered my flashing answer phone.

"Caitlin, this is your mother here." I grimaced, I hadn't yet returned the message she'd left the day before – and, peering through to my kitchen wall clock which read 11.10pm, I realised it was too late to return this one. "I haven't spoken to you for almost a week. What's going on? Are eating properly?"

I thought of the Pop Tarts.

Four minutes later – my mother rarely required a response so my answering machine was the perfect form of communication - I had learned my sister Lauren was threatening to leave her husband (again) and Alan Simpkin (who?) had died of a heart attack at the weekend. My mother's news was always bad. Whenever we spoke she seemed to have some new tragedy to tell me about. Someone was always dying, getting diagnosed with cancer, or getting divorced. Maybe that's why I was so reluctant to talk to her.

I wiped the tape clean and curled up in bed with a pad and pen for a brainstorm on my big story.

It had all started a week before with a mysterious phone call when I was on a late shift. The man asked for me by name, which wasn't unusual, but he said he would give me the scoop of my career, which was. He said his name was Mr Smith and that he worked for a local company, but had to be careful what he said as more than his job was at stake. He hinted at a conspiracy at the highest level and said it had already cost two lives and could cost more. Mr Smith promised to ring back with more information and had since rung twice, but had given me nothing else but hints, although he had admitted that he worked for Fifen Pharmaceuticals, a local drug company with laboratories on the edge of the city.

A week later I had no story and a sneaking suspicion someone was winding me up. I threw my pen and pad down onto the floor in disgust and switched off my bedside lamp. That was it, the next time he rang I was going to make him agree to meet me face-to-face or tell him to get lost and stop wasting my time.

# CHAPTER 2

"McCall, wake Edward up will you?" The shout carried over my computer, from Nina Koslowski, the ebony-haired girl sitting at the desk opposite mine, breaking my concentration in deciphering my shorthand of the previous day.

"Huh?"

She pointed an expertly manicured long red nail at the silver-haired man slumbering peacefully at the desk on my left.

"Edward," I stage-whispered at him.

"Not like that," she said with a shake of her head. "He'd sleep through an air raid."

"He did," added Tony McFadden, the News Editor, as he walked past. "It was a napalm raid. Sent him out with the US troops in Vietnam back in the 70s and he nearly missed all the action."

Nina laughed and I looked up at her questioningly. "Who is he?" I asked. The desk had been vacant since I started.

"I'm sure he will introduce himself when he wakes," she said mysteriously, going back to her computer screen.

Nina had quickly become my closest friend at the *Post*, not least because she was one of the only other reporters under the age of 30. She was petite, skinny, sallow-skinned, and had the kind of cheekbones that could cut glass. Her long, straight black hair gleamed like high gloss paint and she was never without a slick of bright red lipstick and a full-length black leather coat, which she maintained was a Dolce and Gabbana.

I pretended to go back to my shorthand for a minute, but Edward had begun to stir. Intrigued, I turned around, wondering if he was all right, but noticed that the rest of the newsroom ignored him. I gave him a gentle shake.

He sat upright and I noticed he wore a dapper suit, complete with waistcoat and yellow-spotted bow tie.

"Very kind. Two sugars, not too much milk," he said to me, reaching for a handkerchief from his top pocket. "Not machine stuff though, it disagrees with my stomach." He delicately dabbed his mouth and ran his hands over his thick hair.

Unquestioningly, I found myself walking towards the newsroom kitchen and automatically going for the one cup and saucer set which I had never seen anyone else use.

"Darling girl, how kind," he said as I returned and placed the cup on his desk. "Now any help you need, any help at all, you just let me know. I remember the editor when he was just a copy boy, and a lazy one at that," he held out his hand. "Edward Blake."

I nodded respectfully, shook his hand and muttered, "Caitlin McCall."

"Caitlin McCall – very good alliteration. Nice byline. Is it real?"

I nodded and he turned his attention to his computer, hitting the keys with the force of someone used to the resistance of an old mechanical typewriter. I pushed aside my shorthand and went back to the story from the night before. As suspected, the drug dealer had been charged, so most of what I had written would have to be scrapped – or I would face contempt of court. Tony had promised to get three paragraphs into the back of the first edition of the paper so I could rest easy, knowing my facial scarring hadn't been for nothing.

Ten minutes later I had finally worked out that Bankborough's chief fire officer was not resigning to feed arse but resigned to fighting arson, but my stomach told me it was time for breakfast and my shorthand could wait.

Few things were taken more seriously at the *Post* than the morning constitutional in the canteen after the first deadline. The canteen opened at seven to serve bacon and eggs, sausage sandwiches and doorsteps of toast that tasted like a damp flannel. Cereal was also available, although I had yet to see anyone order it.

Looking around the newsroom, I noticed that everyone had already disappeared upstairs and I was the only one left holding the fort. I had two choices: stay behind and break rank or sneak out from under the watchful eyes of Tony – a short Glaswegian humorously nicknamed 'Big Mac' behind his back by some of the more senior reporters. In answer to my dilemma, the newsdesk phone rang and distracted him. I grabbed my cigarettes and purse from my desk and headed for the canteen.

Conversation was in full swing as twenty journalists crammed around a canteen table designed for ten, smoking and eating. Matt, who sat opposite me in the newsroom, devoured the day's nationals, providing full running commentary. The temptation to sit on a more easily accommodating table was crushed by a shout from him for everyone to shift over.

"It won't take the strain!" Lee, a balding loud-mouthed sports journalist who had tried to stick his tongue down my throat on the last work's night out, yelled from the other end of the table. At five foot three inches and weighing in at a little over eight stone, I knew he was having me on so I squeezed in, scowling in the direction of his Titanic-sized frame.

A coffee and a bacon butty later and I was sitting alone among the debris of the others, finishing off my second cigarette of the day and flicking through the papers. My eye was caught by a small story on the front page of the *Gazette*, our daily rival. The *Gazette* had earned itself the nickname 'the Gazelle' because of the speed with which it copied *Post* stories – legend had it that they had even delayed their print times so their editor could look through the *Post* to make sure they hadn't been scooped.

But this time the *Post* had missed out:

*'Rumours of a hostile take-over at Fifen Pharmaceuticals have been denied by senior staff.*

*The rumours began after trouble in the boardroom following the death of chairman Sir Andrew Fifen in November.*

*The company has recently turned its back on its profitable vaccine lines in favour of specialising in cancer drugs.*

*Chief executive Sebastian van der Hoven dismissed rumours that this had made the company vulnerable to a take-over bid from one of the multi-national companies, adding "cancer drugs are the future of the pharmaceutical trade."*

*With a turnover of under £200 million a year, Fifen is by far the smallest contender in the global drug market.'*

I surreptitiously ripped it out – since Mr Smith had told me the name of his employer, I had been collecting information on the company in the hope it might prove useful. Last night's promise to forget about the story was conveniently forgotten.

Returning to my desk, I dropped the cutting into a drawer and turned to find Tony standing over me. He always piled on the crap to junior reporters, believing that it was all part of the rich tapestry of training. Fortunately we had a coffee machine, or he would have had me making that as well.

"Caitlin, we need you in coroner's court. There's an inquest into a pregnant woman found dead in her house out in Bankborough last month. We've written something on it before, have a look in the archive. Her name's Mary Stanshaw. It starts in twenty minutes at the Town Hall. I want a few hundred words for the last edition so ring in with some copy before twelve, okay?" He finally took a breath.

"Yeah," I turned back to my desk and unearthed my pad from a pile of press releases to write down the details.

Tony stood over me for a minute, as if to check I had written it all down right. He obviously hated giving a remotely good story to a trainee. If he knew about my Mr Smith calls, the scoop would be handed over to a safe pair of hands before I could blink.

"Take a mobile with you, and don't forget to ring copy desk with what you've got by noon," he said before finally walking off.

Edward, who had spent the last hour on the phone announcing to his contacts that he had returned - although no amount of eavesdropping on my part would reveal from where, leant over to me. "An inquest already! I wasn't allowed near the precincts of a court for five years when I started out."

Despite questioning my colleagues at breakfast, nobody seemed to know where Edward had been in the four months since I had started working at the *Post* – except that he had remained on the payroll. I smiled and nodded at him, before turning to my computer, clicking into our archive system and finding a report written about six weeks earlier. Mary Stanshaw had been 29 and was found dead in her house by her five-year-old son, Darren. He had wandered downstairs in search of breakfast to find her lying on the kitchen floor. Cause of death was unknown. According to police, there was no sign of a struggle or a break-in.

I got to the coroner's court in time to hear the coroner record the case of a depressed, newly divorced middle-aged man found hanging from a rope in his garage as a suicide. I quietly took off my coat and pulled out my pad and a couple of pens.

The press bench was discreetly placed on the right of the room, next to the coroner's clerk, who was quietly removing the distraught relatives of the hanged man. I shunned the bench in favour of a seat near the door, which would allow me to sneak out and phone through my story halfway through the inquest without having to walk past the relatives.

I doodled on my pad as the room began to fill with those involved in the Stanshaw case, careful not to catch anyone's eye or draw attention to myself in case the relatives took exception to my presence. Inquests were held in public so they had no choice, but it was better not to get into a debate over it with grieving families.

When I looked up, I noticed an immaculately suited man of about 30 with close-cropped jet-black hair, tapping a pen impatiently on a table, normally reserved for solicitors, in the centre of the room. His suit was single-breasted and dark grey, but he had on the most amazingly bright turquoise tie - the exact shade I'd been looking for to decorate my bathroom.

Silently congratulating him on his taste, I wondered whether he was related to the dead woman, or if he was a witness. He didn't strike me as a solicitor.

My attention was snapped back to the case when the clerk instructed us all to stand as the coroner walked back in. Richard Lewis-Desborough OBE was a small man, aged around 60, who spoke clearly, making my job easier. Even with my brief experience, I knew that a coroner's court was not the place to stand and ask people to speak up, even if it was in the interests of getting the facts of the story straight.

He addressed himself to a large woman in her 50s who was sitting at the central desk - presumably Mary's mother. She reeked of respectability and had obviously gone to a lot of effort to dress for the proceedings, in a navy skirt suit and plain white blouse which both looked newly bought. Her salt-and-pepper hair was set in the regimented curls I recognised from my grandmother when she came back from the hairdresser's. With a pang of pity I noticed her red-rimmed eyes magnified by bifocal glasses as she turned sideways towards the coroner.

"We are here today to try and establish how Mary Stanshaw of 36 Bartholomew Close, Bankborough, met her death. I will call witnesses and ask them questions, and give you the opportunity to ask anything you want to know. The business of this court is not to establish blame but to uncover how she died," the coroner addressed Mary's mother directly.

She nodded gratefully. She sat alone and was the only person in the room to identify herself as a relative.

"The first person I will call is Ms Stanshaw's neighbour, Shirley Evans."

A woman in her 30s identified herself as Shirley Evans and under the gentle coaching of the coroner explained how she came to find Mary. While she was making tea in her kitchen she had heard the screams of Darren and had run out of her back door and across to Mary's house, worried that there was something wrong with the baby. Looking through the kitchen window, she said she had seen Mary on the floor and Darren sitting on her, pulling her hair and shouting for his mummy. She got her husband to break through the back door and call an ambulance while she tried to calm Darren.

I scribbled it all down, my ears pricked and my pen poised ready for a good emotive quote that I could get into print for the final edition.

Mrs Evans didn't let me down: "Darren was screaming for her to wake up and all I could think of was to get the poor little thing away from his mummy because I could see there was something seriously wrong with Mary," her voice wavered as she choked back tears. "He's such a lovely little boy and she was a wonderful mother and so looking forward to having another one, it doesn't seem fair."

After Mrs Evans came a uniformed policeman who described how he was first on the scene and tried to resuscitate Mary until the paramedics arrived. Because I would have to dictate the story over the phone, I began to compose it at the back of my pad, keeping out half an ear for anything worth writing down. I was waiting for the post mortem report, which should reveal a cause of death. I was hoping I could include it my story. Checking my watch, I still had half an hour before I would have to slip out and phone in my copy for that night's edition. Plenty of time.

While the mother was being tearfully taken through her daughter's last few days, my attention wandered back over to the good looking bloke in the grey suit. He was tall, his skin was tanned, and his jet-black hair matched strong eyebrows, just this side of Liam Gallagher, with sideburns which stretched down towards his jaw. He didn't seem to be taking any notes and hadn't identified himself as a witness or family member. I supposed he could be a rubberneck interested in hearing the stories of people's untimely demise at first-hand; after all, it was commonplace in courts, where public galleries regularly packed them in. I hoped not. He looked like someone with better things to do than hang around an inquest, but then so did I.

Drawn by my staring, he suddenly turned his eyes towards me, raising a questioning jet-black brow. I only had time to note his eyes were dark and framed by thick lashes before I looked quickly away. Several times throughout the inquest I felt his eyes on me, but managed to refrain from looking round and raising a blonde brow back at him, despite being sorely tempted.

I stayed long enough to hear that the post mortem showed no obvious cause of death – and that tragically the eight-month-old foetus had been a healthy baby girl - before rushing out of the court to ring the copy desk, praying I wouldn't miss anything too vital while I was out.

Ten minutes later I had phoned through what I hoped was enough for an inside lead in the late edition of the paper. With a feeling bordering on disappointment, I saw the dark-haired man had disappeared when I returned, so I turned my attention to the witness who was discussing Mary Stanshaw's work. I bolted upright when I heard the name of the company she worked for. Fifen Pharmaceuticals. It was obviously a coincidence, but the link was all I needed to let my mind wander back into Woodward and Bernstein territory.

# CHAPTER 3

My answerphone was flashing again when I came home, juggling three bags of shopping and two copies of the evening's paper with my story, complete with byline taking up most of page five under the headline *'Mother's Death Remains Mystery'*.

Tony had said it would have made page two if I had managed to get a picture of the dead woman and her son, but when I had approached Mary's mother after the inquest she had refused. Instead she offered a few choice words on what she thought of reporters - not least that I was single-handedly responsible for killing Princess Diana. I tried not to take it personally. She had more serious things to worry about than me. The inquest had returned an open verdict as they had failed to find a cause of death.

In the kitchen I deposited my bags on the draining board and a half-eaten baguette fell out onto the floor as I turned to switch on the kettle.

Two days off work meant I could finally start decorating. Pouring myself a cup of coffee and burrowing down into one of the bags to find milk, I pulled up a chair at my miniature kitchen table and looked again at the colour chart pinned to my wall. Right. Terracotta in the lounge, white in the bedroom, turquoise in the bathroom and white in the kitchen.

My mind made up, I unpacked my shopping, pulling out a leafy green palm plant that had been on special offer at the supermarket. Adding some water, I put the plant on a side plate – one of the many items of gaudy bone china my mother had given me – and wandered into the lounge to find it a new home. I changed into old clothes and thought longingly of the six bottles of Budweiser speed-chilling in the freezer compartment of the fridge but I told myself I couldn't go on living in magnolia hell any longer and compromised by starting on the smallest room in the house, to ease me in gently.

My bathroom served as a hospital for ill plants. Many of them had been with me through three hard years of university, when they were lucky to get a watering that was less than 40 per cent proof, having lived in one of the liveliest student houses in Birmingham. I stuffed *Dean Martin's Greatest Hits* into my stereo and began the long task of clearing plants from around the bath, marvelling at the new foliage on a cutting from a cheese plant that for some strange reason had been tucked, forgotten, behind the toilet.

The turquoise I had chosen for the bathroom walls was supposed to resemble the azure sea of the Mediterranean but after staring at it for two hours, it looked as exotic as the English Channel on a wet Monday morning. I had bought a darker blue to do the floorboards, but after finishing three walls, Dino had stopped singing and I decided a fag break was in order – not to mention making use of the facilities before the bathroom became out of use.

The banging was so muffled from inside the bathroom, where I was desperately trying to finish painting the floor, that at first I assumed it was some drum & bass coming through the ceiling from Helen's flat upstairs. Her musical tastes and the Sunday morning banging of Ian's DIY across the hall sounded remarkably similar to my untrained ear, which preferred easy listening classics and maybe the occasional grunge band. It was only after the dulcet tones of Dusty Springfield had faded that I realised the sound was coming from my front door. Wiping paint down my t-shirt, I ran out to the hall.

Jen Masters, my best friend of fifteen years, stood in the hall holding a bottle of lemon vodka in one hand and a wriggling ginger kitten in the other.

"When one of my friends tells me they are staying in on a Friday night to do some DIY, I know it's time to intrude on their privacy," was all she offered by way of explanation before pushing past me in to the hall.

I stared after her, "I hope that isn't for me."

"The vodka?"

"The cat."

"It's not a cat. It's a kitten and it's a he. I knew you were looking for a new man in your life and here he is – Caitlin, meet Henry." She held the kitten up at me.

"Very funny," I muttered, following her into the kitchen where she set the kitten down and started opening cupboards in search of a bowl to set out some milk. "I'm serious, I don't want a cat."

"Don't be silly, all single women living alone want a cat. It's the rules."

Cheeky bitch. Jen had been going out with her boyfriend Steve for five years and lived with him in a two-up two-down terraced house in Nottingham which was stuffed full of Ikea and Habitat furniture and soft furnishings in matching neutral shades. My love life, like my flat, was more barren.

Sometimes I wondered how we were friends - our lives were as different as our looks. Where I was small with curves, she was tall and catwalk model-thin. I often envied her flat stomach, but never her flat chest. My hair was short, straight and blonde and I had yellow-toned skin that tanned easily, while Jen had long red tresses and the classic alabaster complexion of a redhead. We both had green eyes, but where hers were round and the shade of rich velvet, mine were slightly slanted and the colour of wet grass.

Jen had met Steve while we were sitting our A-levels, which she had gone on to fail spectacularly. Instead of re-taking, she had philosophically shrugged her shoulders, got a job and moved in with him. At any moment I expected her to announce their wedding, her pregnancy, or both.

The past five years of my life involved a frighteningly long list of unsuitable men, not to mention my mother's attempts to pass me around the unmarried offspring of her Women's Institute buddies.

Jen poured out two enormous vodkas and poked her head into the fridge, looking for ice and tonic water. The kitten lapped up some milk, stared at us, stretched, licked his balls and began prowling around the kitchen.

"Anyway, don't be so ungrateful. He's a moving-in present." Jen added lumps of ice and a splash of tonic water to the two drinks, and took a slurp before sighing dramatically.

"Don't you ever watch those RSPCA adverts – a pet is for life, not just for Christmas?"

"It's not Christmas for another nine months," Jen said, picking up her drink and wandering out of the kitchen. I picked up my drink and followed her, with Henry hot on my heels.

I had to admit the kitten was cute. But my past experience with pets began and ended with a goldfish named Martin who had lived to the grand old age of about three hours when I was eleven. I had come home from school to find he had been unceremoniously flushed down the toilet by my mother, prompting a brief but intense Teenage Mutant Ninja Turtles-inspired phobia of using the toilet in case he came back up, hideously mutilated, to get his revenge.

"I can't take him back, Steve is allergic to cat fur, so you two are just going to have to get used to each other." Jen peered into my bathroom on her way to the lounge. "Interesting floor pattern."

I scowled and looked over her shoulder. Henry had decided to investigate the bathroom and had travelled via the roller tray containing turquoise paint, which he had trodden all over my newly-painted blue floor.

"Shit! Come here you bastard cat – it took me hours to do that!" I yelled, pushing my drink into Jen's hand and rushing up to the bathroom doorway, helplessly willing Henry not to do any more damage.

"Typical male," was all Jen said as she took the drinks into the lounge.

"Fuck. Come here you bastard!" I yelled at him as he cowered behind the sink, a slight wrinkle appearing on his ginger-and-white striped forehead.

"No wonder you're single if that's how you talk to men," Jen said, coming back into the hall. Pushing me out of the way, she crouched down in the doorway and made kissy-kissy sounds to coax the kitten from his hiding place. He frowned up at me, standing as I was behind Jen and waving a bottle of paint thinner around like a mad woman, and decided he had experienced all the bathroom had to offer. He made a run for it and Jen deftly grabbed him in one of my towels and began to fuss him, giving his feet a quick wipe at the same time.

"Piece of piss."

I made a disgruntled snort and followed her into the lounge.

Half an hour later, the cat was busily cleaning himself and I was chilled out enough to tell Jen about my mysterious Mr Smith, thanks to another of her liberal vodka and tonics.

"So, basically, what you are telling me is that some bloke keeps ringing you up, spinning you a yarn about industrial espionage, but won't tell you who or what because he thinks his life is in danger. Is that right?" Jen didn't bother to conceal her disbelief.

"That's about right. I think it's about Fifen, the pharmaceutical company, but he keeps saying he'll ring then doesn't."

"You do know about the new girl tricks, don't you?"

"This is a bit more complicated than being sent for a long wait,"

I told her, scratching Henry behind the ears as he lay in my lap, purring.

"But have you considered that it might be someone at work, having you on?"

Only every minute of the day.

"Yeah, but I don't think they would waste this much time."

Jen refilled our glasses. "Your very own Deep Throat! If it's all true, it all sounds pretty exciting."

Having worked in the same bookshop since leaving school, Jen thought everything about my job was exciting. She suddenly stood up. "Shit, I forgot to get the kitten's stuff. I take it he can stay after all?"

She grinned at me, already knowing the answer. I stuck my tongue out at her departing back.

She came back minutes later with a plethora of cat-related paraphernalia, including a litter tray, bag of litter, kitten food and a flea collar with Henry's name and my address engraved on a silver disk.

I fingered the collar. "Sure of yourself, weren't you?" I muttered, knowing I should be more grateful, but I was still pissed off about her earlier remarks on my non-existent love life.

"Are you going to feed me, or shall we order a pizza?" Jen took the kitten stuff through to the kitchen and ripped open the litter bag. "Knowing you it'll be pizza," she shouted, referring to my habit of keeping the fridge empty. It was my only method of dieting and it worked, as long as there was no takeaway nearby.

"Actually, I've just been shopping." Enough strawberry Pop Tarts to sink the *Titanic*. "But let's get a curry."

I pressed the memory key on the phone to get through to my favourite takeaway. Thanks to its large Asian population, Leicester's range of Asian cuisine was endless. The city housed more than a hundred restaurants and I was slowly working my way through them all. Some were vegetarian and little more than canteens - with prices to match — others, like Balti houses, were unlicensed in respect for the religion of the owners and staff, but allowed their patrons to bring their own booze. My favourite place at the moment was the Durbar, which was really a restaurant but did takeaway food on the side. Despite it being only a two-minute walk away, I had only eaten in once. The décor was a combination of lush deep red velvet walls, vivid pink tablecloths and the kind of strip lighting that burnt your retinas. They stayed in business because the food was so good.

Halfway through the call I noticed the answerphone light was still flashing and as soon as I had ordered our food I pressed the Play button.

"Miss McCall, I apologise for missing our date on Thursday, but I'm afraid it was unavoidable." The hushed tones of Mr Smith came from the speaker.

"Jen, it's him," I yelled. I rewound the tape and waited for Jen to come through before pressing Play again. Following his apologies, Mr Smith gave me directions to a dilapidated building in the west of the city and asked me to meet him at 7pm the following night. I rewound and listened again, scribbling down his directions.

"Well?" Jen asked.

"I'll have to go, he might be on the level."

"You can't go there alone. I'll come with you."

As much as I wanted to say yes, I shook my head.

I couldn't help but be grateful that she had offered.

I forced a smile, "Nah, I'll be fine. I'll take Henry with me – anyway, you were probably right – I'll get there and it will be a wind-up by some idiot at work."

She scowled at me, unconvinced by my display of bravery, and sighed. "Well if it is someone from work they must know you pretty well to know you wouldn't have anything better to do on a Saturday night than go traipsing around a derelict building."

Fortunately I was saved by the biriyani and before Jen could argue with me any more, we were sitting in front of a feast fit for a Raj, which had arrived piping hot at my door.

"There is one thing that's worrying me, though," Jen said through a mouthful of garlic naan bread and chicken jalfrezi. "How did he get your home phone number?"

I checked out the contents of all the tin foil trays spread out before us on the floor and settled for an onion bhaji, "Phone book I suppose."

"Are you in it? You've only lived here four months."

I looked at her sharply. "Shit, that's a good point, I don't know. I filled out one of those little form things when I got connected, so you can probably get it from Directory Enquiries." Satisfied with my answer, I helped myself to a liberal portion of aloo gobi and tore up a paratha to mop up the sauce.

"Does he know where you live?" Jen wasn't going to let it drop. She seemed determined to worry me and she wasn't doing a bad job.

"Jen, you sound like my mother trying to scare me into going back home to live. Anyone can find out where anyone lives, you know, you just look at the electoral register. None of us are safe. That's why I have three locks on my front door."

"Which you never use," Jen muttered into her piled-up plate.

# CHAPTER 4

The morning greeted me with a blinding headache and sleeting rain. Opening half an eye, I tried to focus on the prostrate form sleeping next to me. I had just worked out that it was Jen when a ginger ball of fur lunged at me and began trying to pummel at my face. Forcing back a sneeze, I grabbed Henry and took him into the kitchen, noting with mild disgust that he had already christened his litter tray. I opened the fridge and was assailed by the sickening smells of cold curry and cat food. Swallowing hard past the bile rising in my throat, I took out the half tin of Felix and searched for a clean bowl, settling for a hand-painted plate featuring a view of Lake Garda; it could only have come from my mother.

The cat sorted, I turned my attention to my own pressing needs, searched out headache tablets and made coffee.

The sound of the toilet flushing and my favourite yucca plant hitting the floor signified that Jen was up and not feeling very coordinated. Coming into the kitchen, she scowled at the half-empty bottle of vodka innocently sitting by the sink and sat down. I laid out her breakfast – two Nurofen tablets and a black coffee.

"Same time next week?" I joked.

"Shut up. My mother was right about you – you are a bad influence."

"Huh?" My brain was too sluggish to cope with her humour. Having been best friends since the age of eight after I got into a fight in the playground for sticking up for her, we both know it was my mother who disapproved of Jen. My mum had never forgotten her daughter coming home with a torn school blazer, a black eye and a split lip. It took her a while to realise I was quite capable of injuring myself without Jen's help. I touched my scabbed cheek as a reminder.

"I'm supposed to be finishing my decorating this weekend," I told her. "I've only done the bathroom, and the cat's fucked that up." I scowled half-heartedly at Henry who, having finished his breakfast, had got down to the business of cleaning himself.

I sat and nursed my second cup of coffee and thought about Mr Smith. I had eight hours before I had to head off and meet him and I really had planned to get some more decorating done before then. Arguing that she couldn't drive back to Nottingham without soaking up some of the alcohol in her system first, Jen bullied me into taking her out for a real breakfast.

After a quick shower, I pulled on my jeans and a thick green jumper, bypassed my contact lenses in favour of black-framed glasses, and we headed off into the rain to find a greasy spoon. One of the best things about my flat was its proximity to the city centre and the never-ending variety of places to eat food from around the world.

On the other side of the road was a health club, which I had been into only once, to sign up. I turned my back on it guiltily and within two minutes Jen and I were seated opposite each other in the red leather alcove of Franco's Italian Coffee Bar with two steaming mugs of tea set out in front of us. Jen ordered a full English breakfast - bacon, sausage, eggs, mushrooms, fried bread and beans, and I went for scrambled eggs and toast, before lighting up my first cigarette of the day. Jen frowned at the smoke and I exaggeratedly blew it away from her and grinned, "Soz."

Within minutes our food arrived, raising a question mark over the chef's definition of a cooked breakfast, but Jen dug in regardless. I scraped the eggs off my toast and nibbled on it unenthusiastically, pondering the differences with which people deal with hangovers. Three extra pieces of toast later, Jen proudly patted her newly protruding stomach and pronounced herself full so we wandered back to my flat.

Henry greeted us enthusiastically. I was beginning to see how so many single women end up filling their homes with cats. I needed to find a boyfriend – quickly.

Jen settled heavily onto my sofa and switched on the TV.

"Jen, what time are you going to make a move?"

"I'm staying – we agreed last night. I'm coming with you tonight, remember?"

I rubbed my forehead and eventually came up with, "No."

"You know I can't let you go alone, he might be a nutter."

She had a point, but still. "He might get scared off by two of us being there."

"Ah well, I figured that out." She switched off the TV and leaned forward, suddenly excited.

I could hardly wait. "How?"

"We go in separate cars and take mobile phones so we can stay in touch. When you meet up with him, get him to sit in your car and leave the phone open. If he checks you for a wire, he won't find anything, but I can record your conversation from my car with one of those little Dictaphone things." She sat back, looking pleased with herself.

"Don't be ridiculous." Jen had obviously been spending too long in the 'murder mystery' section at the bookshop, although I couldn't fault her method. Except for a few minor points.

"We don't have mobile phones or a Dictaphone."

She frowned at me. "Surely you can nip into work and borrow them? Anyway, I have got a mobile phone." Jen grabbed her bag and pulled out a phone that looked suspiciously like one you might get with those removable covers that are available in twelve groovy shades – presumably to avoid a major fashion faux pas if your phone didn't match your outfit.

I started laughing and grabbed it out of her hand - her dislike for mobile phones was legendary. "Since when?"

She scowled at me. "It's Steve. He kept telling me all these horror stories about lone women who break down in their cars and psychos who chop off their heads and bang them on their car roof." She grabbed the phone back. "It's just for emergencies."

"And taping my conversation with a contact is an emergency, is it?" I wasn't letting her off that easily. I had spent far too long listening to her slag off anybody holding an inane conversation on a mobile phone in a public place. "When was the last time you heard of a mugger, rapist or madman that paused long enough to allow his victim time to call 999?"

Jen ignored me. "Look Caitlin, he could be a nutter. Think about it. A strange man keeps ringing you up and now arranges to meet you in the middle of nowhere, in the pitch black and," she paused to look out of the window, "most likely in the pissing rain. You'd be mad to go there alone."

I had to admit she had a point. I wasn't exactly relishing the idea of going alone, but I had been looking forward to a bit of peace and quiet to get my head together during the afternoon. Love Jen as I did, she still had a tendency to drive me nuts. Not to mention there was a tin of terracotta paint sitting in the kitchen with my name on it.

"Don't you need to get back for Steve?" Steve was a chef and apparently a very good one, although I had never experienced his skills. Despite his obvious abilities in cooking, he seemed incapable of looking after himself when he got home and relied on Jen to make his meals and wash his socks. Jen was waiting for him to earn his first Michelin star so she could give up work, get pregnant, and hire a cleaner.

"I need to nip back to Nottingham to get changed – if he's not in I can leave him a note. Meanwhile you can get your hands on another phone and a recording device for me to use."

I sighed. "Okay."

I spent most of the afternoon in the bathroom due to a mixture of hangover and nerves for my clandestine meeting. In between my visits, I managed to put my sick plants back in their home and decided to leave Henry's turquoise footprints on the floor. This had more to do with my unwillingness to get down on my hands and knees to repaint than a sudden understanding of abstract art. But I had to admit, his little contrasting footprints going into the bathroom, around the back of the sink and back out towards the door again, did look rather good.

I also nipped into work to borrow Matt's ancient Dictaphone and bought a mobile phone on the way home, sticking it on my credit card - which had been acquired for economic emergencies only. There seemed to have been a lot of them lately.

Finding I still had time to kill before Jen came back and we set off to meet Mr Smith, I turned my attention to the lounge. I covered my scant furniture with a couple of hideously floral-patterned sheets - courtesy of my mother - and got to work.

Throwing down the roller, I surveyed my afternoon's efforts. The room was looking pretty sharp, and even better was that Henry matched my walls – not the best reason to have a cat, but still, if you had to have one, why not match him to your décor?

The darkness outside told me it was time to get myself ready for that night's activities. My only points of reference were a few thrillers lounging in my bookcase among the Penguin classics, and the American cop films I had seen over the years. Judging from the films, I knew lots of black was important, but decided to let the weather dictate so, after a hot bath, I went with thick woolly socks, black jeans, a t-shirt, black cardigan, and a black duffel coat. Finally, I pulled on thick-soled black boots, adding a much-needed two inches to my height.

I stuck in my contact lenses and sat down for a cigarette. Jen was due any minute and then we would be off. Henry, sensing my nerves, jumped up and curled himself into my lap, screwing his eyes up at my smoke in disapproval.

"Everyone's a critic," I told him.

True to her word, Jen turned up at 6pm, dressed identically to me except for a pair of black mountain boots and a black cloth cap over her red curls. I could hear the rain still coming down outside and, not wanting to be outdone in sleuthing style, I added a black canvas raver's hat to my outfit.

At Jen's insistence, we emptied out our bags and did an inventory check. Two mobile phones, both fully charged up. A nasty-looking black heavy duty torch. A Dictaphone with batteries and two spare mini tapes, a couple of pens, notepad, a mean-looking Swiss Army knife and a packet of tissues.

Hang on a minute, go back one... a Swiss army knife?

Taking in my wide eyes, Jen shrugged. "Just in case."

"In case of what? Emergency pulled thread?"

"No, if this guy's a nutter, you could use the knife on him."

"I'd have to find it first." I picked it up and pulled out a bottle opener, a fork, pair of scissors, mean-looking nail file and finally a three-inch knife. Still, maybe she had a point. I wasn't sure what damage the knife could do, but it couldn't hurt to have it. I mean, I might break a fingernail. "Okay."

She dropped it into my bag.

"Now I need to add your phone number into my phone's memory so that when we are on our way I can just press One and get an open line with you," she took my amazed silence as agreement. "We'll do it all the way there to keep each other company, but tell me when you've spotted him and use a code word when he gets into the car."

She was wasted in that bookshop. "Like what?"

"What about 'finally'. As in 'Finally we meet'?"

I shrugged.

"We also need an emergency word for when you need help or the police, let's use your name, Caitlin, okay?"

"Whatever you say." I was beginning to feel surplus to requirements. I really should have asserted my authority. After all, I was the one with the press card. But who was I trying to kid? I was quite happy to let her come up with the ideas, at least she had some.

"Let's synchronise watches," I joked.

Jen pulled up her sleeve. "Good idea, what time have you got?"

I was only dimly aware of the dilapidated building Mr Smith had referred to on the phone, but I had checked my *A to Z* just to make sure. It was on a rundown industrial estate called Branton that had been earmarked for regeneration money by the city council for a couple of years. Driving through it, I could see why. The once prosperous manufacturing units had become derelict with enough abandoned and burnt-out cars to resemble a scrap metal yard. Each unit was identical and set back slightly from the road, fronted by small forecourts for customer parking.

At the back of the estate was the building I was looking for. The Edwardian grey stone five-storey building looked like it had started life as a hospital. Perfectly symmetrical, it had a large, grand entrance in the middle. Wooden sash windows flanked both sides and the company name was etched into the stone above the door. It wouldn't have looked out of place as the main house on a great country estate or at least converted into flats in another part of town.

I pulled up a little early, as planned, to give Jen time to get into a suitably well-hidden spot. I saw her headlights in my rear-view mirror as she turned off and drove behind a unit with a dirty sign advertising MOTs for £15 a pop. I sighed and looked around me for another car.

"Just having a fag," I whispered into the phone which was sitting in the alcove between the front seats. The phones were connected, but Jen had insisted we should maintain radio silence until Mr Smith turned up.

I toyed with the idea of putting on some music, but remembered Jen had issued a radio ban to avoid interference. She had a point; I wouldn't be able to hear her if she needed to warn me. Rolling down the window to blow out my smoke, I watched the rain falling under one of the few streetlights that had been missed by air rifle-toting kids from the housing scheme that skirted the estate.

"Someone's coming," Jen stage-whispered over the phone, making me drop my cigarette on the floor.

"Shit!"

"Caitlin? What?" Jen said.

"Dropped my fag." I moved my seat back and fumbled around on the floor, trying to see the glowing tip of the cigarette which my nose told me was burning its way into the rubber matting and making a terrible smell. A tap at my window made me jump so high, I knocked my head on the bottom of the steering wheel. I tried to surreptitiously stamp at the fag burning somewhere on the floor.

A slender man stood outside the car, wearing a dark-coloured raincoat with the collar turned up against the March wind. With my window open, I realised I wasn't going to be able to warn Jen that Mr Smith was here. I had no intentions of saying 'Finally we meet' and hoped a silent prayer would be enough to keep her quiet. I opened the car door and got out.

"Mr Smith?" The man stood away from me. The poor lighting meant I could only see that he was aged around 60, with a slim lined face, intelligent eyes and silver hair cut short and damped down by the rain. He had obviously walked some way. My hand came out to shake his, but he ignored it.

"Miss McCall." There was no question in his voice, which was soft and gave away no trace of an accent. There was no doubt it was the same voice I had heard on the phone. "I hope you were careful. These papers will explain everything." He placed a brown A4 envelope into my hand, which was still half-outstretched in greeting.

"Wait," I took the papers. "What's going on? What do you want me to do?" His body language told me he was going to disappear into the darkness at any moment and I tried to keep the rising panic out of my voice.

"It's all there, I'll be in touch." He thrust his hands into his pockets and turned on his heel, walking quietly away.

I stood for a minute, watching his retreating back, mouth opening and closing like a goldfish, my brain trying to formulate the right words to bring him back and make him explain. After he had disappeared I got back into the car and picked up the mobile phone. "Jen."

"Caitlin? What happened? I could hear you open the door and then some muffled voices. I don't think it will come out on tape very clearly."

"Nothing to hear. Look, let's go home." I started the car engine and reversed back onto the road. "Meet back at the house. I'm going to pick up some pizza and I'll see you there."

I could hear her considering it over the phone. "Okay."

Okay, so it was a little lie. But I was going to pick up pizza, only I was going to go on a little detour around the industrial estate first to try and find Mr Smith. I needed to see him again and explain I wasn't the hard-bitten newshound he seemed to think, that I hadn't a clue what I was doing and maybe suggest he contact BBC Radio Leicester instead.

After ten minutes of driving around the estate, I realised it wasn't going to happen. Apart from a few pre-pubescent kids smoking illicit cigarettes and a few older ones smoking joints, there was no sign of life. Sighing, I punched in the familiar number of Bella Vista Pizza and ordered a large thin and crispy pepperoni, with side orders of garlic bread and fries, to take away.

Timing it just right, I turned up at the pizza place to collect my order and raced around the corner to find Jen stamping her feet exaggeratedly on my front step.

"Hurry up, it's freezing, and I need the loo." She grabbed my keys and opened the door, leaving me to lug our dinner into the kitchen.

Grabbing two cans of Diet Coke out of the fridge, I set out kitchen roll on the table, opened the pizza box, fries and garlic bread, and sat down.

Jen came out of the bathroom, rubbing her hands to warm them, and grabbed the chair nearest the radiator. "So?" she said, rolling a slice of pizza up into a fat cigar and inhaling most of it.

"He said nothing. Nothing. And then he gave me an envelope which he said would explain everything."

Jen added a mouthful of Diet Coke to her bulging cheeks and swallowed hard before speaking. "And where is it?"

I looked down at the kitchen table and faked surprise. "Shit, I left it on the seat of my car."

Jen snorted. "Some fucking journalist you are."

I grabbed a handful of fries and scowled at her. She was starting to get on my nerves in her matronly role as Lacey to my Cagney. After all, it was my fucking story.

"I'll go and get it later," I said, filling my mouth.

I finally got rid of Jen at around eleven and turned my attention to the bombsite formally known as my kitchen. The remaining slices of pizza joined the onion bhajis and pakora from the night before in my fridge. Deciding it was too gross to keep cold chips, I threw them in the bin along with the debris from the kitchen table, restoring order in a matter of seconds. That was the great thing about fast food - not only was it fast to cook, it was extremely fast to clean up afterwards.

Picking up Henry, I bore him off to my new-look terracotta lounge, ignored the mess around me, and slid my all-time favourite film - *His Girl Friday* - into the video recorder.

When Cary Grant had finished being dastardly in getting his girl, it was past 2am. With Jen gone, I had no excuse for putting off opening the mysterious envelope. Except that it was two in the morning and it was a rainy, cold night – surely even Bob Woodward would have chosen the warm confines of his bed over Deep Throat on a night like this.

Promising I would uncover all first thing in the morning, I cleaned my teeth, stripped off my outer layers, and fell into bed dreaming of being Rosalind Russell. Unfortunately I had no takers for Cary Grant, although the dark-haired man from the inquest drifted fleetingly into my head.

# CHAPTER 5

I was so shocked when the alarm went off the next morning, I fell out of bed.

It wasn't until I picked myself up off the floor and looked at my alarm clock that I realised: a) it was after 10am and b) it wasn't my alarm that had woken me, it was the front doorbell. Hastily throwing a black cardigan over the black t-shirt, leggings and woolly socks that doubled as my pyjamas in the winter, I felt for my glasses on the bedside table and ran into the hall. Putting them on as I opened the door, my legendary lack of co-ordination left me holding my right eye in agony after trying to poke it out with the black plastic frame of my glasses.

Eye red and streaming, I peered out at the hallway to be greeted by a familiar pair of dark, thickly lashed eyes. This time my eyebrow shot up of its own accord. Standing on my marijuana leaf-patterned doormat was the man from the inquest, whose face had sent me to sleep so soundly last night.

If he recognised me, he hid it well. "Ms McCall?" He asked.

He knew my name. "Yes?"

"I'm Detective Constable Llewelyn, Tom Llewelyn. I wondered if I might have a word?" He produced a small black leather wallet and flipped it open with a practised flick of the wrist to show his warrant card. I looked at it long enough to note the photo was taken in one of those photo booths with a blue pleated curtain behind it and he had a first initial beginning with R.

Blinking back the tears that were still streaming out of my sore eye, I nodded and backed away, opening the door wide. Forgetting the half decorated mess of my front room, I started to lead him in, but stopped suddenly as I remembered. He walked into the back of me. I turned around. "Sorry, can we go into the kitchen?"

He looked at the other doors leading out of my small hall uncertainly, maybe scared that if he took a wrong turn he'd end up in my bedroom. I pointed the way and he opened the kitchen door only to be attacked by a ball of ginger fur. Stooping down long enough to pick Henry up, I followed DC Llewelyn and pulled up a chair at my tiny kitchen table. My opinion of the police was tainted to say the least. My experiences on the job had taught me they never gave you what you wanted, professionally speaking.

He got straight down to business. "There was a fire last night at the Branton industrial estate. Your car fits the description of one seen in the area at the time."

I resisted the urge to go 'gulp'. Fire? Then I remembered all those empty industrial spaces – and all those bored-looking kids hanging around with nothing to do but commit arson. I knew a story when I heard it. Police didn't act this quickly on an investigation unless it was serious. The fire must have been a big one.

"A green Polo? Must be quite a few of those around?" I tried to keep my voice on a nice even level, with a note of casual curiosity.

"Not with a registration plate beginning A555." His voice matched mine.

Experience taught me he wasn't going to tell me the whole story until he was good and ready, but it didn't mean I couldn't try. "I might have driven through the estate last night, what time was the fire?"

"Fire service got a call about eight."

"Arson?"

"Too early to tell. Maybe."

"So you want to know if I saw anything?" Either that or I was a suspect. I mentally genuflected and crossed my fingers – my religious beliefs and superstition began and ended with cries for help in moments of crisis.

"First things first, was it you?"

"Yeah, I went through there at about sevenish."

"Why?"

"Pardon?"

"What for? What were you doing there on a Saturday night?"

"Is that relevant?" I said, stalling for time, I certainly wasn't going to tell him the truth.

"I can't say at this stage of the inquiry." Every bit the policeman. Arsehole.

"I work at the *Post*. The *Leicestershire Post*, I'm a journalist. Went out to get pizza and wanted to familiarise myself with the area - the estate is earmarked for regeneration cash, you know. Nice to be able to picture what you're writing about." I scratched Henry's ear and looked at the policeman innocently.

"You're a reporter?" He made it sound like 'SS officer'.

"Trainee."

He got up quickly as though the seat had burnt him. "Well, I'll be in touch if there's anything else."

I smiled sweetly and got up to show him to the door.

"Thanks for your time," he said as he went out.

"Up yours." I replied childishly to the closed door.

After he left, it occurred to me that he hadn't asked me if I had seen anything suspicious. Was he crap at interviews, or was I more potential suspect than potential witness? I shook the thought out of my head. I hadn't done anything wrong. I was itching to go and collect Mr Smith's papers, but I didn't want to race outside in case DC Llewelyn was hanging around, perhaps looking in my car for empty petrol cans or sticks of dynamite. To kill time, I went back into the kitchen and switched on the kettle for that all important first tea of the day.

A cup later, my eye was down to mildly inflamed pink and I felt ready to face the world - and whatever Mr Smith had in store for me. The thick brown envelope was just where I had left it on the front seat. I grabbed it, holding it close for fear someone might grab it off me, and slammed my car door shut.

"Ms McCall?" I whirled around to find DC Llewelyn standing behind me, raising a questioning eyebrow. He had been making a call on his mobile phone and snapped it shut as he stood in front of me.

Trying desperately hard not to look guilty, I followed his eyes down to the brown envelope clutched to my chest. "Research," I muttered to him. "Did you want anything else?"

"Not for the moment." He stood and watched me walk up the three steps of the front door to my building and disappear inside.

Leaning against my door with the envelope still clutched to my chest, I hunted for a pen and noted his name and rank down on a scrap of paper. If this cop was going to start harassing me, I needed to find out all I could about him - both from the paper's excellent archive and its even better gossip network.

I ignored the half-decorated lounge in favour of slumping on my bed with Henry and my mysterious package. Taking a deep breath and lighting a cigarette, I opened the envelope and tipped out its contents.

The envelope contained ten A4 photocopies of some sort of scientific paper. There were parts blanked out on the first page where you would expect to find the author and a title and the next pages contained graphs, charts and mathematical equations big enough to make my brain bleed.

"Shit." I sighed loudly and accidentally dropped ash on Henry from the forgotten cigarette clasped in my left hand. I rubbed the ash from his head. It would be an understatement to say that maths wasn't my strong subject - you only had to look at the state of my bank balance to know that. I tried to put the papers in some semblance of order, which was difficult as there were no page numbers and I couldn't tell what was supposed to follow on from what. After an hour, I had put them into three different orders and was sure none of them was right, but had worked out it was some sort of chemistry paper. I recognised a few symbols from the periodic table and it seemed that someone had been testing something on something else.

What I did know was that this wasn't going to be enough for the scoop I had been dreaming of. I was going to have to find someone who could understand it. The only person I could think of with any chemical knowledge was my brother Ben, and that was concentrated in the general area of amphetamines.

Shoving the papers back into the envelope and throwing it under my bed, I assumed my thinking position on top of the covers.

It was dark and cold by the time I woke up, feeling thick-headed and cold. My face bore the imprint of the top of my spiral pad and Henry had disappeared under the duvet – sensible lad.

I sat cross-legged in my tartan pyjamas with my back against the radiator in the lounge, eating leftover pizza while I considered my weekend's activities. So far I had acquired an envelope of papers containing large amounts of gobbledygook, been at the scene of an arson and I had one of the city's finest on my back. And if that wasn't enough, my best friend had turned into Nancy Drew.

Rolling a plastic ball containing a bell into the path of Henry and watching him pounce on it, I half-heartedly made my plans for the coming week. Find out more about DC Llewelyn, find someone who could decipher gobbledygook, finish decorating the lounge. *And finally, stop eating takeaway food,* I added, burping loudly.

Having mapped out my plans, I unpeeled myself from the radiator and decided to give my mother the shock of her life by ringing her. She picked up on the second ring. Ben and I had bought her a cordless phone for Christmas and I am convinced she walks around the house with it strapped to her hip, like those self-important middle-aged businessmen with leather-encased mobile phones fixed to their belt, usually next to unfeasibly large bunches of keys.

"Mother, it's Caitlin."

"Hello, dear. Nice of you to call." Dripping with sarcasm.

"Well, I was just wondering how you were?"

"Can't complain," she said and went on to do just that for ten minutes, by which time I had smoked two cigarettes and needed the toilet.

"When are you coming home? We haven't seen you for a month."

I stifled a sigh. Being only 30 miles away from Nottingham was the only downside to Leicester. "I'm working next weekend."

"Again?"

"I work every other Saturday, you know that."

"Well, Sunday then?"

"Maybe." I couldn't explain to her that Sunday was meant to be a rest day and, love my parents as I undoubtedly did, going home wasn't my idea of resting. I hurriedly ended the call before she could start asking me about my love life. It would only end in tears and they were usually hers, after she worked herself up into hysteria because she was the oldest member of her bridge club without grandchildren.

# CHAPTER 6

Finding myself back at the scene of the crime early on a wet, cold Monday morning was punishment enough. Finding myself face-to-face with DC Llewelyn again was worthy of Machiavelli.

I had carried out the usual round of police, fire and ambulance calls when Paul Andrews, Deputy News Editor and all-round office nice guy, shouted me over. "Caitlin. Nice weekend?"

"Interesting." I raised my eyebrows at him as he turned his attention to the screen in front of him, tapping it with the chewed-up end of a black biro.

"We've got a story here about a fire at that old industrial estate... Branton?"

I resisted the urge to shout 'it wasn't me' and nodded.

"Police are holding a press conference at the scene. Can you go? We've already got a lead, but ring us if they say anything interesting." From his tone I could tell he didn't think there would be. It explained why they were sending me out into the pouring rain when there were two senior reporters sitting around doing nothing – including our crime correspondent, although even from my desk I could see Rachel was in no fit state to go anywhere, she needed a few trips to the downstairs disabled toilet cubicle first.

"Sure." I walked back to my desk to get my coat.

"I'll send you a copy of the story we've got, so you'll know if there's anything that needs adding. We've got pics, but I'll see if we can get a snapper out there with you." Paul turned back to his computer screen.

"Okay."

So it was that at nine o'clock I found myself standing on the road in front of the grand Edwardian building where I had met Mr Smith on Saturday night, looking straight at DC Llewelyn, who was one of several officers standing in front of the building.

Although it had been dark on Saturday night, I couldn't fail to notice the difference 36 hours had made. The building had been derelict before but it had been intact, with only the bottom floor windows and doorway boarded up as though at any minute it would be opened to reveal the latest in city living for trendy young things.

Now it was a shell of a building. Fire had ripped through the lower storeys, travelled up to the higher floors and literally gone through the roof. Its wooden window frames were blackened and panes of glass smashed and scattered, glittering all over the ground. The roof was missing most of its tiles and what had once been a baronial-style front entrance was leaning on one side, gaping open to expose the chaos inside. It had been gutted. According to the story written by yesterday's duty reporter, twelve fire units had attended and battled with the blaze for two hours before bringing it under control.

Standing behind a radio reporter from a local commercial station, I took in the damage while waiting for the police to start talking. Fortunately, I couldn't spot a white outline of my VW Polo chalked onto the scorched tarmac where the car park should have been.

Before I had time to wonder what would happen to the kids who must have done this, a middle-aged, suited man appeared from behind the building and introduced himself to the small gathering as Detective Inspector Clive Barker from King Street CID.

"Thank you for coming, ladies and gentlemen, on this rather nasty day," he said as the wind whipped around us.

We all murmured and stamped our feet in the cold by way of reply.

"I'm only going to say all this once, so listen up. Most of you know about the fire here on Saturday night. The Fire Service has yet to officially confirm it was maliciously ignited, which is partly what we are doing here.

"Unfortunately, that is not the only reason for our presence. Yesterday fire investigators discovered a set of human remains inside the building."

The murmuring around me grew as I struggled to hear him above my furiously beating heart and get what he was saying down onto my increasingly wet pad.

"Ladies and gentlemen, I will tell you all I can for now and then my officers will attempt to answer any more questions you might have individually." He nodded at DC Llewelyn and the other officers flanking him.

I caught DC Llewelyn's eye, ready to nod an acknowledgement to the expected sign of recognition, but he looked straight through me. Was that a good or bad sign?

Before I had time to work it out, DI Barker spoke again. "The remains are thought to be male," he said, pausing as we all wrote it down. "There will be a post mortem examination later today when we hope to establish the cause of death. That's it, folks." He nodded and wandered off back towards the building where he was quickly joined by a couple of senior-looking firefighters.

I followed a general surge forward as reporters clamoured to get at one of the two detectives, desperate for an exclusive quote.

"Is it being treated as murder?"

"Can you ID the man?"

"Any idea how old?"

"What started the fire?"

"Do you have any suspects?"

"Is it arson?"

As the questions flowed, a thought popped into my head from nowhere. Was it Mr Smith? I dismissed it instantly and watched DC Llewelyn deal with the mass of enquiries calmly, taking down some of the answers. Just because I had been there an hour before a fire broke out didn't mean it was anything to do with me, I told myself and decided to let the scrum die down before steaming in with my own questions. In this case I didn't have to as DC Llewelyn worked his way towards me.

"We meet again," he said. Police humour.

"Yeah." Caught wrong-footed, the questions that had been building up in my head disappeared and all I wanted to know was what had happened and if it had anything to with me. Under the circumstances the best I could come up with was, "What can you tell me?"

He smirked. "What do you want to know?"

"How do you think he was killed?" *Do you think I did it?*

"I couldn't say until the post mortem has been carried out."

"How badly damaged was the body, are you checking dental records and Missing Persons?" *Is it Mr Smith?*

"The body was burned beyond recognition and we will be checking dental records and any recently reported missing persons to try and get an ID, yes."

I scribbled down his response in shaky shorthand, "How many officers are working on this inquiry? Is it a murder inquiry?"

"We have four officers working on this case at the moment. It is not an official murder inquiry at the moment."

"Does that mean you expect it to become one?"

"I couldn't say."

"Do you have any suspects?" *Me?*

"I couldn't comment on that at the moment."

I closed my pad and checked my watch. 9.50am – about ten minutes until the deadline for the first edition. "Okay, well thanks for your time." I managed a weak smile and turned to walk off.

"I look forward to seeing you again, Ms McCall," he called out after me.

I carried on walking to my car and tried not to think what he had meant by that. Getting in, I rolled down the window, lit a cigarette, and rang the newsdesk. "It's Caitlin out at the arson scene. You need to add some stuff, there was a body in there."

Paul spun into action. "Right, let me get the arson copy on my screen and we'll change it for first edition and then you can come back and do a full re-write for the next one."

"Ready when you are," I inhaled heavily on the cigarette and flicked through my notepad. "The body of a man has been found in a derelict building destroyed in a blaze at the weekend. Police have yet to confirm that the fire was arson and have refused to speculate on how the man met his death."

I looked at the printed-out story.

"The building in the Branton Industrial Estate has stood empty since its owners Fifen Pharmaceuticals moved to their new multi-million pound complex in Carson Park on the edge of the city two years ago.

"Then we want: Detective Inspector Clive Barker speaking at the scene today said: 'Yesterday fire investigators discovered a set of human remains inside the building. The remains are thought to be male. There will be a post mortem examination later today when we hope to establish the cause of death.'"

I could hear Paul tapping away at the other end of the phone with the classic two-finger typing favoured by most men. "Okay. Anything else of interest happening?"

"No, police are being pretty tight-lipped. They won't confirm that it is a murder investigation, but they have four officers working on the case and will be searching Missing Persons to ID the body. No news on suspects, witnesses etcetera, etcetera." I looked over at the building where DC Llewelyn and his colleague were talking to the remaining radio journalists, who had waited until it was quieter to tape their interviews, and wondered what Paul would say if I told him that I was a potential witness.

"Can you make sure we have a contact for the post mortem results and any other follow-ups?" Paul said. "I'll see you back here later. Your deadline is twelve."

"Seeya." I put the phone down and took another look at the building. Now the adrenaline from getting my copy in by deadline had subsided, my thoughts turned back to Mr Smith and where he had disappeared to after our meeting on Saturday. My stomach twisted in fear as I considered what the chances were that the dead body belonged to him. If it did, DC Llewelyn might be the least of my worries.

I took a slow ride back to the office and resisted the urge to go home and collect the papers I had so carelessly kicked under my bed in disgust the night before because I couldn't understand them.

The body had to be Mr Smith – who else could have been there at that time? The estate was too far away from town to make it an attractive base for the homeless, or anyone else for that matter. My first thought was that kids had been playing around and it had gone tragically wrong and the other reporters seemed to think the same thing. But if it had been kids, surely the police would know who the body had belonged to and they didn't seem to.

I shuddered at the thought of what could have happened to Mr Smith after he left me. *If it was him,* I reminded myself – although now the reassurance sounded hollow. But if it was, maybe someone had been looking for him, maybe watching him and when they caught up with him, he didn't have what they wanted, so they killed him. Maybe I now had what they wanted – and I didn't have a fucking clue what it was. Swallowing past the frustration, I continued my musings. If it was Mr Smith who ended up dead - who did it? And more importantly, why?

Back in the office, I wandered over to the photography department to have a word with the snapper who had been out at the scene. I found Sally Jamieson, crouching over her negatives and choosing her best photographs for the paper, while simultaneously arguing with the Picture Editor about his choice of shot, which had gone on the first edition's front page.

I sat down and waited for her to finish going through the roll of film. "S'up?" She asked without bothering to turn and look at me.

"Just checking you got a shot of Inspector Barker for the next edition."

She pointed to the small screen by the machine she was using to review her photographs and riffled through the film again, stopping when she got to a picture of him with the building in the background. "That do you?"

"Excellent."

She stopped for a minute and looked up at me through her heavy, dark fringe, which was a few weeks beyond being in need of a trim. "Who was the dark-haired bloke you spoke to?"

"Him? Don't worry, we didn't need a picture, I've not quoted him directly."

She shook her head and laughed. "I didn't mean that, he was really fit."

I blushed and scowled at her. "He's a copper."

"Shame. Suppose that puts him off limits."

I shrugged and got up, wandering back to my desk to file fresh copy for the final edition.

As I finished typing up my notes, a shadow fell over my desk and I noticed that a hush had fallen over Matt and Nina, who had been chatting about their weekends.

"Good, good. No, get the murder in higher. You need to build it up if it's going to splash." I recognised the voice of the *Post*'s Editor; a misogynistic, squat Welshman who chewed foul-smelling cigars and only left his office to bark orders at his newsroom staff like a drill sergeant. Although his name was Harry Thomas, I had never heard anyone refer to him as anything other than 'the Editor', usually in the hushed tones reserved for child-killers or cannibals.

"They haven't said it is a murder inquiry yet," I said, suddenly finding my ability to type disappearing.

"So?" he barked back. "They are leaning that way enough for you to go a bit further than speculate in the fifth paragraph. You need to learn when to push a story. It's staring you in the face that by tomorrow this will be a murder inquiry and we want to be the first to say it – even if it is before they have. Especially then."

I turned round and found I had an audience, as Tony had joined the Editor. "Come on Caitlin, we need it now," he sighed impatiently.

I took a deep breath, copied another quote out of my notepad, and gave it a quick spell-check before pressing the Send button. "It's over," I told them.

The Editor walked off towards the sub-editors' desk to see what headlines they were planning to use, stopping only to drop a hand on Edward's shoulder and say "Welcome back" as he sat with his feet up on his desk, coolly watching my panic.

Within minutes, the edition of the paper had travelled down the computer wires to the printers in the basement and the stories that had held the editors captive only seconds before were instantly forgotten as they gathered to discuss new stories for the following day.

The Editor took up his position at the head of the table set aside in his office for the news conference with his reporter's pad at the ready. I watched as Rachel sauntered into his office. Her DTs had disappeared, no doubt along with a couple of inches of gin from her secret cistern stash. The return of her faculties effectively took me off the story. Legend had it she didn't give up a front-page crime story byline without a fight. It suited me. I'd had enough excitement for one day.

I busied myself staring into space, waiting for more information about the fire and the body, but gave up after about an hour when Nina assured me there wouldn't be any further news that day. Following the post mortem, the police would have to search their files and inform the relatives. It would at least take them into the next day.

"Go out and see some contacts," she said loudly for the benefit of Paul on the newsdesk, before mouthing 'shopping' at me with a wink.

Although reporters often worked well beyond their hours, Nina took an anarchic attitude to claiming her time back. With a vague mention of 'popping out to see my contacts', she would happily spend an afternoon out shopping, arguing that the out-of-town shopping centre was geographically within the boundary of her news patch, although I had never known the *Post* to feature stories about the latest French Connection sale.

I switched off my computer and shrugged into my coat. Picking up a copy of the last edition of the *Post*, which had the fire splashed across the front page, I walked down to my car.

# CHAPTER 7

With no plans made for my afternoon, I followed Nina's advice and settled on a drive around my news patch. The city had been sliced up between the reporters to ensure no town council decision, school fundraiser or community group meeting went unreported, no matter how insignificant. My area effectively covered the suburban area of Bankborough.

A couple of miles north of the city centre, Bankborough had its own town council, a busy high street of shops and an active Neighbourhood Watch scheme, which made my job a lot easier. Homes were mostly red brick semi-detached and privately owned, with enough council houses to keep property prices down. It was a nice place to live if you liked the suburbs and your salary didn't stretch to moving to one of the pretty market towns dotted around the county.

Driving through the main street, I spotted a road sign for Bartholomew Close where the late Mary Stanshaw had lived. With nothing better to do, I turned into it, coming to a stop about halfway down. Her house number had been 36 - I remembered it being read out in the inquest court. It was a small house, which the builder would no doubt have marketed as a starter home, perfect for a newly married couple. A newly-erected 'For Sale' sign stood on the small patch of grass at the front which was broken up by a withered-looking bay tree planted in the middle. I briefly considered ringing the estate agent for a look around the house, but discounted the idea - what would there be in the house that could help me?

After a few minutes pondering this statement, it turned into a question. What was in the house that could help me? Looking across, I saw it had no net curtains – surely it couldn't hurt to have a little peek in the windows? My mind made up, I restarted the car and looked for a place to park inconspicuously. The street came to a dead end a few hundred metres further, which gave way to a patch of muddy grass worn thin by children playing football. At this time of day the kids were at school and the street was quiet. I parked, careful not to block anyone's driveway - experience at home had taught me that obstruction was the fastest way to get noticed in a neighbourhood.

I walked back to the house, scoping out its neighbours for any twitching curtains and signs that I was being watched. I walked up the path of number 36 without incident and tried the gate by the side of the front door. It was open and led into a small, tidy yard. Closing the gate behind me, I leant against it for a second, waiting for someone to yell out and ask me what I was doing.

The road remained silent and I moved away from the gate. The back door to the house was a few steps away.

*If this was a film, I would be able to pick the lock,* I thought, leaning on the door handle, thinking maybe I could finally find a use for the credit card-sized health club membership I had in my bag.

Like hundreds of women before me I had hoped the pain of parting with £40 a month for gym membership would be enough to get me fit without having to don tracksuit and trainers and actually turn up and do any exercise. Picking a lock would be the first time the membership card had been used for anything other than scraping ice from my car windscreen.

But it wasn't needed. My gloved hand flew off the handle as though bitten as the door gave without effort - it wasn't locked. I peered in through the open doorway, expecting to see a white outline of where Mary Stanshaw had lain dead. Instead I found a newly-installed fitted kitchen and laminated wood flooring that creaked slightly as I stood on it. Without realising it, I had entered her house. The damage was done and if I was going to go to jail for trespassing, I might as well have a good look around and make it worthwhile.

I closed the door behind me and stood and looked around, waiting for my pulse to drop to pre-stroke level. It was a small box kitchen, neat and tidy with half-empty cereal boxes stacked along the counter and a box of teabags next to the kettle. It had two doors leading off it – one to the hall and one to a small dining room at the side. Deciding if there was anything to find it wouldn't be in the dining room, I went for the door on my left and walked through to a whitewashed hall with seagrass carpeting. Red and orange light flooded in from the stained glass front door ahead of me, reflecting off the high gloss paint of the closed door to the right. Remembering the large window that offered unobstructed views into the room to anyone who walked by and cared to look in, I ignored the closed door and stepped lightly onto the stairs.

Once on the landing I was faced with another choice of doors –

this time there were three. I guessed they were Mary's and Darren's bedrooms, and the bathroom. I opted for the front room, which looked the largest of the three, and crouched for fear of being seen through the window as I opened the door. The room was square and painted a soft blue to match the duvet which was folded back towards the foot of the bed, crumpled, as though its owner had just jumped out, in a hurry, late for work. Ignoring it, I turned my attention to the wardrobes and opened them up, finding a range of clothes and shoes. With a pang, I noted that Mary Stanshaw, before she was pregnant, had been about the same size as me. Closing the doors a minute later, I sat down heavily on the bed, wondering what I was doing, sneaking around the house of a dead woman.

My heart leapt out of my mouth and I jumped off the bed as a shrill ring sounded through the house. The noise was coming from my bag. I rummaged inside it, trying to feel for my mobile phone, eventually upending the contents onto the floor in my rush to find it and stop the noise.

"Hello?" I said tentatively. My voice sounded loud in the empty, cold house.

"Where are you?" It was Nina.

"Shopping," I said, expecting her to disagree, forgetting she couldn't see me.

"Good on you, girl. Anything doing?"

"Nope. Yourself? Heard anything about the fire?" I sat back down on the bed.

"No. Listen, don't let it bother you that they took you off the story." She had misread the fear in my voice as annoyance. "It's Rachel's job, after all. If she hadn't been so keen to keep her appointment with a certain second floor toilet this morning, she could have gone out to the press conference instead of you."

"I know, I'm not bothered. Just interested."

"Good. Well there's no news, won't be until tomorrow, I told you that."

"Okay."

"Listen, I've got to go – there's a Bish's bash on."

"A what?"

"The Bishop is having his annual dinner or tea or whatever it is. I drew the short straw. Got to interview him about his faith."

I laughed. Nina was a self-confessed atheist who claimed she never prayed, even in moments of crisis. I pressed the End button on my phone and jumped again as I heard the unmistakable tap of someone walking across the laminated kitchen floor downstairs.

Shit. Someone was in the house. I dropped to the floor, hurriedly scooping up my belongings from the sheepskin rug on the floor and stuffing them all back in my bag along with half the rug. There were voices, it sounded like two – the estate agent must be showing someone around. No wonder the back door had been open. Fuck, they must have been in the lounge or the dining room all this time.

Kneeling, I looked across at the wardrobes, trying to remember if there had been any space inside where I could hide. The voices were getting louder as the people moved into the hall. I dropped down and looked under the bed for hiding space. If it was one of those divans with drawers in its base I was totally buggered.

I was in luck. It was an old-fashioned wooden base with elaborate springs holding the mattress in place and about a foot between it and the dusty-looking wooden floor. Telling myself beggars couldn't be choosers, I slid under the bed as footsteps started on the stairs. I lay, trying not to breathe, and realised my hand was empty. My mobile phone! Where had I put it? I closed my eyes, trying to remember if I had dropped it on the bed in my panic or had picked it up with everything else. I pulled my bag up but the shortage of space meant I couldn't look in it properly.

I was just working out how to get the zip open and fumble in it one-handed when the door to the bedroom opened, revealing two pairs of feet. One pair was clad in low-heeled navy court shoes favoured by middle-aged mothers across the land and the other in battered brown lace-up brogues.

"Okay, okay, stop going on about it now," it was the man's voice with the practised whine of a hen-pecked husband used to being nagged at.

"Someone could have broken in," the woman's voice rose dangerously close to hysteria. "Haven't I been through enough these past weeks?"

"Love," the wheedling voice again, sounding even more conciliatory this time, "I'm sorry I left the door unlocked. But nobody has broken in and nothing's been taken. No damage done." As soon as the last words were out it seemed he regretted them and tried to take them back. "What I mean is..."

But he was too late. "No damage done? No damage done?" The hysteria turned up a notch as she sat down heavily on the bed, forcing the mattress down on top of my chest. "My daughter is dead, my granddaughter is dead, little Darren here has been left without his mummy," she paused dramatically. "And if that's not enough, that little hussy from the newspaper, harassing me at Mary's inquest."

My heart stopped beating. Oh. My. God. It was Mary Stanshaw's mother! At that moment I realised that if they found me, I was dead. It was as simple as that. No discussion, no chance to explain, she would kill me. Although that was going to happen anyway if she didn't get off the bed soon and stop crushing me, I silently added with a struggled breath.

My attention was taken off the drama going on inches above my head by the sudden view of a small boy, blowing spit bubbles out of his mouth as he played with a battered green Tonka truck on the floor. Oblivious to the conversation going on around him, he intently pushed his truck around on the sheepskin rug close to my right hand and the swollen ankles of his grandmother. All he had to do was look up and he would see me. I held my breath and willed him not to look across. Deciding I shouldn't stare at him in case he had the third eye and felt my gaze, I turned my head away. His grandparents were continuing their discussion above me.

"She was only doing her job," the whining was back as he joined his wife on the bed, this time flattening my stomach.

"Well, she should do something more ladylike. I'd be ashamed of her if she were my daughter. What does her mother say?"

I bit back a sudden and powerful urge to answer her rhetorical question.

"I'd wonder what I had done wrong, that's what I would do."

*She does – every day of her life,* I wanted to reply.

The man was making agreeing noises.

"I don't know how she sleeps at night, I really don't."

I was pulled away from the ironic turn in the conversation by the gentle but unmistakable thud of a Tonka truck hitting the side of my face. With some difficulty I turned my head back to the side, just in time to see the boy's face scrunched up in readiness for a howl. This was it. He was going to start screaming for his truck. One of his grandparents was going to bend down for it and come face to face with me.

But he still hadn't noticed me. I pulled my hand up towards my face and grabbed at the car, turning it around and sending it back out from under the bed with a gentle shove. Without question, the kid grabbed the toy, the howling face disappeared, the spit bubble returned, and he turned away to continue playing.

The woman got off the bed and at last I was able to breathe. Sweat was pouring down the back of my neck, which was still wrapped up against the icy March wind in a woollen scarf. I fought the urge to pull at it for fear of making too much movement or too much noise.

The couple were now discussing whether it was time to move Mary's belongings out of the house. She seemed to think it was. He - obviously sensing it would involve him doing all the work - was less willing.

"Love, you have to give these things time," he told her.

She sniffed. "Time won't heal these wounds." Despite myself I was beginning to like her. Until she sat down on the bed again.

"You've been through enough, what with that newspaper article." I could see him in my mind's eye, gently patting her hand. "I'll pop back at the weekend. I can get one of those 'man with a van' people and you won't have to do anything." And neither would he.

I was willing him on to succeed. If they stayed to sort the place out I was going to get found out, or die of suffocation.

She began to let herself be talked out of it. "Well, I don't want a stranger going through all her things. Her bosses have already been in to take back her computer."

I closed my eyes and mentally sighed. Her computer was gone and with it any chance I had of finding out about her work at Fifen Pharmaceuticals. My trip here had been a waste of time. All I could do now was wait – and pray it wouldn't be too long.

Thankfully God was listening.

"Well, there's not a lot we can do now. Let's get home so you can put your feet up, you've had a hellish few days," her husband said, trying to sound in control.

She made agreeing noises and the weight was lifted off me again. I took in a gulp of air, enjoying the feeling of my chest being able to expand again. That crisis over, another one began to build up in my throat as I felt the unmistakable signs of a cough welling up. My eyes watered with the effort of not expelling the air and I tried to ignore the intense feeling of dust tickling the back of my throat. *Come on! Leave!* I silently yelled at them.

Hovering by the door, the couple seemed to be looking around the room, their feet half-turned towards the door.

"Come on, you," the man turned, grabbing the boy's hand and pulling him up and finally out of my line of vision, the Tonka truck dangling in his free hand. I was going to make it.

Then I sneezed.

The woman halted on her way out of the door and I waited for them to speak, or at least peer under the bed.

"Wipe your nose," I heard her say, but not to me.

The kid! She assumed it was the kid. The trio finally left the room but I'd have to wait till I heard them leave the house before daring to move. They walked down the stairs and out to the kitchen but I waited for the faint scrape of the key in the door and the sound of a car driving off before speeding into action. I rolled out from under the bed, and with some difficulty got up into a sitting position and allowed myself a minute of coughing.

Wiping the tears out of my eyes, I saw my black duffel coat was covered in dust and hair that had gathered on the wooden floorboards under the bed. Ignoring them, I grabbed my bag and checked the contents – pad, car keys, lip balm, assorted pens, but no mobile phone.

Shit. I peered under the bed to see if it had fallen out, but couldn't see it anywhere. Sitting back up I spied it nestling in the crumpled duvet covers on top of the bed. Mary's mother had sat down right on top of it and hadn't even noticed. Grabbing it and stuffing it into my bag, I left the room and raced down the stairs to the kitchen.

Only then remembering the scraping sound of a key turning in a lock.

I was locked in.

Fuck. Could this day get any worse?

Looking around me, I considered smashing a window, but then noticed the little keys sitting in the window locks. A quick peek into the dining room revealed what I was looking for. A set of patio doors behind thick green velvet curtains. The key was in the lock and turned silently. I slid through the doors. I would have to leave them unlocked, unless I locked them myself and pocketed the key. I decided it would be better to lock up and lose the key later. From what I'd heard, Mary's stepfather had enough on his plate, without getting the blame for that as well. I turned the key and pocketed it, resolving to throw it out of the car window on my way home.

# CHAPTER 8

My flat was locked as I had left it, but my stomach still did several painful flips as I slotted the key in the front door and pushed it open. Flicking the light on in the hall, I shut the door firmly and leaned against it, letting out the breath I had been unconsciously holding since I walked through the shared front door of the house. The landlord still hadn't installed an intercom system, despite his promises when I signed my lease. I was the only one who could hear the front door, which meant leaving it unlocked was preferable to me having to play doorman for the whole building.

I quickly walked from room to room, flicking on the lights and checking behind the sofa, under the bed and in the wardrobe. Once I had checked the whole flat, I decided against emptying Henry's well-used litter tray as it would mean going out to the rubbish bins tucked away in a dark corner of the overgrown wilderness that was laughingly referred to as our back garden. Instead, I headed for the bathroom and a hot bath to wash away the evidence and dust of my afternoon of law-breaking. Half way through rinsing the conditioner out of my hair I heard the phone ring and debated getting out of the bath to answer it. I waited for the answer machine to pick it up and sighed with relief that it was only Jen ringing to check up on me.

"Make sure you ring me straight back – I want to hear about everything," she said in a conspiratorial whisper before ending the call.

Ten minutes later she picked up on the second ring. "Caitlin?"

"Do you always answer the phone like that?" The knotted muscles in my shoulders relaxed at the familiar and comforting sound of her voice.

"Only when my best friend's got herself involved in murder and mayhem."

For a second I thought she was talking about my foray into house-breaking. Then I remembered the fire. It had been a busy day.

"You've heard, then?" At least I didn't have to explain everything to her.

"It was on the TV. You made the local news. What's going on?"

"I don't know. I had a personal visit from the police yesterday, who told me there had been a fire at an empty building on the estate. Then at work this morning I got sent out on a press conference at the scene where they revealed that a man's body had been discovered in the fire."

"Shit, McCall, what have you got yourself into?"

"How long have you got?" I sat on the hall floor and lit a cigarette. Henry joined me, curling up in my lap like a furry, ginger hot water bottle.

"So why did the police come around yesterday? Were we seen?"

"Apparently I was. I just said I was getting to know the area, you know - keen trainee journalist and all that."

"Good thinking. Shit, I hope no one saw me."

"Well if you haven't had a call from the police, I wouldn't worry about it. They came to me pretty quickly. Anyway, I'll just say you came with me as a mate."

"In separate cars? Bit weird."

"No law against being weird; if there was, half the population would be behind bars."

"True," she sighed. "Now the most important thing to remember is to act dumb. I've seen how police trap murderers and criminals because they let slip something about the case which hasn't been made public. If I was the police I'd catch you out because you'd put something in your news story that hadn't been made public and the only way you would have known about it was if you were the murderer. Then you'd be done for."

I stared at the phone. "What do you mean you've seen how the police trap criminals? This isn't *Prime Suspect*, you know. And you seem to be forgetting that I didn't actually do anything."

"Well of course you didn't, nobody's saying that," she said briskly. "Although if I was Helen Mirren you'd be at the top of my list. Reporter desperate for her first front page story. Now what was in the envelope?"

"I don't know. Some sort of research paper, I think. Maybe for a drug. I need to find someone to decipher it for me."

"A drug? I expected it would at least have been some incriminating photos. Disappointed?"

"Nah, I just need to get help with it." I slurped my coffee. "Jen, I need to ask you a favour."

"Anything."

"Can I post you a copy of these papers?"

"Why?"

"Well I don't know if this dead guy is Mr Smith. But if it is, fuck knows what that means. They may be after these papers and that means they must be important."

"Cat, I really think you should tell someone about all this. Apart from the fact there may be serious bad guys involved, you could get in a lot of trouble." For the first time during our conversation she sounded serious.

"Jen, I'm fine. Not only have I got Henry to look after me, I seem to have my own personal detective constable."

"How come?"

"This DC Llewelyn bloke, I keep bumping into him, that's all."

"What's he look like?"

"Fantastic according to a photographer at work. Dark-haired, tall, late twenties."

"Just your type."

"Yeah, if you forget the fact that he's a pig."

She snorted. "You could do with the help to keep you out of trouble. What's your day off this week?"

"Wednesday."

"Excellent. Me too. I'll come down."

I tried to convince her there was no need but she was adamant, so I ended the call.

Going back to the bedroom, I fumbled under my bed for the folder. Wiping the dust it had collected down my pyjama leg, I pondered where I was going to find someone who could tell me what the papers meant.

Eddie. Duh! I mentally slapped my forehead. I had gone to journalism college with a press officer at the University of the East Midlands, which was an amalgamation of five different former polytechnics in the region, including one in Leicester. Eddie had taken one look at the pittance being offered to trainee reporters as a starting salary and headed straight for the more lucrative field of public relations, leaving any principles at the door. As our teacher had once said, the field of public relations was where journalists went to die.

Because of its size, the university was a mine of information on everything from sports science to criminal psychology. They were bound to have some chemistry expert there somewhere. And Eddie could be relied on to find them for me. If that failed, I'd give Ben a ring, though I knew that the only thing he was likely to be able to tell me was whether it would make you high.

Resolving to call Eddie first thing in the morning, I wandered into the kitchen and stuck a couple of Pop Tarts in the toaster for dinner.

# CHAPTER 9

By the time I got into work the next morning, I had been up for over two hours, unable to go back to sleep. Today was the day I would find out if the arson victim had been Mr Smith. Maybe.

To keep myself busy, I had cleaned my flat from top to bottom, put my lounge back together, and even ventured outside to empty Henry's litter tray as soon as it was light.

My first job of the day was to copy the research papers - twice for good measure. I left one set in the drawer of my desk, which was such a mess even I would have trouble finding it, stuck the other copy in an envelope and posted it to Jen. I opted for second class and left her postcode off it in the hope it would be safe in the mail for a few days.

Returning from the post room, my heart gave a painful lurch as I noticed a police fax left on my desk. Looking more closely, I saw it was a press release on the launch of a campaign to cut car crime. Tony had scribbled a note on the top, asking me to track down a victim and develop it into a lead for the second edition. Putting in a call to the police press office for help, I switched on my computer to search for the follow-up story on the arson I had covered the day before. Rachel had written an exclusive front page story for the next edition, which said a murder hunt had been launched. The police had confirmed the cause of the fire was arson but the victim hadn't been identified yet. There were a few details about how police were still searching dental records and Missing Persons.

I toyed with the idea of giving Helen a ring at work and pumping her for information, but decided it wasn't really in keeping with our arrangement. She usually came to me and the information she gave was generally already in the public domain, having originated with a 999 call from them. I was going to have to be patient. Instead, I opened up a new file on my computer to write up the lead on the police initiative, wondering what they were calling it this year.

The city's police force had totally given up on giving their campaigns titles that had anything to do with the crime. Instead, they picked any word from a designated 'letter of the month'. The way it worked, according to Helen, was that the letter of the month was set nationally. The only rules were that the word couldn't be in use by any other force. It helped avoid confusion, apparently. Last year's car crime campaign had been the completely irrelevant Operation Opera. I had been disappointed that there was no Operation Orgasm, though I had high hopes that they were saving it for a special campaign to clear the streets of kerb-crawlers.

Halfway through reading the press release, I noticed a few nonsensical quotes and a lack of statistics to back them up, and decided it could wait. Instead, I wandered over to where the Health Reporter usually sat and filched his copy of *Black's Medical Dictionary*. I didn't really know what I was looking for so I started to flick through it – a dangerous thing to do with a book that details every disease and ailment known to man.

After ten minutes I was no closer to unravelling the mysteries of the research paper, but was one symptom away from meningitis. I had no idea there were so many things that you could die from. Deciding ignorance was bliss, I closed the book quickly before I could read just exactly how the Ebola virus liquefies your organs and bleeds you to death.

Back to the pile of press releases on my desk, and a return call from the police press officer. "We can't find you any victims, but we do have an officer willing to talk to you about last year's successful campaign," she paused as she looked at her notes. "His name is DC Tom Llewelyn." I closed my eyes and let out a whoosh of air as she read out his extension number.

"Obviously he was in uniform then – detectives are far too precious for these sorts of campaigns," she laughed.

I put down the phone, pondering how it was that I had never heard of this Tom Llewelyn in four months of working at the *Post*, yet suddenly he seemed to be the only policeman working in Leicester.

I was saved from having to ring him by the return of Nina, who rushed into the newsroom hot from a press conference and breathlessly related how she had just fallen in love at first sight. I had only known Nina for the four months I had been working at the paper, but she had declared herself to be in love on five separate occasions during that time. She lived her life like a soap opera and wasn't happy unless the ratings were high.

Despite her taste for melodrama, she had been the first person in the office to invite me to the pub after work when I started and wasn't without a sense of humour. Stuck to her computer was a collection of bizarre bylines in which her surname Koslowski had been spelt incorrectly by illiterate sub-editors, including one that had earned her the nickname Coleslaw.

Today she was in full flow. "Caitlin, darling, he was the most divine thing I'd ever seen." She sat down at her desk and shrugged out of her trademark leather coat.

"Who? What?" I looked at her uncomprehendingly.

"This man I just met, he was gorgeous." She lengthened the last word until it became a sigh.

Realising it was going to take some time before she collected herself, I steeled myself to ring Llewelyn's extension and got his answering machine.

"Hi," I mumbled after a computer voice with a mid-Atlantic accent informed me he wasn't there. "I'm calling from the *Leicestershire Post*. The police press office suggested giving you a call about a story I'm doing on car crime. I understand you led last year's Operation Orgasm," I stopped. Shit, did I just say orgasm? I quickly righted myself and left my direct line, banging my head on my desk as I put the phone down. Why did I say orgasm instead of opera? A little voice inside me was telling me it was a Freudian slip. I preferred to think it was because I was a moron. At least I hadn't left my name. For all he knew there could be dozens of female reporters working at the *Post* who were stupid enough to leave that message.

Picking my head back up off the desk, I noticed a photograph had been stuck between the keys of my computer keyboard, featuring me looking lightly wind- and rain-swept, talking to DC Llewelyn who was smiling down at me, his looks unaffected by the weather. It was taken at yesterday's press conference. Cursing Sally, I threw it to one side and answered my ringing phone.

"Newsroom," I said distractedly.

"This is DC Llewelyn. I got a message to call someone about Operation Opera." He enunciated the last word carefully.

My heart skipped a beat at the sound of his voice. "That was me," I said, not revealing my name. He didn't ask for it.

With a minimum of prompting, he took me through the details of last year's car crime crackdown, reeling off the facts and figures that had been missing from the badly-written press release.

"We recognise that car crime is something that people worry about," he continued. "Like most crimes, the fear of it is much greater than the actual risk. We wanted car owners to take control by taking more precautions; you know, locking doors, crook locks, keeping personal belongings out of sight," he went on to list them as I scribbled.

"It's not rocket science, but it seemed to work and cut down thefts by about 20 per cent – that's around 300 fewer car stereos being sold in the pubs of Leicester."

"Right. That's great, thanks." I was determined not to push my luck in case he recognised my voice and asked me any awkward questions.

"You're welcome, Caitlin." Shit. He was onto me. I laughed nervously, acknowledging I'd been had and waited for him to say something more but he put the phone down.

By the time I had written in his quotes and sent my story across to the newsdesk, Nina had disappeared off on another story, so I had missed her latest tale of true love. But it was a postponement rather than an escape; we had arranged to go to the pub after work so I knew it wouldn't be long before I was fully briefed.

She arrived back just before 4pm and quickly wrote up her story for the next day as I sat and read it over her shoulder. She had been busy.

*'The body of a man found after a blaze in a derelict building at the weekend has been identified as James Anthony Scott, aged 62, of Manor Street, Bankborough.*

*His badly burned body was found by police early on Sunday morning after firefighters noticed a strange smell as they damped down the former Fifen headquarters on the Branton Industrial Estate.*

*The fire, thought to have been started deliberately, broke out just after 8pm on Saturday night and more than 60 firefighters tackled the blaze for two hours before bringing it under control after 10pm.*

*It wasn't until hours later that firefighters recognised the smell of charred flesh and called police, who discovered the body just after midnight.*

*A post mortem examination carried out on Monday was unable to determine the cause of death, and police checked dental records to uncover the man's identity.*

*Insp Clive Barker, who has been leading the investigation, said that murder had not been ruled out.*

*He told the Post: "As of yet we have no idea what Mr Scott was doing at the building and have been unable to establish how he died. It may have been a prank that went horribly wrong, at the moment we just don't know."*

*Police are now keen to uncover what Mr Scott was doing at the building on Saturday and have urged anyone who was in the area to contact them on 424242.'*

Nina finished the story with a flourish and did a quick spell-check before sending the story to the newsdesk. I wondered what the odds were that Nina's Mr Scott was going to turn out to be my Mr Smith.

"Any photos of him?" I asked Nina, trying to sound casually interested.

"They're sending some through later tonight, that's why I didn't put a description in the story. The late duty reporter is going to have to do a death knock. Rachel is going to be pissed she missed this one," she laughed at her unintentional pun, "Ready for the pub?"

I nodded and wandered around to my desk, switched off the computer and gathered up my belongings. I didn't really feel like going out, but brooding at home didn't hold much appeal either.

Nina followed me around to my desk and gasped as she took in the picture lying next to my computer. "Llewelyn!" she yelled.

I blushed. "Huh?" I asked, following her eyes and rushing to pick up the photograph before her.

She got there first, "Cat, this is who I was talking about earlier! Tom Llewelyn. He is so fit."

She held the photograph to her heart and swooned like a B-movie romantic heroine.

I snatched it back, shoved it in my rucksack, and headed for the lifts. "Coming?"

Five minutes later we were comfortably ensconced on a squashy red velvet sofa in our local, the Rainbow Bar, with two vodka and tonics sweating on the glass table in front of us.

"When did you meet the stud muffin?" Nina asked, flicking back her glossy hair, aware she had already drawn interested looks from two tired-looking men in suits hunched over bottles of Czech lager. Her idea of feminism was to treat men like pretty decorations rather than real people. Apparently she felt they had it coming after doing it to women for so long. She got away with it because of her looks, but the irony was lost on her. I wondered how far she would get with it if she looked more like Bella Emberg.

"At the press conference on Monday morning."

"Why didn't you say anything?"

"He's just a copper." I took a slug of my drink.

Nina snorted. "Cat, that man is not 'just' anything. I chatted to him at the police station this morning at the press conference."

Nina proceeded to relay their entire conversation and attempted to get me to join in dissecting it to uncover any hidden come-ons.

"Nina, I think it's fair to say when a bloke says 'see you around' he is merely being polite and not asking you where he might bump into you of an evening," I told her when she asked me whether I thought he fancied her.

She frowned thoughtfully and took a slug of her drink, "Mmmm, you may be right, but just think what I could do to improve police relations with the *Post*." She giggled.

Within half an hour the pub had filled up with subs and reporters from the *Post* and I was forced to listen to Nina recount her tale several times to other reporters while I quietly reflected on my day. I had spoken to Eddie from the university during the afternoon and he had arranged for me to meet with a Professor Vincent Johanson on Thursday morning to discuss chemistry. Pleading a doctor's appointment, I had talked Tony into changing my day off. I needed to decide what I wanted from this professor and whether to show him the file.

My reverie was interrupted by the arrival of Edward, who walked over to the table carrying what looked like a vodka martini in one hand and a silver-topped cane in the other. "Dear boys and girls, I have missed you all," he said dramatically as everyone stopped talking and turned around. Happy that his entrance had produced the wished-for effect, he sat down on my side of the sofa and leaned forward, "And you, dear girl, how marvellous for you, a front page story. I should buy you a drink to celebrate, but I have my pension to think about."

I took the hint and stood up. "Allow me to get one for you, to welcome you back."

"You're very kind," he smiled at me, all suave charm. "They know what I'm drinking. Ah, to be a reporter in the first flush of youth." He sighed.

I walked over to the bar, wondering if anyone else realised that Noel Coward was alive and well and living in Leicester.

# CHAPTER 10

Waking up in the dark, I sensed something was wrong. My body clock was telling me something my alarm clock hadn't. I was late.

The quick drink after work the night before had gone on longer than planned and I had forgotten to set my alarm when I had finally stumbled home at eleven. I blinked and tried to clear my head with a shake and then winced, wishing that I hadn't. My head was pounding steadily to remind me of the evils of alcohol. I eased myself into sitting position and turned on my bedroom light, feeling for my alarm clock, which read 7am. I decided on a quick bath for medicinal purposes, making a coffee while I waited for it to fill up.

Dragging myself out of the bath after what felt like five seconds, I went into my bedroom to dress. Kneeling down, I felt under my bed for my black bootleg trousers, which I had last seen on Friday. Henry, however, had other ideas and jumped from the bed onto my back and purred into my neck, ready to play. Grabbing hold of something material, I carefully reversed and threw the trousers on my bed, turning around to grab Henry and losing the towel wrapped around me in the process. Deciding Henry was too young to notice, I wandered naked into the kitchen to get my coffee, crouching below the window. I sorted Henry out with his breakfast and gazed blearily into the darkness outside.

I screamed and grabbed a nearby tea towel as a face at the window came into focus. I ran from the kitchen, dressed within seconds, and raced back to the kitchen with my glasses. Henry, unaware that anything was wrong, nonchalantly continued his way through his food as I peered cautiously through the kitchen window. It was now growing lighter but, despite my efforts, I failed to see anything. Glancing at my watch, I realised I was too late to investigate further and grabbed my coat, scarf and gloves.

I stepped out into the morning and paused to look up and down the street as the wind whipped around me. Down at the bottom of the street was a Catholic church. Built in the 1960s, it had rejected the more traditional spires for a squat concrete cross. Its Sunday morning congregation was tiny compared to the number of people who attended its Tuesday night soup kitchen where the city's friendly, but often quite rowdy, homeless gathered for a square meal and a chance to see a GP who volunteered there. Sometimes a few were still sleeping off their meal in the street the next morning, although they had never been into our garden before, plumping instead for the cosier confines offered by the doorways of the solicitors' and accountants' offices across the street.

This morning the street was quiet, with no evidence of the previous night's soup kitchen. I started a brisk walk into the city centre to work. On my way, I tried to put together a photofit of the face at the window but without much luck; without my glasses I had only really seen a blurred outline.

Had I imagined it? I looked into the dark shop windows as I passed and my worried face stared back at me. Had I just seen my reflection? Maybe someone had slipped a tipple of absinthe into my drink last night and now I was hallucinating. I shook my head gently. I was going mad. First I was thinking I'd stumbled onto some sort of conspiracy, which no one else seemed to know about, and next I was seeing faces at my window. I was obviously turning into one of those paranoid old women that are convinced men are after them.

The newsdesk diary was crammed with memos and it took a while to find my name in it, next to the words every junior reporter dreads: 'death knock'. My heart pounded at the thought of cold-calling a grieving family and asking them questions about their dearly departed. It pounded even harder when I saw it was the family of James Scott, the arson victim.

Edward, who sat sipping bone china-encased Earl Grey tea at his desk, said he wished he could do his first one again. "You'll never forget it," he said.

Cue story.

"My first one, a young suicide – and that was in the days when it was illegal – called Aiden Martingale. He had tied a rope around a beam in his attic and jumped off a dining room chair. An antique, if I remember. Dreadful business. His mother gave me four cups of tea and she had a lovely home-made cake," he paused and looked skyward. "Almond, I believe. I was there so long they sent a copy boy out to see if they had blacked my eye. That didn't happen until my fifth death knock. The brute knocked out two teeth – how was I to know his wife had been having an affair – mind you, it came as no surprise when he turned out to be the one who had done it."

With these cheery thoughts I set off and half an hour later I was standing in a pension-day line at a Post Office on Manor Street. I was the youngest person in the queue by a good half century. The old women looked in no hurry to get served and were busily exchanging gossip with each other. Their conversation consisted mostly of who had died, who was currently in hospital, and who was looking ill the last time they saw them. I thought fleetingly of my mother and wondered if this was what I had to look forward to as I grew older - an unnatural obsession with death, along with facial hair and stretch marks.

Given their favourite topic, it didn't take long for them to get around to their recently departed neighbour.

"Dreadful business," one was telling the others. "They say he was burned beyond all recognition." Her audience shuddered with horror, although desperate to hear more.

"Well I heard he'd had his teeth removed to prevent identification," another said, claiming she had the inside track as her son's next-door-neighbour was a traffic warden who knew the firefighter who had found the body.

I considered asking them for his address, but fear over the onslaught of questions I might face if I explained why I wanted it kept my tongue still and my eyes firmly on the floor. Instead I waited for the queue to go down and got to the front, press card in hand, to ask the counter worker if she knew where Mr Scott had lived. It was standard practice for the police to give out a road name but no house number, so it was a question of checking the phone book or electoral register in the office for a house number. If that failed, and all too often it did, it was a question of getting out there and knocking on doors until you got the right one. That was all very well, but having driven up and down the length of Manor Street, unless I got very lucky I was going to be there all day.

At that moment, the sight of the familiar red-and-yellow livery of the Post Office was a godsend. What could be easier than popping in, buying a lottery ticket and asking for an address?

The woman behind the counter frowned for a minute and then grabbed a big book. Turning to the right page, she silently pointed to the name Scott and the full address next to it. I nodded my thanks and left the shop, writing down the number 116 on the corner of my pad.

During Edward's pep talk back at the office, he claimed people often want to talk to the press about their dear departed – that was why the death notices were so popular, he said. At least this way they didn't have to pay and they got more than a naff four-line poem under a surname.

I hadn't really believed him at the time, but sitting ensconced on a chintzy sofa with a cup of tea in my hand an hour later, I realised he was right. I had also discovered that Mr Scott was definitely Mr Smith.

Having rung the bell at number 116, a white-haired woman in her 60s had come to the door. Despite it being only just after 9am, she looked like she had been up for hours. Mrs Scott was only too happy to talk to me about her husband. She led me into her home, made me tea and settled a plate of biscuits in front of me before thanking me for my time.

It was then, sat on the sofa, teacup in hand, that I had looked up at a wall of framed family photographs where Mr Smith smiled out at me over and over again from a variety of locations.

I gathered the necessary information quite quickly. The couple had been married for 35 years, had no children, and had lived in the city for most of their lives. Mr Scott had been a keen gardener and had worked for the same company all his life as a laboratory technician.

I hardly needed to ask her where but she told me anyway.

"My husband started working at Fifen after his national service and stayed with them. He got his 30 years' service medal recently and was looking forward to retiring. He loved working there, he said they had some smart people who would be able to cure cancer, given a few more years." She smiled and proffered the plate of biscuits at me again.

The official biography completed, I put down my pen and pad.

"I'm so sorry, Mrs Scott," I began, "Have the police told you anything about what happened?"

She took a sip of tea, "Only that he was found in the old Fifen building, not far from his old laboratory, actually." Her voice wobbled and she paused to pull herself together. "It was on the first floor near the back. I remember going there for the company's open days in the past. It's not as grand as the new building, but it was lovely, very posh."

I let her ramble before bringing her back to the question. "Did you know he was going there on the night he died?"

"No. He had been having trouble settling over the last few months, something on his mind. He didn't want to tell me about it. I thought he was worried about retiring, you know, having nothing to do. I think he loved being in the cut and thrust of medical breakthroughs – kept him young, he used to say.

"It's so different from our day, two of my sisters died before they were ten from bad chest infections, but now you've got all these treatments on offer and all free." She stopped abruptly, aware that she was falling into clichés of how the young had it so easy nowadays.

I swallowed the last of my tea. "He didn't tell you anything?"

"No, apart from his retirement, I can't think what else it could have been. He loved that job. He's got a study upstairs and everything, he used to get all the medical journals and was even on the Internet – imagine that - a man his age using that. He showed me once, but I couldn't work it, I told him it was for the young, all this technology, but he just laughed at me."

I took a deep breath. I wasn't going to get anything more out of her, but it would be nice to get into his study and see what was there that would tie him to the research paper he had given me. Maybe I could come back.

I stayed and chatted for a few minutes, refused more tea, and left with her thanks ringing in my ears and an envelope of pictures of her husband warm in my pocket. I had told her I would bring the photographs back to her personally as soon as we had finished with them. It was partly to be nice - at the *Post* borrowed photographs had a habit of going missing and it was always the precious, irreplaceable ones that couldn't be found. It also gave me the excuse to go back and talk to her if I needed to.

The story wasn't going in the paper until the next day, so I sat in my car and lit up a cigarette, daydreaming about the story I was going to break and how I was going to get justice for Mrs Scott.

Throwing the butt out of the window a few minutes later, I was snapped out of my reverie by a tap on the passenger window. Looking up, I saw DC Llewelyn peering in. I hadn't noticed him pulling up behind me in his car. Presumably he had come to talk to Mrs Scott again. Either that or he was following me. I shuddered slightly at the thought.

He opened the door and curled his long frame into my passenger seat.

"It's dangerous to sit in a car on your own with the doors unlocked, anyone could just get in," he said.

I gave him a withering look, suggesting they just had, but as I turned I caught a whiff of *Givenchy for Men* – my all-time favourite smell.

"Well?" I said defensively, refusing to let the scent have its usual effect on me. "I do have a right to be here. My editor sent me out on a death knock." I shut my mouth quickly before I said anything else stupid, maybe Jen was right about criminals who talk too much.

He smiled and the humour hit his eyes. He really did have a very nice smile. His teeth were white and even and when his lips curled up he had a very slight dimple in his right cheek.

"I thought, seeing as you were here, you might appreciate a debrief."

I resisted the urge to giggle at the unintended double meaning and dragged my eyes away from his mouth. "I need my pad." I leant down between his legs and grabbed my black rucksack, rummaged in it for my pad and then looked for a pen. Too late, I realised the photograph Sally had taken of me talking to him on Monday morning had floated out of the mess and landed picture-side-up on the handbrake between us.

"Autograph it for me?" I joked quickly before he could say anything.

He picked it up and frowned before handing it back without comment. Pen and pad finally in hand, I shoved my bag back on the floor and waited. I hoped the information he had was going to be worth the humiliation.

"He died from a blow to the back of the head."

I replied with an involuntary sound at the back of my throat, half gasp, half gurgle.

He ignored it. "Blow to the back of the head, blunt instrument, haven't found the weapon yet."

I cleared my throat. "How did you find out?"

"Post mortem. Compressions on the back of the skull."

Yuck. I scribbled down in shorthand what he had told me and waited, pen poised, to see if there would be more.

"So does this mean it's a murder inquiry?"

"Not officially, but it's highly unlikely he wandered in there, accidentally hit his head and knocked himself out just minutes before a fire broke out."

"He worked for them, you know."

He looked up at me sharply. "Who?"

"Mr Scott worked for Fifen, the building is owned by them."

"How d'you know that?"

"His wife told me."

He shrugged. "Well that's all I can tell you at the moment."

"Why?"

"Why what?"

"Why are you telling me?"

He sighed. "I don't know." Opening the door, he climbed out of my car. "Well, I've got to go and tell Mrs Scott her husband was probably murdered," he paused and turned to look at me. "That's off the record by the way." He pressed his card into my hand. "Keep out of trouble."

I watched him walk down the path to Mrs Scott's house. When he had gone I peered into my rear view mirror and cursed. My hair was a mess and I had a big glob of sleep in my right eye. Not that it mattered, I told myself sternly. There was nothing going on and even if there was, every time we met my overwhelming response was one of terror – hardly a solid foundation for a relationship.

# CHAPTER 11

It was after eleven by the time I got back to the *Post*. On the newsdesk Tony paused long enough to flick through the envelope of photographs while I went through a few details of the obit. Without a 'well done' or a 'thank you', he chose a couple of good pictures and sent me over to the Picture Editor who would scan them in and make a final decision on which one to use later in the day.

"Tony, I bumped into a copper while I was there, he confirmed a cause of death on Scott," I said before I left.

He turned back to his screen, unimpressed. "Yeah we know, press release came through ten minutes ago, Edward's doing it. Still aren't calling it murder though."

Turning red, I walked back to my desk, cursing Tom Llewelyn with every step. He had made it sound like he was confiding in me, but it was common bloody knowledge. Arsehole.

Edward turned to me, "I don't normally do anything from a press release," he said, disdainfully holding up a fax between his thumb and forefinger. "But this rather piqued my interest."

I finished off the obituary on Scott in record time. By then Edward had completed his story and gone off to meet a contact, or in his case probably his stockbroker. I grabbed a couple of coffees and dropped one on the desk of my favourite sub-editor Annie, reading Edward's story over her shoulder while she tinkered with a headline and checked the copy for errors. My obituary was going below his story as background.

"You won't believe this." She started laughing.

"What?" I peered closer at her screen.

"This cop they are quoting is called Rupert. I bet he was bullied at school."

I grabbed the press release from Edward's desk and skimmed it to the end. She was right. The last paragraph was an appeal for witnesses to the incident from a Detective Constable Rupert Llewelyn.

His warrant card swam into view and I remembered the mysterious R in front of his name. I giggled as the warm flow of vindictive blood travelled through my veins - finally a chink in his armour. I rummaged in my bag for the card he had given me an hour earlier and dialled the direct line on it.

He answered it within three rings.

"Can I speak to DC Rupert Llewelyn?" I asked innocently.

There was a brief silence on the other end of the phone. "Sorry?"

"I said can I speak to DC Rupert Llewelyn," I dragged out the first syllable of his first name.

"This is Tom Llewelyn speaking."

"Tom? I'm sorry, I must have the wrong number."

There was a pause.

"No, my first name is Rupert, but I use my second, which is Tom. How can I help?"

"This is Caitlin McCall from the *Post*. We met this morning."

"Ms McCall, what can I do for you?"

"I was just checking the facts on a press release we've had through this morning on the Scott enquiry and it quoted your name as Rupert. As you know we like to get our facts straight and I just wanted to check which name we were supposed to put in the paper." I fought laughter as Annie listened with a wide smile.

There was a sigh at the other end of the phone, "I suppose that makes us one-all, Caitlin."

I banged the phone down and through my giggles explained to Annie what had happened that morning.

"Wanker," was her response. Turning back to her computer, she hit a few buttons and a photograph of Mr Scott appeared. It was a relaxed picture of him sitting laughing with a young woman in her twenties.

"Actually, while you are here, you can help me. They decided to use this picture of him with his daughter, but we don't have her name," she tapped the picture on the screen with a long gold fingernail.

"He doesn't have a daughter," I peered at the screen. The young woman had dark, curly hair and a pretty smile.

Annie looked up from her screen. "No? Good job you came over. The caption says it is his daughter. Bloody picture desk. We'll need to use another photo." She stood up.

"I can ring his widow and get her name?"

"No, if she's not related we shouldn't use it. They must have one of him with his wife." She disappeared to sort out another picture and I wandered back to my desk.

It wasn't until I got home that I remembered the face at the window. During the day I had managed to shrug it off as a hangover-related hallucination but going outside to clean Henry's litter tray, I took a look around the garden and checked the back gate – the only way into the garden except through the house. It was firmly locked. Everything in order, I returned to my kitchen and stood there. Dusk was quickly turning to darkness and, switching on the kitchen light, I realised the only face I could have seen was my own. It was the only explanation I could come up with and it was better then any of the alternatives lurking in the back of my mind.

The steady and mildly irritating noise permeating through my ceiling signified that Helen was home and listening to music. Over the months I had got used to the sound and usually managed to block it out. At times it was reassuring to know that there was someone else close by. Living alone could have its downside, especially when I woke up in the middle of the night, heart pounding for no reason, half expecting an axe-wielding madman to crash his way into my flat - not that I would ever admit it out loud.

I made two cups of coffee and went upstairs. It took a few knocks to rouse Helen out of her dance-trance stupor to answer my banging, but she smiled widely at the coffee cup and beckoned me inside. Although one-bedroomed, her flat was larger than mine, with a huge living room that had a wooden floor which occasionally doubled as her dance floor. It was furnished with beanbags and floor cushions and painted a migraine-inducing shade of cerise. Her kitchen was attached to a fire escape that she used to dry clothes and grow a weedy-looking cannabis plant. "You really need to use halogen lights to get them growing properly," she had once explained to me, "but the police have tracked growers down in the past through the size of their electricity bill. To grow it properly around here, your bills would be bigger than Heathrow Airport's."

After that it had come as a surprise to find that she worked for the police as a call handler. Although she would tip me off to things going on in the city, she was careful never to tell me anything that couldn't be traced to a phone call from a concerned member of the public. She had her own, if slightly complex, morality when it came to informing the public on police activity. Not to mention drugs.

"I'm glad you stopped by," she told me, walking into her lounge and dropping onto a faux suede beanbag positioned by a serious-looking sound system, which she leaned over and turned off in my honour.

"Yeah?" I asked, wondering if she was going to tell me it had been her face at the window.

"I have some top gear at the moment and I think it would chill you out nicely."

I slumped onto an orange tasselled floor cushion opposite her and pulled out my cigarettes instead. "Hmmm. Nice as that offer is, I think I need my wits about me at the moment."

"Why?" Helen wasn't used to being knocked back.

I explained about the face at the window and asked if she had seen anything dodgy recently or anyone hanging around.

"Apart from Ian, you mean?" Although in his twenties, Ian spent his Sundays building furniture and sprouted the kind of facial hair normally associated with men twice his age who spent their weekends rambling in the countryside and writing down train numbers. I had spoken to him briefly when I moved in and he had eagerly invited me to dinner, boasting of his skills with a tin opener. I had declined and avoided him ever since. Weeks later, I discovered he had asked out practically every woman in our street at some time or other, including Helen - who had actually gone but refused to reveal any details about their one hot date.

"You know him better than me," I told her, hiding a smirk, "Did he strike you as that kind of man when you went out?"

She shook her head, refusing to be drawn on the subject.

Instead we went through the other occupants of the house, looking for likely suspects, but apart from Ian and the amorous couple downstairs, they were all students and I didn't think they would have been up at that time.

Helen offered to ask around at work about any reports of weirdos in the area. She was pretty sure there had been no new escapees from the nearby secure hospital who could now be camping out in our garden shed.

I thanked her and moved on to my second reason for the social call. "Have you ever met a DC Tom Llewelyn?" I tried to sound casual.

"Doesn't ring a bell," Helen took a long draw on her joint. "This wouldn't have anything to do with your visitor early Sunday morning?"

I paused before nodding.

"I was just getting in from a club and I saw him at your door. Always tell a cop, something about the way they stand. Is he going to be a regular caller?"

That all depended. "He came around to see me about that fire on the industrial estate," I said, ignoring the question. "I was driving around the area just before it broke out."

She let it go and we chatted for a few more minutes before I headed for home, enjoying the buzz from her secondary smoke.

Back in my flat, I resolved to buy a blind for the kitchen – just to be on the safe side. I headed for the fridge. Henry meowed furiously at my feet and I realised I wasn't the only one who hadn't eaten since breakfast. I felt guilty and cursed Jen for giving me a pet when I was so obviously incapable of looking after myself. I gave Henry double-helpings in the hope he would forgive me, and turned my attentions to my own pressing need for food.

The salad I had bought with good intentions on Friday sat inevitably untouched in the bottom of my fridge and was starting to go brown and sludgy in its unopened bag. I threw it all out and settled for yoghurt and a glass of orange juice instead.

Sitting cross-legged on the floor by my radiator in the lounge, I reviewed my agenda for the next day. As well as keeping my appointment with Professor Johanson at the university, I wanted to revisit Mrs Scott and get a look at her husband's study.

My plans made, I surveyed the walls of the lounge. The paint had dried evenly, but jagged-edged where the roller had stopped. Absent-mindedly, I picked up a two-inch paintbrush and dipped it into the tin of paint still sitting by the door. I went off to change into old clothes and had just picked up the paintbrush again when the doorbell rang.

Opening the door and brandishing the paintbrush like a weapon, I peered out to see Tom Llewelyn standing in my doorway. I heard Helen's door open upstairs and could feel her peering over the balcony. That was all I needed, we'd be a hot item by her tea break tomorrow.

"Hello." He looked worriedly at the paintbrush.

I waved him in, splattering terracotta paint on the hall walls as I did so but thankfully missing his suit. He followed me into the lounge where Henry was spread out on my futon. Llewelyn smiled at the cat and perched on the edge of the chair. Henry ignored him. I put the paintbrush down and sat on the floor opposite him cross-legged, aware of my scruffy clothes.

"Sorry, am I disturbing you?" He gestured to the walls, "Nice colour."

"Thanks." Begrudgingly, I got up. "Can I offer you a drink? Tea? Coffee? A beer?"

"Beer would be great."

"Not on duty?" I asked, getting up and going into the kitchen.

"No." He called through.

I handed him a bottle and returned to my earlier position on the floor, waiting for him to explain his presence and squashing down a fantasy that he was preparing to make a pass at me.

"What can I do for you?" I eventually asked, taking a slurp of my orange juice.

"I wanted to talk to you about Saturday night." He reached out and gave Henry a rub on his stomach. Henry curled his paws up around his hand and purred loudly. I scowled at the cat. Creep.

"But you're not on duty," I stalled.

"This isn't official. I just wanted to check what you told me on Sunday."

"I went out for pizza, and decided to take a drive around the estate. I saw a few kids hanging around, smoking and drinking." I stopped, feeling like a snitch.

"What time were you there?"

"About sevenish." I said, deciding it was best to keep it vague.

"How long for?"

"Dunno, about twenty minutes or so. Long enough for the pizza to be ready when I collected it."

Llewelyn nodded and chugged on his beer. Henry sat up and began to prowl around the futon, climbing onto the policeman's lap and leaving a trail of bright ginger cat hairs on his black trousers. Llewelyn didn't seem to mind.

"Caitlin," he began. Before he got any further, my buzzer sounded. I got up and ran out into the hall to answer the door. I wasn't too surprised to see Jen standing in the doorway. I sighed.

"Are you going to let me in then? It's freezing out here."

I motioned for her to pass me before I realised she had started talking about Mr Smith. I went to grab her as she went through my flat door, but missed and could only follow her into the lounge, praying she didn't say anything too stupid.

"So what's happening? Any word from Mr Smith or has he been barbecued?" She stopped as she saw Llewelyn sitting on my futon, playing with Henry. She turned and looked at me, "Am I interrupting something?"

Llewelyn stood up – every bit the gentleman – and offered his hand to Jen, "Tom Llewelyn, nice to meet you."

I scowled at him as Jen took the proffered hand and gave him her sexiest smile. "Nice to meet you, Tom. I'm Jen, Cat's best friend. I thought I would drop in on her as a surprise, but I can see she's the one who's full of surprises." Her twinkling eyes slid around to meet mine.

"Jen, Detective Constable Llewelyn stopped by to ask me some questions about Saturday night, you know when I went out for pizza." I emphasised his police title, hoping Jen would heed the warning.

She ignored me. "So, Tom, you're interested in Cat's movements, are you? You'll have to be pretty quick to keep up with her." She smirked at him and picked Henry up from the futon before sitting down and dumping him on her lap.

"I'm beginning to realise that," he told her, standing up. "Thanks for your time. And the beer." He smiled politely at me and walked towards the door. I followed, to see him out. He paused before opening the front door of the building and half turned around, realising he was still holding the beer bottle.

"Best not drink and drive," I said, taking it out of his hands. I watched him walk out to his car, get in and drive off.

I could hear Jen laughing as she stared out of the window. Turning round as I entered the room, she stood up and ran over to me. "He was gorgeous! Where did you find him?"

What was wrong with everyone? First Sally, then Nina, and now Jen bewitched by him – even Henry had succumbed. He was just a man, for God's sake.

"I told you about him, he's the cop who's been hassling me. Anyway, what are you doing here?"

"I thought I would come anyway – if I waited for an invitation..." she trailed off. She had made her point.

"Humph," I muttered stomping off to the kitchen to get her a drink.

"So what was he doing here and why was he drinking your

beer?" Jen asked as I handed her a bottle.

"I don't know, he turned up about ten minutes before you did, played with my cat, drank my beer, told me he was off duty and asked me more about what I was doing on Saturday night." I slumped onto the futon.

"Ooooh, I wish I had him hot on my tail, what a sexy smile. And did you see his eyes? Mmmm, what I wouldn't give to wake up to those in the morning." Jen swooned. She had obviously been at the romantic fiction shelf in the bookshop again.

Ignoring her, I got up and switched the TV on, tuned into a soap opera and turned up the sound. She grabbed the remote control and switched it off. "Okay, I get the hint. You don't want to talk about him. But I tell you one thing - if he was after me, I wouldn't be sitting here watching *Eastenders* right now."

Hiding behind the sofa would be a better idea.

"Jen, he is not after me like that, he's more likely to want me locked up." I snapped.

Jen put her arm around me, realising how badly I was rattled for the first time. "Cat, chill out. You haven't done anything wrong. Anyway, if you are so worried about getting into trouble, why don't you tell him what happened and hand over the file?"

I shrugged. Jen wouldn't understand that if I did that, I would never get to the bottom of it and I wouldn't have a story. Some journalist. She eventually dropped the subject and offered to help me finish painting the room.

We fell into bed well after midnight and Jen lay looking through the file from Mr Smith – or Mr Scott as we now knew him.

"Well, it doesn't mean anything to me," she said after flicking through it for five minutes.

I rolled onto my stomach. "I've got an appointment with a professor at the university tomorrow afternoon who's going to take a look at it for me. Maybe he can shed some light on it."

Jen sat up, pulled her hair off her face and reached for the glass of water on her side of the bed. "What are you going to do about Llewelyn?"

"What do you mean? Nothing. Did I tell you his first name is really Rupert?"

She choked on her water, coughed and started laughing before humming the theme tune of his famous bear namesake. "I think you should talk to him," she said, breaking off and suddenly serious. "I'm sure he would help."

"Yeah, after he locked me up for withholding evidence," I said.

"Anyway, how about a shopping trip tomorrow morning, to take your mind off it?" she asked. "I mean, if you are going to have a bloke that good looking hot on your heels, you've got to make sure you're looking your best."

I scowled at her and turned out my bedside lamp.

"I'll take that as a yes," she whispered into the darkness.

# CHAPTER 12

I slept through until my alarm went off at nine the following morning. Jen was already up and about, prowling around the kitchen for breakfast. I wandered through and watched her make coffee and toast. She pointed to a stack of brown envelopes. "I got your post for you."

I looked at it without enthusiasm. "Thanks." I knew without looking that it would only be bills.

"And I met your neighbour." She set toast and coffee out in front of me and I picked up the peanut butter.

"Who?"

"Ian, is it?" She frowned. "Big beard. A bit weird."

I nodded and laughed. The first time I had met him, he was in a bright green shell suit and I was wearing a t-shirt and my bed socks.

"Yeah, watch yourself - he's on the prowl for a girlfriend."

"Happy hunting." She raised her mug in a toast to the futility of his exercise.

I carried myself and a cup of coffee off to the bedroom and dressed in a long black dress, my knee-high black boots and long blue leather coat, bought secondhand from Birmingham's old rag market. Jen threw on jeans and cowboy boots along with a baby pink cowl-necked sweater stolen out of my wardrobe. By the time she was ready, it was after ten.

Although it was only March and Easter was weeks away, the summer fashions had begun to appear, making the leftover winter stock hanging limply from sale rails look even more dejected. The rejected sale clothes looked like they had been picked over by thousands of pairs of hands before being tossed aside as the wrong size, wrong colour, wrong shape, or just plain ugly. I knew how they felt - although in my case it wasn't thousands of pairs of hands; not quite, anyway.

Within half an hour we were in the changing rooms of Topshop. Jen was struggling to get into a strappy pink dress, while I was admiring myself in a slinky black number she had convinced me to try on. Getting the dress over her head, and smoothing down the skirt, Jen turned to look at me, her face pink from the exertion and clashing with the dress and her hair.

"Wow! You have to get it." Her face broke into a wide grin.

"You think?" I turned away from the mirror to see that all-important rear view. It was a great dress, stopping six inches above my knee and skimming my frame. Long sleeved, it was split from shoulder to wrist and cut low at the back. I grabbed my bra straps and pushed my bust up and out. It would definitely need my Wonderbra.

Jen went back to her own dress, posed in front of the mirror, drew her red curls up away from her face and sucked in her cheeks, "Definitely a fuck-me dress." She was looking at my reflection in the mirror. I wasn't sure if she meant mine or hers. I turned around to take the dress off, my resolve weakening, I had nowhere to wear a dress like that.

Sensing my change of heart, Jen crawled out of her dress. "If you will, I will," she said. "And you know I need it more than you do. I need something to light Steve's fire after all this time."

I looked at her choice: a floaty bias-cut summer dress with spaghetti straps that lay in soft folds over her flat chest but clung flatteringly tight to her taut stomach. I looked down at my more rounded belly and pulled it in, feeling jealous. If Jen swallowed a sugar lump you would be able to see it. I consoled myself in the knowledge that her dress was totally unwearable for at least another three months and pulled my clothes back on. "Alright."

By the time we left the shop, Jen had talked me into new shoes as well. She had gone for four-inch high strappy numbers that pushed her over six feet tall, while I had insisted on something that I wouldn't break my neck in - black with straps that crossed at my ankles and two-inch block heels. I was still short, but at least I could walk.

I made us salad for lunch in honour of our new dresses, before Jen rushed off home to try out her new look on Steve. I pushed mine to the back of my wardrobe where it would no doubt stay until it was out of fashion.


Professor Johanson was based in the Quad – a square on the campus of the University of the East Midlands at the top of the city's only hill. It featured four identical 1960s concrete towers with a grassy square between them where the architect must have imagined the students would lie around and discuss Albert Camus and Jean Paul Sartre.

But he hadn't counted on the weather or how windy it got on

Leicester's only hill where the tower blocks stood. The area was rarely warm enough to sit outside and the winds were so bad at times that the glass doors were almost impossible to pull open. As I walked through the square, the wind whipped at my skirt, tossed through my hair and fired litter at me, but a weak sun was shining, reminding me that summer was only a few months away. I took a minute to lift my face to the sky, close my eyes, and luxuriate in the feeling of warmth on my cheeks.

All four buildings in the quad were named after local luminaries who had made the largest donations to ensure their immortality and preserve their name, but were simply known as East, South, West and North by everyone who worked there. Johanson was in the East building on the third floor. His office was a typical pokey corner room with drab décor and was just big enough to fit him, his desk, a couple of chairs and a vast array of textbooks as thick as breeze blocks which sat on shelves around his head.

Professor Johanson, however, looked anything but the typical university lecturer. Aged around 40, his blond hair was cropped close to his head to disguise a receding hairline and his suit was immaculately cut - I guessed it wouldn't have given much change from £1,000. Education must be more lucrative than I thought. I could imagine he was a big hit with his female students too – the biggest thing in chemistry since the discovery of the contraceptive pill.

He greeted me with a wide grin and moved some papers from the only other chair in his cupboard-like office. Sitting down, I smiled and began my well rehearsed patter. "Thank you for seeing me like this. I'm hoping you can help me with some files that have been sent to me. It looks like some sort of research paper." I paused and handed over the file. He opened it up and flicked through the pages. "It certainly looks like some sort of drug research, but my specialty isn't really in pharmacology. Can I ask how you got it?"

I looked at him, trying to work out if I could trust him.

By the time I had explained how the files had got into my hands - leaving out Mr Scott, his death and Flfen Pharmaceuticals - we had got through two cups of coffee each and a small packet of plain chocolate biscuits that he kept in his desk for emergencies.

Leaning back in his chair, he peered at me with piercing grey eyes. "I take it this is all extra-curricular?" he asked, referring to the press card I had shown him when I came in.

"At the moment, yes."

He flicked through the file again. "Ms McCall, this is going to take some time to go through. If you leave it with me, I will give you a call when I've got the answer you are looking for."

I sighed and tried to hide my disappointment. I suppose it was a bit much expecting him to read it like a Jamie Oliver recipe and tell me what it tasted like. I left him with the file and my phone number and walked slowly back to my car.

Half-way home, my mobile phone rang. Fumbling for it, I mumbled a greeting into the receiver.

"Caitlin, it's Nina. Nice day off?"

"Yeah, been clothes shopping."

"Good, did you buy anything for Saturday?"

Saturday? What was happening on Saturday?

"You've forgotten, haven't you?" I could hear her tapping away at her computer.

"No. What time is it?"

"It's after six, I'm on lates tonight. So did you get anything?" We were going out for her birthday. It was all coming back to me. I described the dress and shoes I had bought while she made approving noises, before musing her own possibilities. She didn't have an outfit so much as a short list. I thanked God I didn't have the wardrobe to necessitate such a hard decision.

"We're still meeting in the Rainbow Bar at eight and then the plans are to go for a curry after, or maybe clubbing."

"Okay, well, I'll see you at work tomorrow anyway."

"Mmmm, oh, the other thing before you go, your mum rang up looking for you, she sounded a bit pissed off when I told her it was your day off. Just wanted to warn you."

"Please tell me you didn't give her this number," I groaned, before answering for myself. If she had, Mum would have rung me on it by now. I ended the call and threw the phone onto the passenger seat as I pulled up outside my flat, only then noticing that I had a missed call.

"Caitlin, this is your mother," I groaned again and held it away from my ear, still able to hear her faint, slightly outraged voice. "Why didn't you tell me you had a mobile phone? Why is it switched off? Whose voice is that on the answerphone? It sounds like a man." I pressed Delete.

Inside, I lit up a cigarette and tapped in my parents' phone number on my landline. My dad picked up the phone after five rings. "Hi Dad, it's Caitlin."

"Hello. Your mother's not here, she's out shopping. Back later."

"What are you up to?" My dad, like most fathers, left communicating with his children to his wife. "I've been off today, out shopping with Jen," I told him when he made no attempt to answer me.

"Bloody dogs," he said distractedly.

"What?"

There was a long pause. "Caitlin, I've got to go. The bloody dogs next door have got out onto my lawn again."

I said goodbye to the dialling tone.

# CHAPTER 13

The face at the window on Wednesday morning had freaked me out enough that I waited until I was fully dressed before going into the kitchen the next day. Carefully opening the kitchen door, I peered out into the garden and bit back another scream. The face was there again and it definitely wasn't mine. This time he wasn't getting away. I sneaked out into the garden, stepped carefully over the stinging nettles and assorted weeds that grew like triffids around the back door, and rounded on the person still staring through my kitchen window.

Recognising the blue shell suit from behind, I shouted out his name, "Ian!"

"Arghhhhhh!" he turned round and tried to run back into the building to the safety of his flat, but I blocked the door.

"What the hell are you doing?"

He looked at me and shrugged. "I came out to put my rubbish out and thought I saw something in your kitchen."

"You did. Me," I said. "What about Wednesday morning?"

"Wednesday? What?" He tried to blag it, but a sudden red tint to his skin gave him away.

"Ian, you know exactly what I am talking about. I know it was you and if I catch you again, I'm going to call the police. There are laws against perverts like you." I stomped back into my flat before he could reply. How many times had he stood there like that? And how many times had I wandered into my kitchen half undressed and bleary-eyed to make breakfast? I shuddered, shaking the image out of my head.

"You're not much of a guard, are you?" I asked Henry as he tucked into his breakfast, unaware of the soap opera going on around him. I went back to my coffee. I was almost relieved that it was just Ian. A pathetic perv of a civil servant I could handle, but someone who might wield a blunt object at the back of my head before setting the flat on fire was another matter entirely.

A pile of press releases had been dumped on my desk. Tony had apparently decided I'd had enough excitement for one week, with an arson and possible murder enquiry. Little did he suspect I couldn't have agreed with him more. I spent the morning blitzing the pile, stopping only to ring my mother to make sure my father hadn't been carted off to an institution. She refused to discuss it over the phone. In hushed tones she made reference to an uncle on his side of the family who had not been 'all there'. I could see her tapping her temple with her index finger as she spoke. She insisted on coming to Leicester on Sunday when she would take me out to lunch and 'explain all'. I agreed unenthusiastically and told her to say hello to my father, who was apparently holding guard on the front lawn – although against what, I didn't know.

I put the phone down and mused on how long it would take Professor Johanson to come back to me. He had told me it would probably take a few days before he would be in touch. He had his own research to be getting on with. I had to be grateful that he was sparing me any time at all, but it didn't stop me getting annoyed that it was taking so long. The research paper could be the key to why Mr Scott had died.

I was pulled away from my musings by a phone conversation going on nearby. Matt was busy following up the arson inquiry and cursing the police for not returning his calls. My ears pricked up when I heard him speaking to Tom Llewelyn. It sounded like Matt was trying to get him to confirm they were now looking at a murder inquiry, but Llewelyn was stalling. After a brief exchange, Matt looked up at me and said into the phone, "She is, did you want to speak to her?"

I blushed and pretended to continue typing.

Matt shouted over to me, "I've got DC Tom Llewelyn on the phone, he wants to talk to you."

Nina watched me like a hawk as Matt transferred the call and I picked it up. "Hello?"

"Ms McCall, it's Tom Llewelyn."

"What can I do for you?" I asked as another flush of embarrassment washed over me, well aware that Nina and Matt were listening in.

"We've been speaking to some kids who were hanging around the Branton Industrial Estate who say they saw a woman talking to a man outside her green car at 7pm. I don't suppose you know anything about that, do you?"

My cheeks burned as I searched for an explanation. I didn't need one. "I suppose you got lost and just stopped to ask directions?" he said.

"That's right. I'd forgotten about that."

"Description?" he asked me.

"Erm, it was a man, about 60, tallish and local accent."

"That's it?"

"Yes." At last I could tell the truth.

"What did you talk about?"

"I asked him how to get off the estate and he told me."

"That's it?"

I paused. Someone might have seen him hand over the papers, so I decided to hedge my bets, "I got out of the car with my *A to Z* and got him to point out where I was."

It was quiet on the other end of the phone as he wrote down what I was saying. I couldn't believe I was so blatantly lying to a police officer. My mother would disown me if she ever found out.

"Okay. I'm going to need you to sign a new statement."

"You want me to come down to the station?" I asked nervously.

"I thought you would have given your eye teeth to have a look behind the scenes at King Street."

As long as it didn't include the insides of the cells. "About five?"

He paused. "You do know it's a crime to withhold evidence, don't you Ms McCall?"

I put the phone down without comment. Bloody teenagers. When I was their age I was too busy enjoying illicit activities like alcohol, fags and the opposite sex to play neighbourhood watch. What was the world coming to?

Matt and Nina sat watching me, curiosity glinting in their eyes. They weren't journalists for nothing.

"Well?" Nina finally said.

"S'nothing. I wanted to talk to him about another story," I racked my brain, "Car crime."

Matt shrugged and got back to his work, no reason to think otherwise. Nina, however, wasn't going to be that easily put off. She got up and walked around the desk. Picking up my fags and grabbing my hand, she pulled me in the direction of the lifts. "Let's go and have a coffee break – my treat."


We got to the top floor, which housed the canteen, and sat with a couple of cardboard-encased cappuccinos. I sat back and awaited the inevitable onslaught. Nina was beginning to get on my nerves. I was quite happy to let her live her life in public, but why did she think everyone else had to? Privacy was a redundant concept in her journalism handbook.

She sat and looked at me, waiting for me to crack.

Eventually, inevitably, I relented. "You have to promise not to tell anyone," I told her, formulating a lie that would shut her up and get her off my back.

"Okay." She helped herself to one of my cigarettes, lit it and inhaled.

"We're going out."

Nina choked on her smoke. I avoided her eye and took a slurp of my cappuccino, wiping away the frothy milk moustache it left.

"Since when?" Nina, who always conducts her complicated private life before an audience, found it hard to believe I would keep mine so quiet.

"About a week. I haven't told anyone for obvious reasons."

"But he's gorgeous. If I was shagging him, I'd have told everyone."

I sighed. "We're not shagging, we've just seen each other a few times."

That wasn't actually a lie. "Anyway, you always tell everyone, whoever you're shagging."

She shrugged. "Touché. How did you meet?"

At last a question I could answer honestly. "Our eyes met across a crowded inquest. We got chatting afterwards and he asked me out." I had my fingers crossed under the table. "This is top secret, Nina, I mean Top. Secret." I enunciated each word.

She ignored me. "So what's he like?"

"Nice."

"Nice? God, girl, you really don't have a clue, do you?"

I drained my cup and stood up to go. "I'll let you know."

She laughed, but let it go at that.

By the time we had got back to the newsroom, I had sworn Nina to secrecy. Praying she would change her habits of a lifetime and keep to her word, I cursed myself for not coming up with a better story: the truth, for example.

At the end of the day, I turned down Nina's invitation to the pub, with a wink that suggested I had better things to do. Maybe having a non-existent boyfriend could have its uses. I called into King Street CID on my way home to sign my statement. Leaving my name at reception I waited to be picked up and taken to DC Llewelyn, hoping he would change the habits of this week and be too busy to see me. I was unprepared when the man himself came through the electronically locked doors a few minutes later and let me through to an interview room.

The room was brightly lit by strip lighting and encased in roughcast walls. The pockmarked linoleum on the floor bore the scars of thousands of cigarettes smoked on both sides of the desk as confessions were sweated out of the good, the bad and the innocent. It was sparsely furnished with a desk and two plastic chairs. There was an old-fashioned recording device on the desk with two microphones pointed at the two chairs. The digital age had yet to reach Leicester police. I considered myself lucky when Llewelyn didn't press the Record button as we sat down.

He passed me a single-page typewritten statement and watched me silently as I read through it. I finished and put my hand out for a pen, which he produced from his jacket pocket. He watched as I signed the bottom as instructed.

"Anything else?" I asked, getting to my feet.

"Yes. Pull up a chair."

I sat back down, folding my arms belligerently and fixing him with a glare. A heavy glass ashtray, which was screwed down to the table in front of me, had me reaching for my cigarettes.

"As from now this is a murder inquiry," he told me.

"A press release is no doubt winging its way to our newsroom as we speak."

He smiled, and my anger dissolved. He really did have nice eyes. They were the colour of dark chocolate, with flecks of amber sprinkled around the pupil. I wondered again why he had become a policeman. I had a hard time picturing him in a uniform with one of those ridiculous hats.

"Probably," he eventually answered. "But that's not why I asked you here."

*No kidding,* I thought, deciding he wasn't that good looking after all.

"The chances are that the man you spoke to was Mr Scott and you are the only lead we've got on what he was doing there and how he came to end up dead."

"I was only asking him for directions," I lied. "If I had known he was going to get himself murdered I would have stopped and asked him a few more questions." That bit, at least, was true.

He sat back in his chair, changing tack, "This is your first job on a paper?"

I nodded.

"How are you finding it?"

"S'okay," I said defensively, wondering where this line of questioning was going to lead.

"Not really two professions known for seeing eye to eye, are they?"

"What?"

"The police force and the media."

I shrugged and stood up, unwilling to get into a debate as to the reasons why, mostly out of fear I might let something slip. He let it go and opened the door for me. The quicker I got away from him, the better. When I was with him I seemed to spend half my time terrified he was going to arrest me and the other half terrified he might make a pass at me – or, worse still, that I might make a pass at him.

Like a reformed exhibitionist, my answerphone was resolutely refusing to flash when I got home, signalling there was still no word from the professor. It was worse than waiting for a potential boyfriend to ring. To make sure my phone was working and to fill her in on the latest, I called Jen. Unfortunately I caught her in the middle of something with Steve and, giggling, she promised to ring back later. Presumably the new dress had worked its magic.

I sat down on my bed and inwardly bemoaned my single status. Maybe going out with a cop wouldn't be that bad after all. Anything had to be better than sitting at home alone on a Friday night while everyone else was out and/or having sex. My last relationship had ended just before I had moved to Leicester to work at the *Post* the previous November. Jon had been 28 and studying for his PhD when I met him in a Nottingham nightclub in the summer. He had also been a complete tosser, something I'd realised after he cheated on me. I tried to picture him, but found Tom Llewelyn's face swimming into view instead. Not a good sign.

I picked Henry up and sat with him on my lap, staring at the wall for a few minutes. "There's nothing wrong with being single and there's nothing wrong with me," I told him, deciding I was going mad.

# CHAPTER 14

Getting up for work on a Saturday felt wrong. My body clock was screaming at me to get more sleep. Saturdays were for lounging around watching kids' TV in my pyjamas before meeting friends for lunch.

I had woken up starving and decided to walk to work so I could call into one of the bakeries around the corner to sample some of the goodies I could smell from my front door.

After a hot bath that my body didn't want to leave, I got dressed and went out in search of chocolate croissants and coffee. The smell of baking French bread was going straight up my nose and into my empty stomach. I gazed at the array of pastries filled with glazed fruit, crème anglaise and chocolate and gave a moan of greed. After feasting my eyes for a few minutes, I ordered an extra large coffee, two chocolate croissants and egg mayonnaise in a still-warm-from-the-oven baguette. Saving the pastries for pudding, I began munching on the baguette, pausing only to slurp coffee from a hole in the top of the cardboard lid.

The office was always quieter on a Saturday when there were fewer staff and those there were keen to finish so they could get home and begin their weekend. I offered Matt a croissant and watched him eat it in three bites, as I waited for the baguette to go down and make room for mine.

The big story of the day was the launch of the murder inquiry and Tony had asked Matt to go out after nine and speak to Mrs Scott. Matt, looking for an easy day that would get him home in time for the 3pm football kick-off, reminded him that I had already spoken to her and would be the best one to go, as she already knew me.

Muttering that he didn't give a fuck who did it as long as it got fucking done, Tony stomped back to the newsdesk. I raised my eyebrows at Matt for an explanation of the sudden expletives.

"Rangers went top of the Scottish Premiership yesterday," he explained, leaving me none the wiser. "He's a Celtic fan," he added by way of illumination.

Still I looked blank.

"You are aware of the existence of a popular sport called football?"

I shrugged and Matt went back to his computer, disgusted. Apparently the rivalry of the two Glasgow clubs was legendary and had very little to do with actual football.

Thankful that I could get out of the office, I also realised it had given me a legitimate reason to go back to Mrs Scott. I picked up the envelope of photographs of her husband that I had promised to return and set off, wondering what excuses I could make for getting into his study.

Mrs Scott opened the door and motioned me in, rushing off to the kitchen to make tea, "And I've got some nice ginger cake to go with it."

We sat opposite each other at her dining table and she dished out a generous slab of ginger cake. Having polished off the chocolate croissant in the car on my way, I looked at it unenthusiastically and took a small bite to be polite.

She seemed to sense my discomfort. "It's only shop-bought cake, but it's from Jones' up the road and they make it on the premises, better than I could."

Assuring her it was lovely, I waited for her to disappear into the kitchen for milk and pushed the cake into my shoulder bag, careful to pull out the envelope of her photographs first. The woman had been through enough without me insulting her hospitality.

She sat down and, refusing more cake, I took her gently through the last few days. I needed to find out how she felt about her husband being murdered, but it seemed such a stupid question.

"You must be devastated," I began, hoping she would expand.

"Yes. It's been dreadful. I can't imagine who could do such a thing to my Jim. He didn't have any enemies," she sniffed into a tissue. "I keep thinking it's all been a dreadful mistake and he'll come walking through the door at any minute." She looked at me, as if hoping I'd agree. I looked down at the floor, unable to acquiesce.

"Now I suppose you would like to have a look at his study," she said, suddenly brusque and back to business.

Looking up, surprised, I nodded.

"I thought so. That nice policeman has already been up there and had a rummage around, but I don't think he found anything."

I took a sip of tea before being led upstairs to a small room at the back of the house, which must have been meant to serve as a box bedroom. It was painted a cheerful blue and, unlike the rest of the house, there were no net curtains or knick-knacks dotted around. This had obviously been Mr Scott's domain.

Sitting on a fake mahogany desk was a slim black laptop. Underneath the desk was a filing cabinet, which Mrs Scott told me had been emptied out by 'that nice policeman'.

No prizes for guessing which one she was talking about.

I booted up the computer and had a quick look at the files on it. None of them looked like they contained the files Mr Scott had given me, most were just letters and articles on Fifen's drug treatments that had been downloaded from the internet. Mrs Scott hovered over me, keen to help. "There were some of those little square things that go in, disks, is it?" I nodded and she carried on, "But they were taken away by..."

"That nice policeman?" I guessed. She nodded.

I switched off the computer and told her I had seen enough. She led me back downstairs, made more tea and offered me more cake, while we chatted some more about her husband. She seemed to be taking it all quite well and I was beginning to wonder if she wasn't glad he was gone, when she pointed to a mass of sympathy cards she had received. "Honestly, I haven't stopped," she said. "What with the police popping around and people from his work coming to offer their sympathy. And I've got the funeral directors and the vicar coming around this afternoon. I shall have to pop out and get more cake for them," she paused and looked at me. "Do you think pine or mahogany is better?"

It took a minute to realise she was talking about coffins rather than cake. "Mahogany is nice."

"That's what I thought."

I said my goodbyes and thanked her for her time.

"The funeral is on Wednesday. At St Peter's at three. You will come, won't you?" she called to me as I walked down her garden path. I turned and told her I would try.

Mrs Scott seemed to be enjoying the attention created by her husband's sudden fame. I only hoped she would take it in her stride when all the attention stopped and she had to face life alone as a widow.

Getting to my car, I realised I had forgotten to give her the photographs which were still clasped in my hand. I got out and walked back down her path. She answered immediately and I handed them over. Instinctively she pulled them out for a quick look. The picture of him smiling with the young dark-haired woman was on the top.

"Who is she?" I asked, remembering the picture editor's fuck-up that had almost put her in the paper as their daughter.

Mrs Scott shook her head sadly and tears sprang to her eyes. "That was Mary."

I was nonplussed. "Mary?" I probed, hoping for more.

"She worked with my husband. She died," Mrs Scott replied.

My heart contracted painfully as I took in what she was saying.

"That's Mary Stanshaw?" I tried to get my voice to sound normal, my mind racing through all the possibilities.

"Yes. Lovely girl. My husband's assistant. He was so upset, well we all were. That poor little boy of hers, too." She pushed the photographs back into the envelope. "Now I must get on. The vicar will be here soon."

She closed the door on my barely spoken goodbye.

What did this mean? What were the chances that two people who worked together in a company would be killed within a few months of each other? I reined myself in. But Mary Stanshaw hadn't been killed, I reminded myself. There was no active police inquiry into her death. The inquest had recorded an open verdict, but there had been no sign of forced entry and there had been no evidence of any unnatural cause of death.

I drove back to the office in a trance, my brain turning over all the possibilities, trying to work out what it all meant but coming up empty every time.

The first edition of the paper was out, announcing the launch of a murder hunt into the death of Mr Scott on the front page. It included some of the information that I had written in the obituary from earlier that week and a quote from Fifen Pharmaceuticals saying what a great worker he had been and how much he would be missed by colleagues. Those that were still alive, that is.

I sat and toyed with the piece I was doing on Mrs Scott's reaction to the murder hunt. Knowing I couldn't really put 'Mrs Scott is enjoying her new-found fame and plans to bury him in a mahogany coffin', I put together 400 words to go under the ready prepared headline: *'Find My Husband's Killer: Widow Pleads For Witnesses'*.

Leaving work at three, I had four hours before I had to meet Nina for her birthday. She had rung at lunchtime, just to remind me. I went straight home to find the professor still hadn't returned my call. Rummaging in my bag, I found his card and rang his direct line, only to find he wasn't there. I left a message asking him to ring me back when he could.

"It's really important," I said mysteriously before putting the phone down.

I lay on my bed, staring out of my window and watching the weeds in the back garden swaying in the wind. It had finally stopped raining.

My brain turned over the puzzle surrounding James Scott's and Mary Stanshaw's deaths. I felt like I was in the middle of some giant game of snakes and ladders and every time I thought I'd reached a turning point, I hit a brick wall and slid down to where I had started from, none the wiser. I needed to talk to someone about this, but the only person I could think of was the last person I wanted to deal with. Tom Llewelyn.

Fixing myself a liberal vodka and tonic, I put it out of my mind – there was nothing I could do now, except go out for Nina's birthday, and first I needed to get ready.

Looking in the mirror an hour later, I wondered if I would be better off in jeans. The new dress I had bought looked even shorter than it had in the changing rooms of Topshop and there was a definite outline of chocolate croissant and ginger cake around my stomach. I had teamed the dress up with the new shoes and sheer tights, but decided I looked too tarty – and cold. It was freezing outside and this year the mottled look was definitely out.

The phone rang and I raced to get it, thinking it might be the professor. It was Nina. "You're chickening out, aren't you?"

"Huh?" I asked.

"The dress, I bet you were just deciding to wear jeans instead."

"Was not," I lied and put the phone down, annoyed she thought she could read me so well. I kept the dress on, but added thick opaque black tights and my battered knee-high boots, giving them a quick going over with a black permanent marker bought specially for the task of hiding scuffs; it lasted longer and was quicker than actually using polish.

I was far too lazy to wear make-up at work – it would mean

getting up ten minutes earlier – so I kept it simple. After rubbing in some foundation, I coloured in my eyebrows using a little brush dipped into Vaseline and mixed with brown eyeshadow. It had been a tip from a friend at university who, in the manner of a scary department store make-up counter woman, had told me fair-haired people needed to 'bring out' their brows. I added too much to my left eye and grabbed a tissue to rub it off. It spread across my forehead and refused to budge, forcing me to reach for the eye make-up remover which also took with it a layer of foundation, leaving me with a visible patch of pale skin around my eyebrow. Turning on the hot tap, I washed it off and started again. Maybe it was a sign that I should stay in.

Within ten minutes, however, my face was complete. I added some powder to stop the make-up from sliding off my face as soon as I left the house and peered at the finished result in the full-length mirror in the hall. Unfortunately some of the powder had come off on the black cardigan I was planning to wear with the dress. Fuck it, it would be too dark in the pub to notice but just in case, I brushed on some black eyeshadow to mask it before grabbing my scarf and gloves and pulling on my long blue leather coat.

By the time I got to the pub, the damp air had ruined my hair and the cold had given me a runny nose and red eyes. Looking around, it didn't take me long to spot Nina, who was holding court around a long trestle table filled with people from work and a few unfamiliar faces. I ordered myself a Bloody Mary and dropped a card and present on her lap as I squeezed in next to her on the velvet bench.

Nina gave me a hug and a 'thanks', before diving straight for the present. It took about two seconds to unwrap and she pronounced herself delighted with a copy of *Sex And The City*, before it joined a pile in the middle of the table.

I lit a cigarette and let the rowdy conversation wash over me for a few minutes, with Nina having a heated discussion about fake fur with photographer Sally and Fashion Editor Nicole. While Nicole considered it passé, Nina was extolling its virtues and Sally, a vegetarian, was firmly in favour. Quickly removing my leather coat and squashing it up behind me, I changed the subject by asking what our plans were for the evening.

Nina gave me a mischievous grin, "Well since it's my birthday and I get to choose, I decided we should go somewhere different."

"Really?" I was having a hard time coming up with a pub that Nina had never been in.

She winked at me. "I've decided we should all go and try out Porky's."

There was a groan from around the table as everyone absorbed this shocking news. Rumour had it that Porky's was aimed at attracting police clientele. A stone's throw from King Street police station, no one I knew had ever been in, so I couldn't answer for its success. That said, I had my doubts that the police possessed enough self-irony for frequenting such a place.

Within an hour, we found ourselves huddled outside the stained glass double doors of Porky's waiting for Nina to go in first - after all, it was her idea. She teetered up to the entrance in unfeasibly high-heeled boots, which stopped at her calf. Her trademark floor-length leather coat covered a turquoise Lurex dress - which didn't have enough material in it to make a tea towel, as my mother would say. She pushed through the doors and grabbed my arm, pulling me in after her.

The pub had wooden floors, low lights and white walls with squares of reds and oranges to add some warmth. The windows had black bars over them to give the impression you were in a cell - something I could have done without after my activities over the last few days. A couple of behemoth black leather sofas slung against the walls completed the pseudo-bondage theme. Tables and benches filled the rest of the room and a large, long bar took up most of the back wall. It was quiet with just a few suited men sipping pints at two of the tables.

A good looking man in his 30s, with thin dreadlocks tied into a loose ponytail, stood behind the bar, chalking up wine prices on a blackboard. He turned to smile at us as we walked in and his smile got wider as we continued to flood in through the doors.

"I'm in the mood for cocktails," Nina said. "Let's drink vodka martinis."

I nodded agreement along with Nicole and Sally and she marched up to the bar, while the others bagged one of the low comfy-looking sofas. Nina came back as the barman prepared our drinks and sat down with a wince. "These new boots are killing me," she whispered.

"I'm surprised you haven't been arrested for carrying a lethal weapon," I said, eyeing the mean-looking six-inch metal spikes that passed for her heels. We leaned back and drank in our surroundings.

"I was expecting it to be filled with fit coppers," she told me, looking disappointed. "But he's not bad." She pointed to the barman, who looked up to meet our eyes and smiled.

Throughout the evening, Nina kept the drinks flowing and the group got rowdier. I looked past Nicole, who was deep into why brown will never be the new black with Sally, and worked out why. The birthday girl was chatting up the barman. I started laughing and nudged Sally.

She helped herself to my cigarettes and shook her head with mock disapproval. "Apparently he owns the bar. His name is Norman."

I stood up to go to the loo, swaying slightly. My green eyes glinted back at me in the brightly-lit bathroom mirror where I ran my fingers through my hair and applied lipstick with exaggerated care. I checked there was none on my teeth and that I hadn't tucked my skirt, such as it was, into my knickers before I hauled up my Wonderbra and stared back at myself in the mirror.

An image popped into my head of Mary Stanshaw doing exactly the same thing in front of her dressing table in her whitewashed bedroom. Until today she had been just a name. I thought of the picture of her laughing with Mr Scott like she didn't have a care in the world. Unaware that she would be dead within months. Nobody knew why or what had killed her and, sadder still, nobody seemed to be looking. Why had she died? She hadn't had cancer, no heart problems or any other diseases – a perfectly healthy person and yet she was dead. I pushed myself out of the bathroom, suddenly gripped by alcohol-induced urgency. I had to find out why she had died.

I got back to the table to discover that Edward had arrived and was holding court. I sat down next to him and he took a slug of his drink.

"That's his third," Nina whispered. "And he still hasn't put his hand in his pocket."

"He's probably saving for his retirement."

"He must have millions squirrelled away."

Edward finished his drink and told me of the time his mother took him to see a man hanged during the 1950s.

"I swear I can still hear the crack of his neck breaking," he told me with a camp shudder.

At the end of the evening, Nina had given up any pretence of coyness and had perched herself at the bar to bat her false eyelashes at Norman, leaving me to get a cab home with Edward.

"Take me home first," Edward told the cabbie before turning to me. "You don't mind do you, dear girl? At my age you need your beauty sleep."

I smiled and shook my head. I was curious to see where he lived. I wasn't surprised when, a few minutes later, we pulled up at a grand three-storey Georgian villa set back from the road in a part of the city which, surrounded by parklands, was mostly inhabited by plastic surgeons and businessmen.

"Thank you darling," he said, getting out. "I'll settle up with you in the morning."

Resolving not to hold my breath, I gave the cab driver my address and sat back, searching my pockets for some cash to pay him.

# CHAPTER 15

My eyes refused to unpeel themselves, despite the persistent noise of someone leaning on my buzzer competing with the pounding inside my head.

I crawled into the bathroom and waited until I had flushed away the contents of my stomach and splashed cold water on my face before finally opening my eyes. Then I shuffled through to the kitchen in search of painkillers, drowned four soluble aspirins in a gallon of water and downed the lot in one go. It was Sunday and, with nothing better to do, I decided to go back to bed.

I had just pulled the duvet back over my head when the buzzer started again, this time singing a duet with the ring of my phone. I sat back up, holding my head in agony, and tried to work out which was more urgent.

Going to the front door, I don't know who got the bigger shock. My mother at seeing her daughter looking like an earthquake in pyjamas, or me seeing my mother and father standing on the step all done up in their going-to-town-on-a-Sunday best.

"What have you been doing? We were ringing for ages." My mother pushed past me, brandishing a mobile phone. "And I've brought you some towels," she added, rustling an ancient Marks and Spencer carrier bag in my direction. "But I want the bag back."

My father followed after her, leaving me to close the door and remember what on earth they were doing there. I settled them into the lounge and left my mother examining my decorating while simultaneously running her finger along an available surface to check for dust and evidence of my slovenly ways while I went into the kitchen to make tea.

I rummaged in a cupboard, looking for the teapot my mother had bought me for Christmas, and switched on the kettle. My mother followed me, tutting when she saw me add teabags to the pot. "You should warm that first."

I took the bags out again and squinted out of the window, blinking at the bright sun shining directly in through my east-facing window and scorching my retinas.

"So how are you?" I asked, wondering where my sunglasses were.

"Where are we going for lunch?" she asked, ignoring my question.

"Erm, I don't know really," I said, thinking I would have trouble keeping any food down at the moment.

"There must be somewhere we can go, the promise of a Sunday roast cooked by someone other than me was the only thing that got your father out of the house today."

"There's a pub around the corner that serves a Sunday roast that is supposed to be quite nice," I told her vaguely. I had no idea where you could get a Sunday lunch from at this time of day – it was still too early for breakfast. But there had to be a few pubs in the area that offered it.

The tea made, my mother rooted in my fridge, looking for milk.

"What is all this?" I heard her ask in muffled tones.

"What?" I asked her navy Anne Harvey-clad rear.

She backed out and came up for air with two withered-looking onion bhajis that must have been left over from the weekend before. Taking them over to the bin, she threw them in and went off to the bathroom to wash her hands, muttering about bleach.

I took the tea through to my father, who was sitting in a director's chair in the bay window, looking thoughtful.

"How are you, Dad?" I asked, passing him a mug.

"Bloody dogs," he muttered in response.

"Sorry?" I said, waiting for more. When none came, I went over to the window, thinking he was talking about something going on in my street.

"They leave their mess on the lawn, you know," he finally added by way of explanation.

The pounding in my head wasn't making me think very straight, but even so, I knew there was no greenery in my street. It would take up precious car parking space. "Dad? What?"

He turned away from the window and took a slurp of his tea. "And I'm not talking about small dogs either," he continued, failing to notice that I had no idea what he was talking about. "It could fill a wheelbarrow some days."

My mother came out of the bathroom and rummaged in her handbag, before vigorously rubbing in hand cream. "For God's sake, John, Caitlin does not want to hear about it." She picked up her tea and suddenly noticed Henry curled up on my futon.

"I have to go out there and clean it up," he said.

"Caitlin, where did that come from?"

My mother, a compulsive cleaner, was not a big cat fan – too much hair, not to mention all those germs.

"It's not a *that*. This is Henry," I said, picking him up and sitting him across my lap.

"I thought I could smell something when I came in," my mother's perfect little nose wrinkled with disgust, "and it wasn't just rotting food in your kitchen."

"Maybe I could get a shotgun, sit outside with it and wait for them to do it, sort of catch them in the act and then who could argue? I would be well within my rights," my father continued to muse.

My mother and I both stopped talking and looked at him. "Whaat?"

"John, you are not going to kill the next-door-neighbours' dogs," my mother told him in her no-nonsense tone, usually reserved for children who were about to behave very badly. I had heard it a lot growing up. She turned to me. "He's obsessed by the dogs next door. Two setters, I think they are. The woman next door lets them out in the morning, to do their you-know-what and they seem to like our lawn. Your father's obsessed. Out there at all hours of the day and night, like a sentry keeping guard over something precious. It's just a lawn."

My father responded with a deep frown in her direction.

I slumped onto the sofa and drank my tea in silence, racking my sore brain for an excuse to forego dinner, without success. I picked up the ancient Marks and Spencer carrier bag from the floor and tipped out towels featuring classic 1970s brown and yellow swirls. Helen upstairs would love them – her flat was filled with kitsch Seventies memorabilia.

"What are these for?" I asked my mother.

"They're towels," she said redundantly. "I had a bit of a sort out and I knew that you could do with some guest towels."

"I've only got one bedroom. Where exactly am I going to put a guest?"

My mother was of the make-do-and-mend generation, which should have meant she didn't replace things until they were on their last legs. She circumnavigated the theory by palming off anything she wanted to replace on me, telling herself that I needed it. And so what if this also freed her up to make use of her department store cards? She was just helping her daughter set up home.

Of course she would never admit that. "You can never have too many towels, dear," she said.

I nodded at her vaguely and went off to get dressed. They might come in useful if I ever had to bath Henry.

Looking in the mirror, I resisted the urge to scream. I had make-up streaked down one side of my face and my hair was the consistency of candyfloss on one side of my head and chip pan fat on the other. I attacked it with spray gel and my hairbrush and calmed it down.

In my bedroom, I found my mother sitting on my bed, going through the piles of clothes scattered on my floor. She picked up my dress, discarded from the night before, and sucked air through her teeth in disapproval at its lack of material.

"What?" I asked, mentally preparing myself for the onslaught. She dropped the dress on the floor without comment; her face said it all. Instead, she went over to open the curtains.

"Phew, what a fug," she opened my windows wide open. Ignoring the blast of icy March wind that blew the curtains horizontal to the ceiling. "That's better, you just need a bit of fresh air in here."

"Any more fresh air and I'd catch pneumonia," I muttered, waiting until she left the room before shutting the windows, closing the curtains and getting dressed.

I pulled on jeans and a black polo neck jumper, all the time with half an ear to the door listening to my mother wonder where she went wrong with me. "The state of her windows, John. Black they were, absolutely black," she told Dad. I fought an urge to make a run for it out of the flat and pushed my way into the living room.

"Finally," my mother sighed, looking at her Pierre Cardin watch. "It's almost twelve. You know how your father likes his lunch on time." She bustled out of my flat, taking her antique M & S bag with her.

The pub was mercifully dark and dingy, which would hopefully prevent my mother from noticing my green complexion and bloodshot eyes. Once seated, I escaped for a sneaky cigarette in the ladies' loos, leaving my mother to explain she wanted her gravy served in a gravy boat, not on her plate, to a harassed-looking waitress. Mum also wanted to make sure that the mustard was Coleman's before she would commit herself to the roast beef.

By the time the waitress came back and assured her it was Coleman's, my mother had changed her mind and wanted the chicken. "As long as it's breast and there is no dark meat," she said as the waitress nodded and ran off to the kitchen before my mother had the chance to enquire whether the stuffing was Paxo.

By two, I was back in my flat, weighed down by a large portion of Sunday roast followed by apple pie and custard. I had also wrapped up the remains of my mother's chicken for Henry, who wasted no time getting it down his neck, much to the disgust of my mother who had followed me in to use the bathroom because she refused to use public toilets.

"Absolutely full of germs, dear," she tutted by way of explanation. I neglected to tell her the last time I had cleaned mine. She'd have held it in all the way home.

On her way out, she picked up my bag and rummaged in it for hand cream, instead coming up with a lump of stale ginger cake. I opened my mouth to explain about Mrs Scott, the chocolate croissants, and not wanting to hurt her feelings. But my mother peered at it, shook her head and muttered "Shop bought!" disapprovingly before walking into the kitchen to wash her hands.

There were times when I believed my mother had spent her youth in a Swiss finishing school. Waving her goodbye, I could see her mouth moving exaggeratedly. No doubt ruminating on all the ways I was failing as a woman and as a daughter.

In need of light relief, I picked up the phone to ring Jen and fill her in on the gossip. I hadn't heard from her since I interrupted her and Steve mid-coital on Friday. She picked up after three rings.

"How's it going?" she asked when I said hello.

I filled her in on my Saturday night out and she murmured in sympathy with me over my mother. Jen was the only person I knew who wasn't afraid of her. She had even once swapped things around in Mum's regimented larder, just for fun. Of course I had got the blame for it.

I moved on to my meeting with Professor Johanson. I decided to leave out telling her about my theory that Mr Scott and his assistant were selling research off to other companies, until I'd had a chance to speak to the professor again.

"What if he's in on it?" Jen asked when I had brought her up to date.

"What d'you mean, in on it?"

"Maybe he's a bad guy."

"Don't be ridiculous," I told her, with more confidence than I felt. "He was far too good looking."

# CHAPTER 16

My desk phone was ringing when I walked in the next morning. Picking it up, I cradled it under my chin as I took off my coat and switched on my computer.

"Caitlin, is that you, dear?"

"Yes. This is Caitlin McCall," I said, not recognising the voice.

"It's Margaret, dear, Margaret Bishop."

"Uhh?" My memory clicked through anyone I had met of that name, stopping when it got to the woman I had interviewed two weeks earlier about moving from a high-rise building earmarked for demolition on St Joseph's Estate.

The council planners had decided sometime in the 1990s that the Sixties' dreams of cities in the skies hadn't worked and it was now finally getting around to demolishing the hideous high-rises that had instead become penal colonies for single mothers. The well overdue decision was to everyone's delight, except for Margaret Bishop who had lived in her top-floor flat for 37 years - moving in the day they finished building them, with her now deceased husband.

"Mrs Bishop. How are you?" I doodled on my pad as she went through her life story of the last two weeks. The council had a nice bungalow lined up for her in the suburbs, apparently, with an emergency pull cord, a warden and bi-weekly bingo sessions.

"But I've decided I'm not going."

"Not going? Where?" I asked absent-mindedly.

"From this flat. They will have to take me out in a, oh now, what do they call them on television?" She paused while she searched for the right word. "A body bag. Yes, that's what they call them. They'll have to take me out in one of those."

I stopped doodling and began taking notes. Shit. What had she been saying? The council was coming to collect her and she wasn't going to move. The 78-year-old was staging a sit-in. I began waving maniacally at the picture desk, trying to get the attention of the duty photographer.

"What time are they coming to move you out?" I asked her, as the photographer finally noticed me and came over.

"I think they said ten. Now what have I done with that letter? You get to my age and you can't remember what you had for breakfast. Here it is. Yes. Ten o'clock today."

I looked at my watch – an hour to go. "Can I come and have a chat with you?" I asked, my stomach fluttering as the adrenaline kicked in. I checked her address and grabbed my coat, shouting to Tony a few details about where I was going.

"Get something for the next edition," he yelled as I raced to the stairs.


Mrs Bishop's block was huddled with two others on the edge of St Joseph's council estate, close to where the gunman had been dragged out of his house last week. There were a few burly builders milling around, already set up for the demolition. I walked to the front with Simon, the duty photographer, and went straight in the entrance. A burly middle-aged man stopped me and asked where I was going.

"Visiting my nan, Mrs Bishop, flat 156, top floor. Moving out today," I said, walking towards the lift.

"Last one to go," he said as the lift doors closed, enveloping us in the pungent smell of stale urine that seemed to come as standard in council tower blocks.

Mrs Bishop was waiting at the door when I got to her floor. Walking through, I noticed the heavy-duty front door, complete with several dead bolts, put in by the council several years ago as an added security measure to keep out undesirables. I smiled at the irony. The council was going to have a hell of a job getting the door open, if Mrs Bishop chose to be stubborn.

Although every flat in the block was identical in size and layout, Mrs Bishop's was unique. Most tenants in the blocks had been stuck there trying to earn enough housing points to move into a house - the flats received little tender loving care from residents desperate to get out. The majority of the flats had spent the last decade in dire need of decoration, with bare bulbs, uncarpeted floors, and furniture that should have been consigned to a skip. Mrs Bishop's, however, was positively palatial. Scrubbed clean linoleum in the hallway gave way to a beige carpeted lounge filled with over-stuffed furniture, perfectly plumped cushions and a glass cabinet filled with porcelain figurines and a china tea service.

"Now, I've got enough supplies for a month or two," she said, leading us through to her spotless kitchen, opening her pantry door and pointing at rows of canned soups, packet meals and potted meats.

"You certainly have," I nodded, noting down how many things she had bought and nudging Simon to take some pictures.

"Of course the milk will only last a few days, but I have that powdered stuff - it's like the blitz!" Mrs Bishop smiled, "Although of course we never really had much of that here, only a fortnight of it or so."

We sat in her comfortable lounge with a pot of tea and china cups, and I got out my notepad, asking her again why she didn't want to move.

"I kept thinking about my Stan. He would have been proud of me, you know. We lived our whole married life here," she pointed to a framed photograph of an old man with a kind smile and black-framed glasses. "He died in 1995."

I scribbled down some notes, ignoring Simon as he took photographs of her, her flat and her well-stocked kitchen. "How long are you planning to stay up here?"

"I don't want to move. This is my home. Why can't they wait until I'm gone, instead of ripping my home from under me? It's not right," she paused to pull a tissue from her cardigan sleeve. "I just want to live out my final days in my home, not shoved off to a little bungalow somewhere. I remember moving in like it was yesterday. My Stan said it was like living on top of the world." She delicately dabbed her eyes and looked up as the clock on her wall chimed. "Now dear, you'd better go. I don't want to have to open the door again in case they try to overpower me."

I checked my watch and had a quick read-through of my notes. "Okay. Good luck. I'll ring you later and see how you are getting on," I said.

"You can be my eyes and ears on the outside." She smiled, gave me a thumbs-up and pulled her heavy front door closed. I waited and listened as she pulled the deadbolts into place.

With perfect timing, the lift doors opened and two men came out, heading for her flat. Banging loudly, I heard them ask her to let them in, before one turned to me and asked what I was doing there.

"Came to see Mrs Bishop. She's locked herself in. Not coming out until you promise to let her live out her last days there. I'm from the *Post*, any comment?" I pulled out my press card.

The two men walked away from the door, and one pulled out his mobile phone with a sigh.

"This building is now closed for demolition. You're trespassing," the other said.

I stood my ground. "But you still have a tenant."

"Not for long."

The first man came off his mobile phone and they pulled on yellow hard hats.

"You're violating safety regulations. No-one is allowed on site without a hat."

"Better tell Mrs Bishop," I said with a smile.

Simon, who had been hiding behind me, bobbed up and took a quick picture of them over my shoulder as they came towards us with menace, before we both turned and headed for the still open lift. Getting to the bottom, we collapsed on the steps of the building and I fumbled for my mobile phone.

By the time I had filed my first version of the story, two police vans had appeared and we were told to move behind a set of barriers that had been erected. Simon had disappeared back to the office to print up his photographs, leaving me to wander around looking for someone in charge.

After ten minutes and a few offers of dates, I managed to illicit a few quotes out of a housing manager who didn't want to be named, but said it was costing the council £1000 a day for the demolition crew.

Finding somewhere out of the way to stand where I could see the entrance, in case they went in, I tapped in Mrs Bishop's phone number on my mobile. She picked it up after one ring.

"Mrs Bishop, it's Caitlin from the *Post*, how are you holding up?"

"There's a few men standing outside talking to me, but I can't hear them properly. I'm watching *This Morning*. I do like that John Leslie. Such a trusting face."

"There's a few police vans down here and they've got a couple of loud hailers, but I haven't seen a battering ram yet," I joked.

"If they damage my front door, they can pay for it," she said stoutly without a trace of irony.

We said our goodbyes and I sat on the bonnet of my car, waiting to see what would happen next. A group of policemen separated from the crowd near the door and walked over to me.

One of them introduced himself as Sergeant Andrew Owen before asking who I was. I told him.

"Press? Where did you hear about this?" he asked.

"Straight from the horse's mouth." I pointed up to Mrs Bishop's flat.

"You've spoken to her today?"

"Just come down from her flat."

"What was her state of mind?"

"Defiant."

He sighed. This just wasn't going to be his day. "Look, we could just go up, break in and remove her by force."

"A 78-year-old woman? Doesn't look very good, does it?"

He grimaced. "We're hoping we can talk her out. We have a trained negotiator on his way now. I'm sure it will all be over in a few minutes."

He walked off and I got into my car, running the heater to warm up, awaiting further instructions.


My phone chirped and the Editor came on the line. "What's happening?" he barked.

"There's a police negotiator on his way to try and talk her down."

"Good. Good. Are they going to break in and grab her? What about cutting off her power supply? Might snow tonight. Old thing like that, frail, she'd catch pneumonia in a matter of hours." He sounded hopeful.

"Not planning it at the moment."

"Well, there's time," he sounded disappointed. "Come back to the office. She trusts you? Ring her and stay on the line. We don't want anyone else getting through to her and stealing our story."

Taking one last look at the high-rise, I started up the car and drove back to the office. A copy of the front page for the second edition had been left on my desk with a banner headline:

*'I Shall Not Be Moved: Plucky Pensioner Defends High Rise Home*

*Exclusive by Caitlin McCall'*

I began tapping away at my computer to update the story for the final edition. A graphic designer had been asked to come up with something that would enable the *Post* to count the days as Mrs Bishop continued her protest, if she lasted beyond the first night. Tony and the Editor had already come up with a headline to use with the story tomorrow if she made it: *'They Won't Freeze Me*

*Out: Pensioner Keeps Home Fires Burning'*, instructing me to suggest to the council's housing department that they cut her power supply off. Fortunately Mrs Bishop was ready for them, having rented a gas heater and a bottle, so I tapped away happily.

The story written, I grabbed a few copies of the paper and waltzed out of the office at six, my troubles momentarily forgotten, and enjoying the buzz from a rare journalistic high. Reaching my car, I discovered it was mercifully ticket-free, despite having been parked on yellow lines in the city centre all afternoon. Looking at it, I wasn't surprised. Any traffic warden worth his or her salt would go after richer pickings than my green 1981 VW Polo, held together with luck, love and a lot of rust.

I settled for a bacon and egg sandwich for dinner to keep up my cholesterol level, followed by a large glass of freshly squeezed grapefruit juice as pudding to redress the balance. By the time I had finished it was after eight and it was only when I went through to the kitchen that I noticed the answerphone light flashing. Juggling my dirty plates, I pressed Play.

"Ms McCall, this is Vincent Johanson here. I am sorry it has taken me so long to get back to you, but it took longer than expected. So far I haven't been able to find out what you wanted, but I am going to speak to a colleague in the industry today, and will call you later."

The professor had left the message at 9am according to the display on my machine, so he should have had his meeting. Cursing myself for not giving him my work phone number, I wiped the message and went in search of a nice calming snack.

Deciding it would be bad for my health, I lit up a cigarette instead and sat in the kitchen with Henry curled up on the table, surveying the damage from the weekend. My mother was right, there was a bad smell coming from the direction of the fridge. I added it to the mental list I keep of things to do, right below cleaning the toilet and taking my clothes to the laundry.

That done, I checked the locks on my doors and went off to bed, grabbing a paperback copy of Raymond Chandler on the way – it was practically research.

# CHAPTER 17

Humphrey Bogart was telling me something vitally important about Fifen Pharmaceuticals, but I couldn't hear him over the planes flying overhead. His trademark cigarette hung from the corner of his lips as he pointed silently up to the sky and smiled.

The planes got louder and louder until they disappeared altogether and I awoke to find myself lying naked in my bed with the light still on from the night before. The buzzing continued to get louder and louder and I reached out and hit my alarm clock, which must have been ringing for some time. I had fallen asleep reading at some point in the early hours of the morning in a vain attempt to take my mind off the murder inquiry.

Grabbing the last of my clean underwear, I threw on a black skinny rib jumper, woollen tights and a long red skirt. The bath was still filled with water from the night before, along with about a litre of Body Shop tea tree oil which now floated on top of the cold water like an oil slick. My plastic bath duck resembled one of those seagulls caught up in an oil spill.

I didn't have time to hose him down so I emptied the bath water, ignored the black-and-white scum ring left around the bath and turned my attention to the bathroom mirror. My hair had dried while I was in bed and closely resembled a large bird's nest. I grabbed a tin of styling wax and attacked it with my brush. A few minutes later it was calmer, partly from the wax, but mostly because half of my hair was now residing in the bristles of my hairbrush. My eyes were watering from the pain, so I bypassed my contact lenses in favour of glasses and wrapped myself up ready for the brisk walk into work.

The local police force had started a new press-friendly assault, holding a press conference every day at 8am to fill in the media about crimes and current investigations. The idea was to drag reporters away from the warmth of their desks and the ease of the telephone in an effort to improve relations between the two. Rachel was rarely around at that time of the morning to attend, which left the general reporters taking turns. We all had bets on how long the conferences would last for and very few of us had gone beyond the first week.

When I got into the office, Nina was being sent out to cover, leaving me to steal her freshly-bought cup of coffee and ring Mrs Bishop to see how she was holding up before the paper went to press. The phone was eventually answered by a man's voice.

Thinking I had rung the wrong number, I got ready to make my apologies, but he identified himself as a police officer. Had the police and council waited until the dead of night before breaking in and stealing Mrs Bishop away? I identified myself and demanded to know what was going on. The phone clicked again and began ringing.

"Hello?" It was Mrs Bishop's voice on the line.

"Hi. This is Caitlin McCall from the *Post*. How are you this morning?"

"Fine, dear, fine. I'm just watching *Kilroy*. Reminds me a lot of my Stan. Silver-haired old smoothie that he was. Pity you didn't meet him. He always liked the blondes."

I heard faint clicking on the line, "I think the police are listening in on your phone, Mrs Bishop." I waited and heard another series of clicks before the line suddenly went louder, signalling the police had disconnected. "Have you had any more calls?"

"Well, I've been talking to a nice man from the police. He was telling me that I should give it all up now, that I've made my point and I should come quietly. What do you think?"

Tony loomed over me with a questioning glare and I gave him a thumbs-up to indicate she was still sitting pretty and our front page could run as planned. "I think you are doing fine, but it's up to you," I paused. "What do you think Stan would say?"

She giggled, "I've not caused enough trouble yet."

"Well, there's your answer then."

I promised to call her later and opened up a new file on my computer for day three and an in-depth interview commissioned by the Editor, *'The Pensioner Behind The Protest: Margaret Bishop Talks Exclusively to the Post'*.

Nina was back from her press conference within the hour with a hit-and-run to write up and plenty of new four-letter words with which to describe the police's incompetent press officer. I grabbed my bag for another trip across town to Mrs Bishop's flat, while Nina rushed off to a death knock for her hit-and-run story of that morning, with a backward glance and "You owe me a coffee, McCall."

The scene that greeted me at St Joseph's council estate was manic. Although more police were milling around, it was hard to spot them for all the TV vans that had sprouted up overnight. I counted six different channels, including two nationals, and stood watching while the crews plugged in to the tower block's electricity supply. At least while they were there, there was little chance of Mrs Bishop losing her power.

Tripping over some of the cables, I moved forward to try and spot the *Post* photographer who had been dispatched to get some shots of the mayhem. A melée of TV, radio and newspaper reporters had gathered around the front entrance of the building, where a harassed-looking housing officer was answering questions. Looking somewhat conspicuous in an ill-fitting suit and gleaming yellow hard hat, he was relaying the story to reporters that a 78-year-old council tenant was refusing to move from her 18th storey flat, to allow demolition work to begin.

I wandered over to a police van and grabbed the most senior officer I could – a sergeant – to find out what was going on.

"When will you begin thinking about forcing her to leave?" I asked him, pulling out a notepad from my rucksack.

"Negotiations are continuing, but obviously we will have to think about other means if this is not successful," he gave me his best paternal smile. "Of course we haven't given up hope yet that this will all come to a peaceful end."

"Thanks." I noted down his name and rank number in case I wanted to quote him and wandered off. Most of the reporters milling around seemed to have a copy of the *Post* tucked under their arm. I was keen to avoid them in case they realised I had a hotline to the protester so I waited until I was safely inside my car and out of earshot before I gave Mrs Bishop another call. She was still holding firm, although there had been talk of moving her whole flat out of the building and setting it up elsewhere.

"But they can't give me the same view," she told me. "We're at a bit of an impasse."

Back at the office, Tony was dividing his time between issuing orders at me and at Nina, whose hit-and-run had turned out to be someone worthy. I finished off my interview and wrote up a story on plans to recreate Mrs Bishop's flat in an OAPs home, tracking down a museum curator who could guess at how much this kind of thing – usually reserved for dead artists' workshops or great examples of architecture – would cost.

My phone was ringing off its hook, as every few minutes a new TV show, news programme or magazine rang for the inside track on Mrs Bishop. A few already had her phone number, but the police intercepted their calls and when she refused to speak to them, they wouldn't put them through. The Editor was in ecstasy and even went so far as to promise me a pay review at some point in the future. Unbelievably large sums of money were being offered to me to sell the story - a daytime TV programme even offered me a job as a researcher, which would double my salary, if I gave them what they wanted. Tempting as it all was, I turned them down, knowing that once the story had died, so would the offers. Instead, I told them they would have to read all about it in the *Post* tomorrow. The Editor would have been proud.

Matt helped make sure I didn't completely miss out. For a ten per cent commission, he helped me earn £200 by selling the quotes I hadn't used to one of his mates on a national tabloid that would use them under a staff reporter byline in the next day's edition. I bought us coffees to toast my first national story, even if it was anonymous.

During a moment of calm, I remembered I still hadn't spoken to Professor Johanson. In his message he had said he planned to speak to someone later that day. I searched through my pad to look for his direct line. Failing to find it, I dialled the university's press office instead.

Eddie didn't seem surprised to hear from me and before I could ask him for Johanson's number, he told me to grab my pen and he would dictate it.

"Dictate what?" I asked him, grabbing my pen anyway.

"Our statement."

Not wanting to sound thick and ask him about what, I dated a new page in my shorthand book and told him I was ready.

"Okay. Staff are shocked and saddened to hear of the death of Professor Vincent Johanson. Our vice-chancellor led the tributes..."

My pen stopped in tandem with my heart when I heard the name. "Whaaa-at?"

"McCall, your shorthand is crap. I've only just started, you can't have fallen behind already," Eddie said, misunderstanding my outburst.

"Did you say Vincent Johanson?" I enunciated his name carefully, keen to clear up any misunderstanding. "As in the guy you put me in touch with?"

"Yeah. Oh God, I forgot about that, you wanted to interview him, didn't you?"

"Look, Eddie, I think you'd better fax over that statement," I laughed weakly. "With something like this, I wouldn't want to misquote you."

He took down the fax number, made me promise to buy him lunch the next week on my non-existent expense account, and hung up.

I spotted a copy of the late edition of the paper sitting on the newsdesk and found a corner of the canteen to read it in peace. The story was splashed across the front page, pushing Mrs Bishop on to page two. Nina had given the story serious spin, compared to the few paragraphs that had gone in the first edition. Under a headline that read: *'Prof Mowed Down in City Street'*, she had written:

*'World renowned chemistry expert Professor Vincent Johanson has been killed in a hit-and-run incident.*

*Police are hunting for a black four-wheel-drive vehicle believed to have run Prof. Johanson down in the early hours of this morning before leaving the scene.*

*The professor, who has held a chair in chemistry at the University of the East Midlands for 10 years, suffered multiple injuries.*

*He was found lying yards from his home in Mountfield Street in the city by two men returning home from a late shift at a nearby factory and rushed to hospital but was pronounced dead at 3.30am from fatal head injuries.*

*Police believe it is impossible that the motorist could not have known they had hit Prof. Johanson and are treating this as a hit-and-run.*

*Witnesses say they saw a four-wheel-drive black Jeep-style vehicle speed off down the road just before 1am and police are keen to trace the owners of this vehicle.*

*Chief Inspector Michael Peterson from the force traffic department said: "We believe the motorist hit Prof. Johanson and panicked and left the scene.*

*"At this time we cannot rule out the possibility of joy riders and are keen to trace the owners of the black four-wheel-drive vehicle seen in the area at the time."'*

This was followed by a lot of gumph about studies and research the professor had carried out while based in the city and finished with a quote from one of his research peers about what a great guy he was.

I took a drag of the cigarette in my hand, before realising I hadn't lit it. Getting out my lighter, I lit up and waited for my head to clear. Professor Johanson had left a message on my answerphone the previous day and within hours he had been dead. Mowed over by a mysterious car, whose driver didn't stick around to see if he was alive or dead. I tried to remember what he had said in his phone message and wondered what the chances were that his death was linked to me.

I shook my head. His death probably had nothing to do with me, just a tragic coincidence. That's right, I told myself, half-convinced, the driver was probably pissed, it happened all the time. I wrote about one in January. The driver knows they've hit someone but is shit-scared of being breathalysed and ending up in prison. Maybe it was a jilted girlfriend that had killed him, I thought hopefully. Maybe he was messing around with his students and his wife found out.

I inhaled heavily on my cigarette. Who was I kidding? Everyone who touched that file seemed to end up dead. Except for me. I shook the thought from my head, unwilling to dwell on what that might mean.

Whatever else, I knew that it meant there was no way I could go to the police. Two people dead, maybe even a third if you included Mary Stanshaw. Fuck. I had to find out what was going on before someone else was killed, like me. I was going to have to think of somebody else who could help me. It didn't take long to come up with a name.

Jon Mills, PhD. The ex-boyfriend-asshole-fuckwit-tosser who had shagged half his students behind my back.

During the few months that he and I had gone out, before I had moved to Leicester and used it as the perfect opportunity to dump him, he had explained in dreary detail the premise of his PhD research. I didn't understand it, but it was to do with viruses, medical rather than technical, so he had to have some knowledge about chemistry. I decided to wait until I got home to call him, in the hope that something else would overtake the need. I wasn't fussy - alien abduction or a raging case of Ebola would do. Sadly, by the time I got there I had encountered neither. I filled my coffee machine with water and sat down heavily at the kitchen table, trying to work out what to say.

Five minutes later, the coffee had brewed and I was no closer to an approach. Fuck it. It wouldn't matter what I said, having not spoken to him since I dumped him, Jon would know I was after something, and as long as he realised it was his mind and not his body, I didn't care. I found his phone number in my address book. It had been scored out but I could still read it. Checking my watch, I saw it was after 5pm. I dialled his number, praying his answerphone would pick up.

God wasn't listening. "'Lo?"

"Hi, is that Jon?"

"Speaking."

"Hi. It's Caitlin. McCall. How's it going?"

There was a brief pause before he answered. I could almost hear the wheels slowly cranking around in his Neanderthal skull. "Fine, what can I do for you?"

"Well," I said, relieved I was going to be able to get to the point, "I was wondering if I could buy you lunch tomorrow?"

"Why?"

"I wondered if you could look over something for me, it's a research paper and you are about the only person I know smart enough to understand it." I decided I'd lay it on thickly.

"What research?" he asked, refusing to commit himself.

"It's in connection with a story, and I don't understand it. Would you take a look?"

Another pause. "Where are you taking me?"

"How about the Villa restaurant, two o'clock tomorrow?" It was his favourite restaurant – a football-themed pub.

"Okay," he said heavily before putting the phone down.

"Well that wasn't so hard, was it?" I said to Henry, who ignored me in favour of using his litter tray. I knew how he felt.

I fell into bed, tired but unable to sleep. My mind having trouble switching off. I finally dropped off around one but woke up after an hour, my heart pounding. I lay holding my breath, tensing myself, half expecting my bedroom door to fly open to reveal

Leatherface, complete with a chainsaw bloodied from working his way through the rest of my building. After what felt like a decade, my pulse slowed down and I got up, picking up Henry and brandishing him in front of me like a weapon. He wasn't likely to last very long against a live chainsaw but it made me feel marginally better.

The flat was cold, but mercifully psycho-free. Listening in the dark, I couldn't hear anything. I dropped Henry on the floor and went to my front door. I held my breath and listened. All was quiet. I silently slid the bolt on the door and turned the key. Another deep breath and I quickly swung the door open.

"Arghhhhhh!" Standing in front of me was Ian, mouth open, shirt off to reveal a pelt of ginger hair running across his chest and onto his shoulders, making a similar noise.

I was relieved to note he was still wearing his trousers.

"What the fuck are you doing?" I screamed, remembering I was standing in my bra and knickers.

"Ermm," he stared down at my state of undress, and I pulled the front door slightly closed so I could hide behind it. "I heard a noise, but it's gone now."

He bolted across the corridor back to his flat.

"Pervert," I yelled. Slamming the door, I went back to bed. As if I didn't have enough to worry about, now my neighbour was stalking me. I settled down and turned my mind to more cheery thoughts, like what I could spend my £200 on.

Neutering my neighbour would presumably be out of my price range.

# CHAPTER 18

Putting my hand into my underwear drawer the next morning, it came back empty but for a pair of red satin crotchless knickers, bought for me by Jon, and I'm sorry to say not for a joke. The rest of the contents of my underwear drawer was sitting in, on top of, and around my full-to-bursting laundry bag in the bathroom, along with half my wardrobe. I had been stepping over it for days as part of my strenuous efforts to avoid a job I hated. Yet again laundry day had been and was long gone.

My lesson learnt, it took mere seconds to decide that bareback was preferable to a pair of pants with no gusset. At least I wouldn't have to worry about visible panty lines.

My ringing mobile phone dragged my thoughts away from below my navel. A muffled voice on the other end of the line said my name.

"Nina?"

"Yeah." Her voice didn't sound quite right.

"Where are you?"

"I won't be in today. Can you tell the newsdesk for me?"

"Yeah, but I'd better not tell them why. Get yourself home and get into bed with some Anadin Extra."

She sobbed in reply. Shit, I hoped nobody had died. "What's wrong?"

"I'm fine, everything's fine. I stayed at Norman's house last night and I got back to my flat to change before coming into work this morning and some bastard's broken in. I can't believe it. They smashed a window at the back of the house and have pulled everything to pieces. It's such a mess."

"Nina, I'm so sorry. Has anything been taken?"

"My laptop. I don't know what else, it's such a fucking mess, I can't tell. I'm waiting for the police to get here. They told me not to touch anything."

"Is there anything I can do?"

"Well, you could use your influence to get them here a bit quicker – I've been waiting for an hour."

"I'll see what I can do. Look, I'm hoping to get a half day, do you want me to come by and help?"

Nina sighed. "Thanks Cat, that would be great. What time?"

"Four?" That would give me time to meet Jon for lunch.

"Okay."

"And you can come back to mine when we've finished and stay over."

"Thanks Cat, you're a star. Look, I've got to go, there's someone at the door. I'll see you later."

I put down the phone and pulled out the card Tom Llewelyn had given me. Maybe I could ring him and ask him to help, I considered, forgetting that I was avoiding him. Hmmm. I tapped the card against the wall for a few seconds before putting it back in my bag. Every time I saw him, there seemed to be another crime committed.

I delivered Nina's message to the newsdesk on my arrival, but only after I had secured the afternoon off, pleading emergency dental decay.

Margaret Bishop had again been relegated to page two, so I put in a quick call to see how she was. The country's press had disappeared off the estate – no doubt London staff too precious to waste for long in the provinces - but they had left a fair number of council workers better off, judging by the number of anonymous quotes littering the stories in the nationals.

Apart from boredom, Mrs Bishop seemed to be holding up well. Her front door was still intact and the council and police were still working on ways to get her to open it peacefully – including getting a distant relative to plead with her. "Stan's cousin, never did like her – all fur coat and dirty knickers," she whispered conspiratorially.

I involuntarily looked down. Better than no knickers at all, I thought.


The Villa was named after the famous football team and was the star attraction in an entertainment park on the outskirts of Birmingham, which also featured a bingo hall, multiplex cinema, several family pub chains and a DIY superstore.

Unfamiliar famous faces grinned down at me from the dining area's hall of fame, which featured examples of every hairdressing crime committed in football over the past 50 years. Wet-look perms, frizzy hair bleached to virtual transparency and comb-overs, where the side parting starts at the ear, surrounded me. I sipped my Coke and pondered the origins of the footballer's fashion favourite: the mullet. You'd think naming a haircut after a fish would be enough of a warning to anyone, yet it dominated the pitch during the 1980s more than Maradona and lingered into the 1990s like a stubborn stain.

I smoked a cigarette as I waited for Jon to show up. Considering our last conversation, I had to grudgingly admit that it was good of him to agree to see me, although the fear remained he would think this an elaborate set-up to get back together. Tall and dark-haired, Jon had looked just my type. When I had met him in a nightclub, I had been impressed by the fact he was doing a PhD.

Throughout my degree I had toyed with the idea of being an English Professor, wandering the hallowed halls of some ancient university and writing important critiques on Virginia Woolf which nobody read, whilst endlessly studying for more academic accolades.

I had thought being with Jon would give me the chance to savour that world — which it did, in a way, although his habit of sleeping with his students wasn't quite what I had in mind.

After a few short months, we parted company. I'm ashamed to say our final date consisted of me throwing a steak tartar in his face in the middle of a restaurant. For pudding I called him a fucking cunt, much to the consternation of the other diners, especially a large group of senior citizens who were celebrating a golden wedding anniversary. At the time I had felt utterly humiliated, but I came to realise it could have been worse. I had nearly ordered the bolognese.

I'm still barred from the place, but at least Jon will never again take a woman to a public place to tell her he had slept with someone else in the belief that she wouldn't make a fuss because she might embarrass herself.

Jon arrived in the middle of my musings and sat down opposite me without a word, waiting for me to offer him a drink. He had decided I owed him a meal, after I threw the last one back in his face. When the waitress came, he ordered a large steak and chips, side portions of onion rings, garlic bread, barbecue wings and a salad.

I ordered a tuna melt, another Diet Coke, and handed him the brown envelope without ceremony. He flicked through its contents and I waited for him to ask where it had come from. He didn't. For a scientist, he had the curiosity of a gnat.

Our food arrived as he was still looking through the file. He picked up a handful of chips and shoved them in his mouth as he continued to read. Eventually he came up for air and picked up his knife and fork to tuck into the steak.

I picked at my food. I was feeling too tired and edgy to eat. Too much coffee, too many cigarettes, and too many dead people. "Is it okay?" I asked him as he shoved half a cow into his mouth, adding a couple of onion rings as an afterthought.

He grunted at me and took a slug of his beer. Master of small talk. We continued to eat in silence, and before I was halfway through, he was wiping up the remains of his ketchup with the last of the garlic bread. Leaning back from the table, he burped loudly and patted his sated stomach. I pushed aside my food and waited for him to earn his lunch.

"What you have here, Caitlin, is the results of a research project."

No shit. "I hope you aren't expecting me to stump up for pudding if that's all you can tell me."

He eyed the dessert menu on the table with disappointment. "Well, it's missing the details of what the research actually was. All I can say is, whatever the authors set out to prove it looks like they were right."

He stopped as the waitress came to clear our plates. She looked disapprovingly at my barely-touched lunch and asked if we wanted anything else. I plumped for a coffee and after a swift look at the menu, Jon chose an apple and cinnamon pie warmed up, with cream and ice-cream. The man was evidently trying to spend half my pathetic salary in one sitting.

The waitress left and Jon looked at the file again. "To be honest, I don't know what else I can tell you," he paused and smiled before delivering his last crushing line. "You've been had, babe. It's meaningless."

The waitress returned with my coffee and his dessert. I looked at it longingly, imagining Jon wearing it. As if reading my mind, he protectively drew his plate closer. Instead of reaching for his plate, however, I reached for my cigarettes and lit one up, inhaling deeply before I let the smoke drift over his way.

"Well, thanks for your help anyway," I said.

He smirked and dug into his dessert, finishing it in the time it took me to smoke my cigarette. Getting up to pay the bill, I grabbed my bag and the file. "I have to go. Thanks again, Jon. Nice to see you." I went over to the bar and paid up, before walking quickly out to the car park.

The whole lunch had taken less than an hour, but he had managed to eat his way through the best part of £40. Stifling a yawn, and wishing I had used the loo before stomping out of the restaurant, I got back into my car and headed towards home and Nina, berating myself for putting my pride before a full bladder.

By the time I got back to Leicester, I was close to tears and had to ease myself out of the car carefully before running to her front door, hopping from one foot to the other and pressing her bell insistently until she answered.

"Need the loo." I grimaced and raced to the back of her flat to make full use of her facilities. As I came out and down the hall, I realised she was talking to someone in her front room. I also noticed the mess for the first time. Like Nina, her flat was anything but understated. Instead of wallpaper, her walls were covered in boudoir-style blue velvet, which had now been shredded and ripped down. Frosted glass shelves which had held her books along the wall of her hallway were cracked and leaning dangerously, having been relieved of their load by the callous swipe of someone's hand. The books lay in piles, with pages torn out and front covers missing.

I surveyed the damage, before walking into the lounge to find her sitting on her red velvet sofa next to Norman, who was looking at her with concern and holding a jam jar full of coffee. Both were looking at the figure in the window. He turned towards me just as I put a name to the back of his head.

"DC Llewelyn."

He nodded in greeting. I pulled up an upturned director's chair, which had been ripped down the back, and perched on it, while Nina went over what had happened that morning. Llewelyn made a few notes and sipped some coffee from a bright orange plastic beaker, which I recognised as that which normally housed Nina's toothpaste and toothbrush in the bathroom. I looked from the beaker to Norman's jam jar full of coffee and deduced Nina's crockery had also fallen victim to the vandals. In the kitchen I unearthed a plastic measuring jug normally used for watering plants and made some tea.

Back in the lounge, Llewelyn had put away his notepad and was sitting in the director's chair, quietly surveying his surroundings.

"Have you been to question the neighbours?" I asked him. "Did they see anything?"

"Yes and no," he replied.

I watched him drain the beaker and wondered what coffee and Colgate tasted like. Nina got up and took the beaker from him, "More coffee?"

He smiled at her, his eyes softening. "A little too minty for my taste."

She giggled and followed him to the door, apologising. I heard him tell her he would be in touch and to make sure she contacted her insurance company as soon as possible. "Take some photographs for them, it makes things easier," he told her as he left.

"Nice bloke for a copper," Norman said from his place on the sofa as Nina came back in.

She slid a sneaky glance at me. "You're not the only one who thinks so."

I let her have that one. She'd had a bad day. "Nice to see you've not lost your sense of humour."

She sat down heavily on the sofa. "How am I supposed to take photos if my camera's been nicked?"

"Sally?" I suggested, thinking the staff photographer would be happy to help out by popping in with her Nikon on the way home.

"Good thinking, I'll do it later," she surveyed the chaos. "I still can't fucking believe it. Look at this place."

"What did Llewelyn say?" I asked her.

"He seems to think they were looking for something specific, and he's not sure if they found it. All they took was my laptop – must have been after my future Pulitzer Prize-winning novel." We all smiled at her weak joke.

"They got in through a window at the back and pulled everything apart, that's why the police think they were looking for something. Probably cash and jewellery or small things they could sell for drugs."

"Well, do you want to get started?" I asked her, motioning to the mess, ready to keep my promise of helping her clear up.

"Well," she looked coyly at Norman. "The thing is, Norman has offered to help and then take me back to his place to stay the night. So if you want to go off home, don't worry about it."

I drained the measuring jug and nodded. I know when three's a crowd.

"I'm off tomorrow anyway, so I'll give you a ring." She walked me to the front door, "The glazier is coming around to fix the window sometime today and then I can start clearing up the mess." She gave me a quick hug and I walked back to my car.

I took a slow drive back home. It was only five, but I decided on an early night. I needed at least eighteen hours' sleep. Maybe I could get away with handwashing some knickers. My plan sounded good until I pulled up outside my flat to find Tom Llewelyn leaning insolently against my wall. I did some breathing and stealthily kicked my copy of the research file under my passenger seat before I got out of the car.

"Maybe I should just give you your own key," I told him as I walked past to open the front door. He ignored the sarcasm and followed me in.

"Coffee?" I asked him, heading for the kitchen, surreptitiously noting my flashing answerphone.

"Please."

He followed me in and sat at the tiny table. I busied myself with the coffee and opened a can of food for Henry. Hearing the familiar sounds of his dinner being prepared, Henry opened one eye and stretched, aiming a shot of evil cat breath at Llewelyn through a jaw-cracking yawn, before using the policeman's suited knee as a step down from the table. I sent up a silent prayer that Llewelyn wasn't going to stay long and sat opposite him.

"Well?" I asked, reaching for the ashtray on the side of the sink just for something to do with my hands.

"I just wanted to make sure you got home okay," he said, his eyes hidden under drawn-in brows. Impossible to read.

"So you got that coffee under false pretences," I said.

"There was something else," he paused and took a sip of his coffee. "Have you seen anyone hanging around your flat, anyone suspicious?"

Apart from my pervert neighbour?

"No, but then I haven't really been looking," I lied. "Why?"

"No reason, I just wanted to warn you to be careful. I don't have any proof of anything."

"Proof about what, what do you suspect?"

He opened his mouth at the same time as the phone started

ringing. Great. Perfect timing. "It doesn't matter. Your phone is ringing."

I got up and picked it up. "Hello?"

"Where have you been? I've been ringing and ringing you," snapped a voice down the receiver.

"Jen?"

"Well?"

"Well what?"

"Where have you been?"

"Out. What's wrong?"

"Out? Is that all you can say to me? Out? I have been ringing your phone every twenty minutes for the last four hours. I rang you at work and they said you had to take the afternoon off for an emergency, and I panicked that something had happened to you."

"Dentist appointment. Emergency dentist appointment," I lied. Telling her I had been to see Jon would do little to calm her down. She thought even less of him than I did.

"Dentist? Fuck's sake, tell that moron who picked your phone up I will be suing him for unnecessary stress."

"It was probably Matt, you know us journalists, always economical with the truth," I joked, trying to calm her down. "What was it you wanted?"

"Just checking in to see how you were, wish I hadn't bloody bothered now. You completely fucked my day up."

"Huh?" I asked, my eyes sliding over to the kitchen door where Llewelyn was fussing over my cat.

"I said you're out getting root canal and I'm sitting at home panicking that you've been abducted or something."

"Well think of it as good training for when you and Steve start breeding."

Jen laughed, and I could hear her tension dissolving.

"Look, Jen I'm going to have to go. I've got DC Llewelyn here, I'll give you a call back tomorrow." I put the phone down before she could make any lewd suggestions. "Everything alright?" he asked as I walked back into the kitchen.

I stood staring at him, momentarily speechless. Henry was sprawled out on the table on his back, legs high in the air, displaying his wares like a hooker promising a good time. Llewelyn's left hand was covering Henry's belly, his fingers splayed, scratching and tickling him under each leg.

I pictured myself in Henry's place and squeezed my upper thighs together, suddenly aware I wasn't wearing any knickers. "Everything's fine," I croaked, shaking the image out of my head.

Llewelyn went to move his hand, only to be grabbed in Henry's vice-like grip.

"Was there anything else?" I asked.

"You could help me out of this one," he said, motioning towards his ginger glove before tentatively picking his hand up with Henry firmly attached.

I pulled Henry's legs one at a time from Llewelyn's hand, noticing the cat digging in for dear life with his claws. I couldn't say I blamed him. If I had got Llewelyn's hands between my legs, I might not be so keen to let him go. I squeezed my thighs together again at the thought, a steady pulse throbbing in me, and busied myself slowly unhooking Henry's claws. I was aware as I bent down, intent on my work trying to free the man from my cat, that his mouth was only inches away from my ear. If I turned my head just a little, it would be my mouth.

After a minute Henry let go and I saw he had drawn blood. Putting him on the floor, I threw him a felt mouse to play with instead. "Hold on," I said to Llewelyn, and ran to the bathroom for my medical kit.

Coming back into the kitchen, I got out the TCP, cotton wool balls and plasters. Opening up the bottle, the familiar smell hit the air, distilling the tension.

"Hope you didn't have a hot date tonight?"

Llewelyn laughed in answer and I fought the urge to ask him again. Shaking his head at the proffered plaster, he examined his wounds. "It'll be fine," he told me.

I threw the cotton wool in the bin and closed up the TCP bottle, replacing it in my medical bag, keeping myself busy to avoid his eye, scared he might read something there.

"Nice bag," he said.

"My mother," I said by way of explanation.

Llewelyn got up, "Well, thanks for the coffee, and remember what I said, take care."

"Always," I told him, following him to the door. "Sorry about the cat."

He stopped and turned towards me, "No problem."

He gave me a smile before bending down to give Henry a quick scratch to show there were no hard feelings. I closed the door and fastened the chain quickly to stop myself chasing after him.

Halfway through the night, something Llewelyn said jolted me awake with a snap. He had asked if someone was hanging around, someone suspicious. He suspected I was at risk of getting burgled. Why? Because Nina had been? Fuck. Was he onto me? I fumbled for my light switch and got out of bed, tipping the contents of my shoulder bag onto the floor and searching through the debris and cake crumbs for his card.

It included a mobile phone number. He picked up after five rings and it was only then I stopped to look at my alarm clock. It was after 2am. Half tempted to put the phone down, I realised he might know my number.

"This is Caitlin McCall."

I heard him cough as he tried to wake himself up and prayed I wouldn't hear him talking to a woman lying in bed next to him.

"Good morning. Checking on your patient?"

"You think Nina was burgled because of her job and they might come after me?" The words tumbled out breathlessly. Why else would he have answered a routine burglary that should have been dealt with by a beat bobby?

"Have you been worrying about this all night?" he asked.

"No. Well, sort of. Well, do you?"

"There's no reason to think it is connected with your work, unless there is something you are not telling me. Are you working on anything which could be connected to any crime?"

"I could ask you the same thing." Crisis over, I was now wishing the call over quickly, so I could do something less stupid, like put my head in the oven.

"Was there anything else?" I could hear him yawning and felt a pang of guilt at waking him. The police worked long hours – or they did on TV, anyway.

I fought the urge to ask if he was alone. "I'm sorry for interrupting you... I mean, waking you."

"No problem. Any time." He pressed the disconnect button on his phone and I stood, waiting for my breathing to return to normal. Was Nina's break-in related to this story?

Did they come after her because of the missing file? I crawled back into bed, feeling no more reassured.

# CHAPTER 19

"Two fillings," I said breezily to no one in particular as I walked past the newsdesk the following morning, my left jaw padded down with cotton wool for added effect.

A peek in the diary saw I was marked down for the funeral of Mr Scott after lunch. Shit. I wondered if it was blasphemous to go to church without knickers. Events had overtaken me the previous night and for the second day running, I found myself going bareback.

I didn't have the heart to tell Mrs Bishop she had been downgraded to page five, but fortunately the police weren't letting her paperboy go up and deliver her *Post* – a fact which the Editor made sure I included in the latest story on her protest. By mid-morning, I had begged a couple of hours at the Magistrates' Court as evidence of the *Post*'s continued commitment to journalism training. For legal reasons, reporting restrictions on magistrate court hearings were so tight you were lucky if you could squeeze two paragraphs out of the first appearance of a mass murderer, but it was all good experience.

On the way, I stopped off at a supermarket to track down some emergency knickers - a three pack of cream-coloured nylon pants to keep me going until the weekend. Racing home, I ripped open the packet and headed for the bedroom. It was only as they unfolded themselves that I realised I had bought the wrong ones – they were the size of a bed sheet.

Looking more closely at the packet, it dawned on me that I had managed to buy knickers for a heavily pregnant woman. But these were desperate times. I pulled off my tights and put a pair on. It wasn't that bad, they almost stayed up. All I had to do was put my tights back on and pull the top of the pants over them. I looked in the mirror for a final check. They were fine, as long as I didn't lift my hands above my head to reveal an expanse of baggy skin-coloured pants. As a journalist, I knew I should always be dressed and ready for anything, but I was pretty sure I wouldn't be called upon to do a Mexican wave at Mr Scott's funeral. If I did, maybe I would get lucky and someone would just assume I had a freakishly baggy stomach.

Promising myself some quality time with the launderette later, I headed off to court.

The Crown Court had joined the central police station on the edge of the city, but the Magistrates' was still in the city centre. Following Nina's advice, I parked in a visitor's slot of King Street police station, which was practically next door to the court, and nipped in to log my name and registration number at reception as a visitor. When it came to writing down who I was visiting, one person sprang to mind and I scrawled DC Llewelyn's name in my most indecipherable handwriting.

Magistrates were not legally trained and the ones sitting in judgement that morning seemed to know less about the law than I did. After ten minutes there, boredom set in and I wondered what possessed these people to leave the safety of the suburbs and join the bench. Civic responsibility would no doubt have been the answer, had I stood up and asked them. Personally I thought they were just bored of rotary clubs and bridge nights, and thought time in court was an easier way of getting an OBE than fundraising for charity. Fortunately, anyone who committed a serious crime was sent up to Crown Court to be dealt with by a judge who at least had some legal training, even if most of it had been 50 years ago.

I sat for another half hour before my rumbling stomach reminded me of the prawn mayonnaise baguette that was sitting on the passenger seat of my car. With the funeral an hour away, I decided to sneak out early and scoff the sandwich before driving over to St Peter's Church. Mrs Scott had said she would save a seat for me in the chapel, but I didn't want to be late.

I walked down the steps and across to King Street to pick up my lunch, pausing to light a cigarette and remember where I had parked my car. In the far corner away from the building, I spotted a small group gathered around a vehicle. Out of the corner of my eye I saw a man carrying a large yellow triangular object towards it, which could only have been a clamp.

"Stop!" I yelled, throwing my cigarette away and running across the road. "That's my car!"

The group turned around and I recognised one of them as the receptionist I had blagged a space from earlier.

I ran up to them, out of breath. "What's... going... on?" I panted, pushing my hand into my side where a stitch was beginning to take hold.

"Miss, is this your car?" the receptionist asked.

"You. Know. It. Is." I panted back, resisting the urge to bend double and throw up. God, I really needed to stop smoking.

"I'm afraid it's parked here illegally and we are going to clamp it," he said, motioning to the traffic cop with the clamp to carry on.

"No. Please. I'm. Supposed. To. Be. At. A. Funeral." I said, still gasping for air. One of the police officers laughed before muttering, "Yeah, right."

"Wait. I'm. Not. Parked. Illegally. I. Came. Here. To. See DC Tom. Llewelyn. Honestly." The three officers looked at each other, before the receptionist looked at me, "Well, where is he then?"

"That's. What. I've. Been. Trying. To find out. He stood me up," I lied, finally getting my breath back. I rummaged in my rucksack and pulled out my press card. "See," I said, in an effort to convince him.

He nodded slowly. "Alright, this time I'll believe you. Go on."

I smiled and thanked him, got out my keys and got into the car. He tapped on the window and I turned and rolled it down.

"I'll tell DC Llewelyn you were after him then, shall I?" he said.

I concentrated on not blushing. "Oh, erm. No, don't bother."

"It's no bother," he replied with a smile, walking back to the building.

"Bollocks!" I said to no one in particular, pulling out of the car park and resolving never to listen to Nina ever again. I turned my attention to my lunch and drove with one hand on the wheel towards St Peter's Church, alternating a mouthful of prawn mayonnaise with a mouthful of crisps all the way.

Arriving at the church with minutes to spare, I paused to brush crumbs from my black polo neck jumper when my passenger door opened and DC Llewelyn peered in.

"You have prawn mayonnaise on your cheek," he said. I blushed and wiped at it with my sleeve.

"I missed you at King Street, was there something you wanted?"

That bastard receptionist. "Nothing, it was a misunderstanding," I said, trying to sound vague, feeling the heat rise to my face. "What are you doing here?" I changed the subject.

"Standard procedure." He climbed into my passenger seat.

Was this standard procedure too, I wanted to ask. Instead, I lit up a cigarette and cranked the driver's window open to let the smoke escape.

"She's nice. Mrs Scott," I said, trying to make conversation.

"Hmmm," was all he replied. He stared out of the window, watching people going into the church, deep in thought, as I sat and finished my cigarette.

"Right, are you ready to go in?" he asked, turning to me as I rolled my window back up.

"What is this? A date?" I asked sarcastically, pulling on my coat, careful not to lift my arms too high and accidentally reveal an expanse of baggy off-white knickers.

He turned around, his dark eyes assessing me, making me squirm, before turning to open the passenger door.

I watched him walk quickly towards the church and sat debating another cigarette, before realising the hearse had pulled up outside the church.

"Shit." I scrambled out of my car, almost slipping on the wet grass in my hurry to get into the church before the coffin. Inside, I headed for an empty pew at the back and stood waiting for the coffin to come in to the sound of Louis Armstrong's *It's A Wonderful World* being piped through a decrepit PA system at the front. As always, it was freezing in church and I pulled my coat around me and huddled into it, wondering if Christians depicted hell as a burning pit of fire because they preferred the cold.

Llewelyn stood at the back of the church near the door, flanked by another police officer. His dark eyes bored into mine for a moment before looking away.

I did a silent head count of how many people were in the chapel and noted it in my book. I reckoned it was around 40 – not a bad turnout, I supposed. At my funeral I'd be lucky to get more than a dozen. My parents would be there, my mother no doubt telling everyone how I only had myself to blame for being a corpse. My brother Ben would arrive late from Manchester, having overslept from clubbing the night before, and my sister and her husband would travel up from Kent, bickering all the way. Jen would be there, dragging a reluctant Steve along for emotional support - and Nina, who wouldn't pass up the opportunity to buy a new outfit. I wondered who else would come. Would Tom Llewelyn be there? Inform my parents it was standard procedure? Maybe he would look at the framed photograph on the coffin – my mother would pick my graduation one - and feel a slight pang of, what? Loss? Regret? What might have been?

I swallowed past a sudden lump in my throat and pulled myself together as I became aware that the proceedings at the front of the church had ground to a halt. There was the unmistakable tinny sound of a mobile phone ringing to the theme of *Love Story*. I tutted in disgust, as the people on the pews in front of me shuffled around, trying to locate where the sound was coming from. Who would leave their mobile switched on at a time like this? I looked down at my bag on the floor in horror. Me, that's who.

The chest pains soon ceased, as I remembered that my phone had a normal ring tone. I hated those tunes you could install. They were annoying.

However, my confidence dwindled as everyone in the church seemed to agree it was coming from my direction. In horror I bent down to my bag and pulled out my phone, the sound getting louder. In panic I pressed an array of buttons to try and shut it up.

"Caitlin, is that you?" My mother's voice suddenly echoed throughout the church. Fuck. I had somehow put it on to speakerphone by accident.

I pressed another button and it went quiet. The priest returned to the service and slowly everyone stopped glaring at me and faced front again.

"I'm at a funeral," I hissed down the phone. Scared she might ring back if I put the phone down without explanation.

"Funeral? Whose funeral?" my mother continued, unmoved. "Do I know them?"

I crept out of the church, face flaming. I passed Llewelyn and glanced up at him. He seemed to be struggling with a straight face. Great. I was now officially a laughing stock. If any members of the congregation complained to the paper, I would probably be sacked.

Outside, my mother was unsympathetic.

"It's the modern world," she told me, assuming a lecture was just what I needed. "You young people can't do anything without technology."

I muttered goodbye and put the phone down, aware that a policeman was standing nearby, waiting for me to finish, probably planning to arrest me for a breach of the peace. He walked over and asked if I needed help. Llewelyn had dispatched him outside to offer me assistance.

I stuck my mobile phone under his nose.

"Do you know how to turn this off?" I asked.

He nodded and pressed a few buttons before handing it back. I walked back inside behind him and hid out of sight behind a marble column for the rest of the service, which thankfully passed without incident.

It was soon time to file out of the church to the burial site. I hung back with Llewelyn to give Mr Scott's family and friends privacy at the graveside, where it was almost warmer than it had been in church. Within a few minutes it was all over and people were rushing to get back to their cars and out of the cold March wind. I turned around to join the stampede but saw Mrs Scott left alone at the graveside and felt compelled to speak to her.

I walked forward hesitantly, embarrassed by my performance in the church. "Mrs Scott."

She turned with a sniffle, but her eyes were dry. "Oh, hello dear," she said, taking my outstretched hand. "Thank you for coming, my Jim would have appreciated it."

"I just wanted to say hello and how sorry I am for your loss," I said. "And I am so sorry about my phone going off," I was suddenly compelled to come clean. "It's new and I don't really know how to work it."

She smiled mistily. "I remember when we went to see that film at the cinema. They had love seats at the back and we cuddled all the way through it."

My conscience cleared, I said goodbye.

"Are you going?" She looked concerned. "I have sandwiches and cake back at the house for everyone. You will come, won't you?"

I smiled through my embarrassment, "I would love to, but I really have to get back to the office."

She nodding understandingly and I felt mean. I could have gone but I wanted to get my story written up and get home on time. I also didn't want to get caught out with my knickers hanging at half-mast half way down my legs during such a sombre occasion.

I felt Llewelyn walk up behind me as I reached my car. "Don't say a word," I said without turning around. I got into my car, hiked up my pants, and drove off without a backward glance.

It was almost five when I got home and I stuffed my washing into my car. At the laundry, I filled three machines with clothes, adding washing powder and conditioner as an afterthought. The cycle took 70 minutes, plenty of time to get to the office and write up my story.

Edward was sitting at his desk and wasted no time describing the first funeral he had covered as a cub reporter. I made us both a cup of coffee and cut him short with an apology, saying I had a hot date. I didn't bother adding that it was with twenty pairs of knickers down the local launderette.

40 minutes later, without bothering to use the spell check, I pressed the Send button on the story I had written, fully expecting it to be sent back to me by the News Editor the following morning for a soft focus re-write. As far as the world was concerned, Mr Scott's death was just a tragic story of a bloke in the wrong place at the wrong time and the trail had gone cold.

On my way out of the building I wandered over to the Health desk, where the newspaper's Health Correspondent was tapping away. Lewis Gilbert was around 40 and had the fake tan and generous moustache of an ageing porn star. Despite his looks he was a happily married man with three children, as the soft focus studio portrait on his desk testified. He was tweaking the next day's front-page story on a £100 million new hospital to be built in the area. I watched him type 'exclusive' in capital letters on the top of the story before he turned to me.

"Do you know a lot about Fifen Pharmaceuticals?" I asked, pulling up a chair.

He shrugged, "The usual boardroom shuffles and shenanigans you get in companies. Their PR man is a bit of a prick, very self-important about the work they do – doesn't see anything morally reprehensible in making huge profits out of human misery, disease and death." He stopped and turned to a pile of faxes on his desk, flicking through the top few, before finding the one he was looking for. "There's a lunch tour there tomorrow. I can't go, but if you're interested you can go in my place?"

I nodded. Tomorrow was Thursday, my day off. "Okay, thanks."

"Is this anything I should know about?" he asked, sniffing for the aroma of a story on his patch.

"No, not really. Nothing, probably," I said, taking the fax and scrunching it up into my bag. "I'll let you know."

I got back to the launderette in time to see the three washing machines end their cycle one after the other. Back home, I put my central heating up full blast and crammed wet clothes onto every available radiator space – giving my knickers pride of place. Within half an hour the rooms were steamed up enough to light my aromatherapy candles, put on my dressing gown and pretend I was in a sauna. Instead I settled down with Henry to watch *Breakfast at Tiffany's.*

Henry watched it long enough to meet my namesake in the film before slouching off unimpressed to the corner of the room to have a good wash. Once Audrey Hepburn had got her man and my knickers were well on the way to being dry, I rang Jen. Her phone was engaged, but she had 'call waiting', so I waited a few seconds for it to connect.

"'Lo?"

"Jen, it's Cat."

"Oh, I'm glad you rang. Listen, I've got my mother-in-law on the other line, can I ring you back in about twenty minutes?"

I looked at my watch. It was after eight. "Okay, but let it ring for a while, I'm going to take a bath." Through careful deduction I had worked out that Jen must have fiddled with my mobile phone. She had been only too happy to help programme numbers into its phone book when she stayed last week.

The line went dead as she clicked back to Steve's mother. While I waited for the bath to run, I emptied my bag and found the crumpled fax from Fifen Pharmaceuticals. The invite was addressed to the newsdesk rather than the Health Correspondent. It was from Sebastian van der Hoven, the acting Chief Executive of Fifen Pharmaceuticals – or rather his secretary - and the RSVP was to a Richard Kirkland, Press and Public Relations Executive Officer. Every journalist I knew hated these kinds of meetings. They never yielded any stories. You spent hours talking to people you would never meet again, telling them what kinds of stories you want, handing out business cards. They in turn would offer up some promising glimpses of decent stories, but when you tried to hold them to their word they never returned your phone calls.

I was just testing the bath water when the phone rang. Without waiting for her to speak, I told Jen to hang on a sec while I got into my bath, slipping on the half a bottle of bath oil I had dumped in it and dropping the phone as half the water splashed out. I righted myself and grabbed the phone. "Right. Sorry about that," I said, carefully holding the phone out of the water.

"No problem," said a distinctly male voice.

I sat up in the bath quickly and more water ran over the side. "That's not Jen, is it?" I asked rather redundantly.

"No, it's not."

"DC Llewelyn?" I guessed.

"Yes."

With horror I saw my nipples were erect, despite the heat of the water. I resisted the urge to put the phone under the water but found myself trying to cover my naked body with a flannel instead. "What can I do for you?" I asked, lying still in the hope he wouldn't realise I was lying starkers in the bath.

"I understand that you knew Professor Johanson."

"Well I wouldn't go that far, I only spoke to him once." I faltered.

"He rang you at home the morning before his death."

My mind raced as I tried to think of a simple answer. "Yes?" was all I could come up with.

"We've looked at his phone bill. There is a call to you at this number that lasted 55 seconds at about 9am on Tuesday."

"Yes?" I said again.

"Can you tell me what it was in connection with?"

"Erm yes, I spoke to the press officer at the university about a story I was working on and he suggested I speak to Prof. Johanson. I met with him once and he rang and left a message on my answerphone in reply to a question he couldn't answer at the time." I was getting good at this. That hardly even registered as a lie.

"Can I ask what the story was?"

Bugger. "Yeah, erm, sure. It was to do with some of his research projects," I said, thinking back to what Nina had written about his interests. "Cancer drugs and stuff like that."

"When is this story going in the paper?"

"Well, since he died, it isn't."

Silence stretched over the phone line and I wondered if this was his interview technique, working me into a panic so I would speak first, preferably with a full confession.

"Was there anything else?" I finally asked, praying he wouldn't mention the funeral.

"No."

"Bye."

I angled out of the bath enough to put the phone down, closed my eyes and slowly slid my head under the water, the sound rushing into my ears drowning out my thoughts. I pushed back up with a gasp when the phone rang again.

"Hello?"

"Cat. It's Jen. Who were you talking to?"

I sighed. "You wouldn't believe it. I thought it was you, so I picked it up and got into the bath. And then I found out it was Tom Llewelyn."

Jen giggled, "Did you put the shower head on?"

"Not my type."

"The shower?"

"The policeman."

"Pity."

I didn't want to think about it. "How is everything with you?"

"Do I sense you want to change the subject?" Jen asked.

"Yep."

"Steve made me get rid of the file you sent me."

"Shit. What did you do with it?"

"Burnt it. Steve doesn't want me to get involved with your hair-brained schemes." I could hear the quote marks around Steve's words. "So he made be barbecue it. Sorry, Cat."

I sighed. "That's two down and one to go," I joked.

"Why don't you send me another and I will send it back to you and you can send it to me and we could keep going like that until you find out what it is."

I laughed and said no. It wasn't that it was a bad idea, but the way I was going we would be doing it for the next ten years. And that was a lot of stamps.

She changed the subject, asking me about Llewelyn, trying to suss out his potential as a boyfriend. Was I remotely attracted to him? Did I sense that he was after more than just answers to his questions?

"No, no, no, no," I said in answer, adding a few more just to make the point. I had lost the energy to row with her over fiddling with my phone.

"Methinks the lady doth protest too much," she quoted, unaware she had narrowly missed out on a bollocking. "Anyway, you don't need a man. You're Henry's Cat now."

# CHAPTER 20

I was vaguely familiar with the new headquarters of Fifen Pharmaceuticals but pulling up outside the main entrance I realised it was the first time I had seen it without the blockade of animal rights protestors and their accusing placards. The gleaming glass-and-steel building was the main attraction at a grand new industrial estate on the edge of the city, known as Carson Park.

There were a few weedy-looking trees in the tarmac car park which had probably looked bigger in the architect drawings that had convinced the city's planners to bulldoze the woodland it had replaced. But I still thought calling it a park was pushing it.

It took ten minutes to get there and another five to find a parking space. I supposed being seven miles outside the city in the middle of nowhere forced people to come to work in their cars, at least that's what it looked like judging by the large, empty bicycle park on the side of the building.

Pulling open the glass doors, I felt the heels of my shoes shrink into the deep navy pile of the expensive carpet and took in the fake marble walls of the grand reception area. I walked over to the receptionist at the far wall, feeling my calves doing most of the work to pull my feet out of the quicksand-like floor. The receptionist flicked back her auburn hair, which hung like a silk curtain around her shoulders, and gave me a thousand-watt smile that didn't reach her eyes.

I returned the smile but could only manage about eight watts and I fought the urge to ask her what hair products she used as I handed over my grubby-looking invitation. She tapped perfectly manicured colourless nails on the slim computer keyboard in front of her and then spoke into the barely-there microphone of her near invisible phone headset. I busied myself picking at my chipped nails as she finished her call and gestured for me to take a seat on a navy sofa that looked like it was made from the same material as the carpet. Fearing I would be sucked into it and never seen again, I plumped for one of the ladder-backed chairs next to a thin glass coffee table.

I was busy people-watching out of the spotless plate glass window when an outstretched hand suddenly appeared before me. Startled, I gripped the hand and stood up, looking up into the beaming face of a man who could only be Richard Kirkland.

"Hi. Ms McCall. Hi. Very glad you could come," he said, slightly breathlessly, "We had hoped of course that Lewis Gilbert would have been able to come, but any member of the press, especially our very own *Post*, is very welcome. We are a little community here and we think of the *Post* as our very own community newspaper."

Hmmm. I bet he didn't say that to the reporter who covered the last animal rights demo. I stood up and looked him up and down. In his 30s, he had thinning hair, the translucent skin of someone who didn't get out much, and the stooped posture people get from years of bending and scraping before their superiors.

He smiled again. "I'm Richard Kirkland, Press and Public Relations Executive Officer for Fifen Pharmaceuticals."

I fought a sudden image of him saying the same thing to his wife and kids every time he went home and picked up my bag, waiting to be led off down a corridor.

"Right, Ms McCall, we are very lucky today because our chief executive Mr Sebastian van der Hoven has agreed to take a few minutes out of his busy schedule to introduce himself before we begin the tour." He beamed at me again and I faked a smile at such an honour.

He looked disappointed that I didn't wet my pants with excitement and smiled again. "I'm afraid he won't have time for an interview, but hopefully I can answer any of your questions adequately."

I nodded vaguely, still concentrating on not being sucked into the carpet. The backs of my knees were in danger of cramping up if all the floors were covered in it.

After a five minute walk down a rabbit warren of corridors, we came to a dead end. With a flourish, Kirkland pulled at a red sash and a pair of elevator doors slid open in front of us.

He walked in and smiled at me. "Executive lift," he whispered reverentially.

I stared at the floor and coughed back a laugh. The lift shot up to the top floor and the doors slid open to reveal a lobby of real marble. Following Kirkland, I noted a water feature like a mini Trevi fountain and wondered if anyone had ever done an Anita Ekberg in it after getting drunk at the firm's Christmas party. A water fountain in the *Post*'s newsroom had suffered a worse fate last year when a few advertising managers mistook it for a urinal.

"Business must be booming," I said, wondering if the company had an executive harem to go with the lift.

Kirkland ignored me and we came up to a door at the end of the corridor. He knocked before we walked in. The office was the size of the entire newsroom at the *Post* and featured a large oak desk in one corner and two Le Corbusier leather sofas by a large plate glass window. Outside there was an uninterrupted view of the fields that separated Carson Park from the city boundary far off in the distance. There were two sets of doors on one wall of the office, presumably leading to a private sauna and the master bedroom. Kirkland installed me on one of the leather sofas and disappeared through the doors to go and find his lord and master.

Just like Mr Benn, as Kirkland disappeared through one door, another suited man appeared through the other. He was about 45, with a shock of silver hair on top of a deeply tanned face, and looked a little like Richard Gere. He looked about five foot ten, but could have been well over six foot without the carpet.

He turned to look at me and started slightly. "Hello?" The accent was pure Eton and his tone wiped away any welcome in the word.

I stood up and walked towards him with my hand outstretched. "Caitlin McCall, I'm a reporter with the *Post*," I said.

He ignored my hand and walked over to his desk.

"I'm here as part of a tour. With Richard Kirkland."

He turned around and finally smiled. All fake charm. "Ahh. Yes. Sebastian van der Hoven," he said, finally holding out his hand. It was smooth and tanned like the rest of him. I shook it and we sat on opposite leather sofas, waiting for Kirkland to reappear. A door opened behind me, and van der Hoven looked past me. "Ahhh, Richard."

Kirkland came into view on my left side, looking flustered. "Mr van der Hoven, I am so sorry. I was just speaking with your secretary who assured me you were not here yet."

Sebastian van der Hoven smiled, "Don't worry, Richard, I came up in my private elevator – Katie didn't see me this morning. Anyway, we have met now and," he looked at a heavy gold Rolex watch on his wrist. "I'm afraid I am due at a meeting." He stood and held out his hand again. "It was nice to meet you, Ms McCall. Perhaps next time we can have a much longer chat."

I shook his hand again and smiled before Kirkland pushed me out of the office, telling me we were heading for the Research and Development area. "It's where the real work is done," he whispered reverentially, despite the fact that R & D were housed at the back of the complex in cheap pre-fabricated buildings. Presumably staff working in this area were too busy to worry about the views or the décor.

Afterwards, I was rushed off to the boardroom for coffee. Kirkland seemed to expect me to take copious notes on everything he was saying and I took to scribbling nonsense whenever he spoke, confident he wouldn't be able to read my shorthand.

"You see, Caitlin. May I call you that?" I nodded. "Thank you. You see, we are doing vital work here. Every day there is the chance that one of our scientists could uncover the cure for anything from AIDS to cancer," he paused for a moment's reverential silence. "Imagine what that would mean to the world." He whispered, to add gravitas to his words.

I bit back questioning them on their dubious sales policies in developing countries and nodded dutifully. If this visit was going to be worthwhile, I needed him relaxed and expansive. Questions like that would just make him defensive.

Kirkland eventually stopped talking and encouraged me to ask 'anything, absolutely anything' I wanted.

Finally what I had been waiting for. "There is some ambivalence towards pharmaceutical companies and the huge profits they can make from drugs," I said as he nodded. "What happens when the drugs you develop replace drugs on the market, and take away business from other companies?"

He frowned and rubbed his chin thoughtfully. He looked faintly ridiculous. "Well to some extent that's a natural progression of the business and it is why companies invest huge sums of money in research and development of new drugs. You see, you can spend a billion pounds researching a drug, which can be replaced within a few years. This is why the drugs are often expensive for the NHS to buy at first. We have to reap that one billion pounds back and we have to do it quickly because new drugs are coming out all the time. The alternative is to go out of business and then there will be no new drugs to help people." He paused, allowing me time to catch up with scribbling his words. For the first time since I had met him I actually wrote down what he said.

"At the end of the day the people working at Fifen want to find that cure or that new wonderdrug more than anything else. To make sure we stay ahead of the game, Fifen will be working on a dozen or more new drugs at any one time so that when one drug is replaced by another, there are other drugs out there making money to ensure the business stays afloat."

I nodded, pen poised, hoping for more. "Of course, we also pride ourselves on getting the best quality laboratory staff so that we find new treatments all the time. We have people moving over to us from other companies, other countries, even universities and the NHS, because the work we do is so vital."

I changed tack. "What about the costs of drugs, how are they set? Some seem to cost pence while others cost thousands of pounds."

"That's a very good question," he told me, smiling approvingly. "There are two types of drugs - branded and generic. You might buy aspirin for a few pence from the pharmacy but will pay more for a new branded painkiller. The cheap drugs are generic. Lots of drug companies make and sell them and there is no," he looked upwards and searched for the right word, "*copyright*, I suppose you could call it – or patent. There are thousands of drugs like them available over the counter and on prescription. New drugs coming onto the market are released by one company. They developed the drug and hold the patent and they can set the price. Of course we also rely on market research."

I nodded and flipped my pad shut. I had heard enough. We shook hands and Kirkland extended an open invitation to 'pop in any time', along with handing me his gold-embossed business card as he walked me back to reception.

All the talk of cures for cancer had made me desperate for a cigarette, but I waited until I had pulled out of Carson Park before lighting up. At home I shrugged out of my suit and replaced it with a pair of jeans and an old rugby shirt I had swiped off my dad. I sat at my tiny kitchen table with a coffee and reviewed my notes. I was now convinced the deaths were linked to some sort of industrial espionage – hadn't Kirkland admitted they poached staff from other companies? And the staff must bring their research with them, even if it was just what was in their heads. If I had invested millions in research and then the scientist decided to take himself and his findings off to another company, I would be really pissed. But angry enough to kill? Who knew what people would do when it came to billions of pounds.

I leaned on the table and stared out of the kitchen window at the sky, which was streaked with shocking shades of purple and orange as the setting sun moved over to light the other side of the world. I continued my musings. Where did market research end and industrial espionage start? Maybe Mr Scott had been a gofer between two companies, got caught giving away sensitive information, and that's why he died. Maybe his assistant knew and that's why she had been killed. But why had the professor died? Was his death just a coincidence? Try as I might, I couldn't make it all fit. I needed to talk to someone who knew what was going on. But I wasn't sure I actually wanted to meet whoever knew what was going on, as they appeared to have killed at least two people.

The grim turn of my thoughts made the shrill ring of the phone a welcome interruption.

"Cat. Nina."

"Hello. How's the flat?" I tucked the phone under my chin and slid to the floor of my tiny hall.

"Okay. Almost back to normal. The only thing stolen was my laptop and that was insured."

"Good. I'm glad. So are you back at work?"

"Late shift tomorrow. Which is why I'm ringing. How about going out and getting riotously pissed tonight?"

"I'm at work tomorrow morning," I told her.

"You're young, you'll recover." So said Nina, who only arranged to go out drinking during the week when she didn't have to stumble into work the next morning.

"How about starting early?" I asked, thinking I could leave at ten, if we kicked off at six.

There was a pause. "Okay, how about seven?"

Good enough. "Okay, deal. Where shall we meet?"

"Porky's?"

Now I got it. "Nina, are you just looking for someone to tag along with you until you pick Norman up?"

I heard her gasp. "No. I'm outraged at the suggestion. Anyway, I'd have thought you would have wanted to go so you could see that delicious cop who's guarding your bod."

Hmm. I was going to have to level with Nina, this was getting out of hand. "I'll see you at seven." I stubbed my cigarette out in a makeshift ashtray - a soap dish which featured a picturesque scene of Bournemouth – one of the more useful presents from my mother.

Porky's was quiet when I walked in and a quick look around confirmed my suspicion that Nina hadn't yet arrived. I was wearing slinky silver-grey bootleg trousers teamed with a two-tone purple shirt with huge lapels and cuffs that I had bought from a secondhand shop during my last trip to London. The barman served me too quickly and I was left wondering whether to grab a table on my own or whisk off to the Ladies to touch up my make-up.

A tap on the shoulder saved me from the decision and I turned around with a smile to see Norman standing before me with a wide, welcoming grin. He said hello and pointed over to a table. I picked up my drink and followed him over.

"Not working tonight?" I asked.

"No, night off."

"It's a nice place," I said. "Where did you get the name from?"

He laughed. "It's a long story. Basically it was funded by the police."

I spluttered. "Really?"

"Well, police compensation, anyway."

"Shit. What happened?"

"I got pulled in one night when I'd borrowed my sister's car. She was a trainee lawyer and had a nice set of wheels, a two-year-old beemer. I explained this to the boys in blue – but they weren't ready to make the leap that a black man driving a BMW could be anything other than a drug dealer. My sister was out at the time and I couldn't prove anything so I got locked up for the night."

"And you did them for wrongful arrest?" I finished.

"Nah, I had a bit of a row with one of them and he helped me down the stairs. Broke my arm in two places."

I gasped and took a glug of my drink, waiting for him to continue.

"My sister argued I was lucky that they hadn't killed me. They settled out of court for £50,000 plus costs. I decided they needed a constant reminder of how foolish they had been so I set up this place."

I laughed and pointed to the doors. King Street Police Station was less than 100 feet away, "You mean it happened over there?"

He gave me the wide grin again in answer.

"Excellent." I gave him a toast and downed my drink.

"Funnily enough, it's proved quite popular with some of the younger cops. I'm not sure if it's to piss their bosses off, or because they know it's the one place they can go where they won't bump into any of them."

I laughed and Norman went off to get more drinks. I was starting to think that I could get used to the VIP treatment when the doors to the bar opened and Nina walked in. I gave her a wave but she turned behind her and I realised she wasn't alone. My eyes met with a familiar pair of dark eyes over her shoulder.

"Of all the bars in all the world," I said to myself as Tom Llewelyn returned my wave.


"Fancy meeting you here," my voice was dripping heavily with sarcasm.

"Would you like a drink?" he asked, ignoring it. I suppose he was used to being made to feel unwelcome in his job.

"Norman's sorting me out."

His eyes followed mine over to the bar where Norman was taking his time kissing Nina hello. "He could be some time. It might be quicker if you let me get you one."

"Vodka and tonic."

Within a few minutes he returned and I thanked him with my coldest smile. I wasn't quite sure why I was being such a bitch. He seemed to bring out the worst in me. Maybe it was because I had made a fool of myself at least twice in his presence - that, of course, and the fact that he had the power to arrest me at any moment for withholding evidence in at least two suspicious deaths.

Nina finally noticed me. "Here she is," she told Llewelyn.

I tried to return her smile but my jaw had frozen. Was the prospect of jail for withholding evidence a better option than death? Only just.

Nina didn't seem to notice my internal struggle. "I managed to drag Tom out for the night," she told me, batting false eyelashes at him.

"Shit," I said again.

Llewelyn silently watched my reaction as Nina got up and returned to her station at the bar. He eventually leaned forward towards me and I looked around for my coat, just in case I had to make a quick getaway.

"Your friend," he motioned to Nina who by now was deeply engrossed in conversation with Norman.

"Nina," I told him.

"Yes. Nina," he looked mildly confused. "She seems to think we are…" he paused, exaggeratedly searching for the right word, "That there is something going on between us?"

I looked ahead and tapped my disposable lighter on the table, feigning boredom. "Hardly surprising. I'm beginning to wonder myself, the way you keep popping up."

He was saved from making a response by the return of Nina and Norman, who slipped me a large vodka martini with the instructions, "Get that down you, girl, you'll soon thaw out."

I followed his instructions to the letter and drained it quickly, nibbling on the olive left at the bottom of the glass.

Llewelyn was soon entertaining Norman and Nina with tales of dodgy arrests, which was 'all most definitely off the record'. Nina, ever the journalist, began to ask him about some of his cases.

"Have you ever seen a dead body?" she was asking.

"Yeah," he looked at each of our horrified faces in turn as we sat and considered what grisly sights he must have witnessed in his job and awaited the gruesome details. "My granddad's."

We sighed in relief.

He laughed. "Policing in this country is not like America, there just aren't enough mutilated corpses to go round."

"But you attend the post mortems, don't you?" Nina persisted.

"Don't have time. We get the reports afterwards and occasionally we might go down to the morgue to see the pathologist, but that's about it. I suppose if you were curious you could have a rifle through his drawers."

"Well?" Nina asked, waiting for more.

He shook his head and Nina looked disappointed.

The drinks and the conversation continued to flow. A jug of vodka martini sat on the table, half empty, and Llewelyn was telling a story about some bloke who had been caught red-handed in a burglary, but insisted that he lived there and had only broken in to check the alarm system was working.

"He was outraged that we wouldn't believe him," he said. "Even when he couldn't produce any evidence that he lived there - like a house key."

Nina began trying to convince Llewelyn that reporters had an important role to play in crime-fighting. "Look, most of your crimes are solved because some member of the pubic walks up to you and says," she paused and looked around the table before pointing at me, "'She did it.' And the only way they can do that is if we spread the word around."

I fought back the temptation to shout back "No I didn't!"

I turned to Llewelyn, desperate to change the conversation. "So what is going on at Fifen then?" I asked. I bit my tongue. Where had that come from?

He shrugged. "What makes you think there is anything?"

I took a slug of my drink. "Well that inquest I saw you at - Mary something..." I pretended to struggle to remember. "Stanshaw, she worked there. Mr Smith worked there. Bit weird."

"Don't you mean Mr Scott?" He asked.

I flushed at my mistake. "Yeah. Isn't that what I said?" I feigned ignorance.

"No. You said Mr Smith."

I tapped my temple. "Professional hazard, so many names, so few brain cells." He smiled at me but said nothing.

"Are you never off duty?" I asked, suddenly crotchety.

"Are you?" he asked.

"Touché." I smiled and picked up my drink. "So between you and me, what is going on?"

"Caitlin, you know I can't tell you that." His tone was casual but there was a warning in his eyes.

"You could. You just aren't going to." I got up and squeezed past him, concentrating very hard on not stumbling and falling into his lap, scared that if I did I might never get up. Either that or I might start sobbing into his chest and admit everything.

Nina pulled me aside to ask my advice about Norman. Was he serious about her, she wanted to know. I shrugged. Who was I to be offering advice? The only bloke who had shown any interest in me tonight was more bothered about getting me down the station than into bed.

I sat back down, my drink untouched. Lack of food meant the vodka martinis had gone to my head and I was feeling slightly sick. I pointed to the door and told Nina I was going home. She broke off her conversation with Norman long enough to say goodbye and I pulled on my coat, in a hurry to get some fresh air.

The cold air hit my stomach the second I got outside and I quickly looked around for somewhere that I could surreptitiously throw up.

Too late, the door opened behind me and I realised I had missed my chance. Llewelyn took my elbow and steered me over to the police station.

"Didn't do anything," I said desperately as I realised where he was taking me.

"I know, I'm going to make you some coffee before I take you home."

I shook my head and found myself whimpering at the thought of going inside.

"You're just saying that to get me in there. Once I'm there it will be push, bang and clang," I motioned the cell door being closed, locked and the key being thrown away over my shoulder, accidentally throwing my glove with it.

Llewelyn turned around and picked it up for me. "You're being ridiculous. How can I lock you up? You haven't done anything wrong."

I wagged my finger at him. "Ah-ha! That's what you think."

Llewelyn ignored me, pushed me through the doors of the police station, and we headed for the lift. We came out on the top floor at a dimly lit empty canteen. Llewelyn frog-marched me up to a table and sat me in a chair before going up to the coffee machine and emptying his change into it. He lined up two cups of black coffee and waited for me to start sipping. My eyes were drooping but I knew that closing them was out of the question if I wanted to hold onto the contents of my stomach. To take my mind off the spinning I took another slurp of coffee and pulled out a cigarette.

"You've had enough," Llewelyn took the cigarette from me. "It'll only make you feel worse, trust me."

I scowled at him, but couldn't speak as I was having difficulty swallowing the coffee in my mouth. Instead he put the cigarette in his own mouth and lit it.

"What were you doing there anyway?" I asked, halfway down my second cup.

"You don't know?" He sounded surprised.

I shook my head, gently.

"Invited by Nina."

I nodded at the inevitability of it. It took me five minutes to finish both cups of coffee, by which time I was feeling better but desperate to get out of the police station. I stood up and walked towards the lifts.

"Well, I'll be going now," I said, getting in one. "Thanks for the coffee."

"Surely you aren't going to walk home on your own?" he asked, following me into the lift. I got out at the bottom and walked out to the street.

Llewelyn followed me. "You work for a newspaper and must be aware of the risks, especially at this time of night."

Not something I needed to be reminded of at that moment.

"I'm more concerned about harassment," I told him, trying not to look too grateful for the company. If it came to a choice between being with him and walking home alone to an empty flat where someone could be waiting, he won. But only just.

He ignored my sarcasm. "I'll walk you home."

"I'm perfectly capable of getting home, I don't need my own personal police officer to do it." I answered. *Yes I do, I do,* I thought.

"Please, I'd feel better if you'd let me." He began walking off in front of me before turning around. "Are you coming?"

My feet were cold and I was beginning to need the toilet. "Don't have much choice." I muttered ungratefully.

Llewelyn pushed his hands deep into the pockets of his dark brown suede coat as we left the building and I waited for the inevitable small talk about the weather. It didn't come.

"Why are you so interested in Fifen Pharmaceuticals?" he asked.

I shrugged, carefully weighing my words before I spoke. "I'm a journalist, I don't think there could be a more nosy profession."

"Except the police, probably," he said.

"Ah, but you like to have all the answers, and keep them to yourselves. My profession is all about spreading the truth."

He laughed. "Or gossip. The police can't afford to spread the truth until they know for sure it is just that. The truth."

"Oh, please. Nina was right earlier, you do catch most people because of help from the public."

He paused before speaking. "You have to admit there are times when a police officer and a journalist can get in each other's way. Say you got a tip-off about a crime, would you go straight to the police or would you try and investigate it yourself to get a story first?"

I was saved from answering by the fact that we had reached my flat. Looking up, I was relieved to see Helen's light on. If I needed help I could just scream.

I turned to Llewelyn and held out my hand, "Well thank you for walking me home. I did appreciate it."

He ignored the hand and followed me to my door.

# CHAPTER 21

The first thing I saw as we entered the communal hall was Henry sitting at the bottom of the stairs, looking bad-tempered, ruffled and wet.

"How did he get out..." Frowning with incomprehension, I turned to where my flat door should have been. It was hanging off its hinges and I could see a chaotic trail of clothes and crockery lying in my small hallway. Llewelyn held his arm out to stop me rushing forward and motioned for me to join Henry on the stairs before disappearing into the flat.

I heard a muffled crash and someone shout out, "What the fuck?" before a man streaked out of the flat and up the stairs. Out of instinct, I grabbed at his foot and pulled him down, realising as I did that it was Ian. He turned to free his foot and fell down the steps, landing on his head. Llewelyn was now standing at the flat door.

"He fell," I told him as we stood over Ian, waiting for him to regain consciousness.

"That's my line," he said and pulled out his mobile phone to call for an ambulance and a police squad car. I sat back down on the stairs and snuggled up to Henry for warmth, trying to work out why the hell Ian had broken into my flat. I told Llewelyn all I knew about Ian, explaining that he lived in the flat next door and that I had caught him spying on me a few times.

"A stalker? That would explain these." Llewelyn pulled out a piece of scrunched up cotton from his pocket. "I take it they're yours?" he said as he unravelled a pair of my knickers with the word 'Monday' emblazoned across them.

I nodded and went to grab them but Llewelyn put them back in his pocket with a shake of his head. "Evidence," he explained, a smile tugging the corners of his lips, "I caught him trying to steal them."

"But then I won't have any Monday pants," I told him, "I'll have to wear Tuesdays and then on Tuesdays I'll have to wear Wednesdays and I'll never know what day it is." I stopped abruptly and bit down on my tongue, aware I was talking nonsense. I suddenly wanted to kick Ian very hard in the balls. Sadly, the sound of sirens reminded me that it was probably not a good idea to do it in front of a police officer, especially when I had already knocked the man unconscious. I grabbed Henry, who seemed to be enjoying all the excitement, and went off to examine my flat. Now I knew it was Ian who had broken in, I was confident there would be very little damage.

I was in for a surprise. The flat was in chaos. Kitchen cupboards had been swept clean and everything was lying on the floor, smashed crockery mingled in with cutlery and tins of cat food. In the bedroom my neatly piled-up washing had been thrown all over the floor and the two framed Mark Rothko prints were smashed across my bed. Even my plants had been uprooted and pulled out of their pots, the soil sprinkling every available surface.

My second thought was that I would have to revisit the launderette again. My first that I should have kicked Ian in the balls when I'd had the chance. Going through into the lounge I saw all my books and CDs had been pulled off the shelves and lay in a heap with the shelves themselves pulled off the wall and lying on top of them.

Trembling, I collapsed onto the sofa, trying to take in the mess. I could hear Ian having his rights read to him as he was loaded up onto a trolley by a couple of paramedics. Two uniformed police officers got into the back of the ambulance with him and drove off. Llewelyn eventually came into the lounge.

"I take it he'll live?" I said without turning around.

"Yeah, but I think he'll have a worse head than you in the morning. I'll need to take a statement from you at some point."

He walked through to the kitchen and I heard him put on the coffee machine and search for something to drink out of. Luckily Ian had missed a couple of china cups and saucers that my mother had given me. We sat drinking coffee in the kitchen and surveyed the damage.

"Why the hell didn't you report him?" Llewelyn wanted to know.

"He seemed pretty harmless, you know, just a sad, pathetic little man," I answered, sipping my coffee.

"That's what they said about Dennis Nielson," he answered. "Of course they were right. He was a sad little man – serial killers are rarely the charismatic criminal genius that TV dramas would have you think." He paused and I pondered the kinds of bad people his job had brought him into contact with – not that mine had been much better so far.

"I've called out someone to come and fix your door first thing in the morning, but in the meantime you need somewhere to stay." He stood waiting for an answer with his mobile phone in one hand, ready to make a call at my request.

"I'll be fine. Thanks."

"I can't leave you here. If you have nowhere to stay, I can put you up for the night."

I resisted the urge to go 'gulp' and shook my head. "I need to stay for Henry. I can fix something up for the door, and besides, Ian won't be coming back tonight."

If I got really scared I could drag my duvet upstairs to Helen's sofa.

He began to argue, but checked himself, stopped and shrugged. "Well, it's up to you."

I stood up and picked my way through the junk, leading him out of the flat. "Thanks." I stood at the door, waiting for him to leave.

He walked out and turned around. "Are you sure you're okay?"

I could read concern in his eyes and resisted the urge to break down and start bawling in front of him. "No problem," I told him. "Thanks for walking me home."

He turned around and gave me a slow smile. "Anytime. You are upping my clean-up rate single-handedly."

If only he knew.

After he left, I pulled the door shut and put the chain on, which was intact. Unfortunately the hinges only needed one good kick to bring the whole thing crashing down, but I was hoping that someone would overlook that. Besides, how likely was it that I would get burgled twice in one night?

I couldn't believe Ian had broken into my flat. Two days ago my biggest concern was a taxman wanking outside my front door. Now my front door was hanging off its hinges. With that thought, I picked up Henry and walked into my bedroom, crawling into bed with all the lights blazing and a large umbrella within reach to deal with any unwelcome visitors.

I realised two things when I woke up: the lights were no longer on and a man was sitting on my chest of drawers.

"There's coffee by your bed." I snapped on my bedside lamp and looked straight at Llewelyn.

"Jesus. Don't you ever sleep? What the fuck are you doing

here?" I asked, feeling for my glasses while simultaneously trying to remember if I was wearing anything under the duvet. Glasses in hand, I realised I was still wearing my shirt and trousers and sat up to reach for the coffee.

"Smartarse," I muttered, spotting the bubble pack of headache pills lying in the saucer.

He stood up. "It's after nine, your door has been fixed, your cat has been fed and I need to take a statement from you when you're ready." He walked out of the bedroom and into my lounge.

"I need to tell work," I said, getting up and bounding over to the phone.

"Done it, you've got the day off," he said without a backward glance.

I closed the bedroom door, quickly flung off my clothes and grabbed a pair of jeans and a rugby shirt. Praying my hair wasn't too frightening, I walked into the lounge, taking a quick look at my new front door as I went.

"I thought you could take me out for breakfast and I could fill you in," Llewelyn said.

I nodded and tramped off to the bathroom to clean my teeth.

Twenty minutes later we were sitting opposite each other in the familiar, friendly surrounds of Franco's coffee bar with a red leather booth all to ourselves and two mugs of steaming hot coffee sitting between us. I ordered us both the full fry-up with extra toast and lit my first cigarette of the day.

"Right, fire away," I told him, blowing smoke behind me.

"Your neighbour claims your flat was already broken into when he came home around eight. He says the door was hanging off its hinges, pretty much as we found it, and he went in to investigate." He paused to take a sip of his coffee.

"And the knickers?" I asked.

"Couldn't help himself. Apparently they were just lying there and he picked them up."

I put my hand up to signal that I didn't need to hear any more. "Is he lying?"

It was hard to imagine how much I wanted it to be Ian who had broken into my flat. If it wasn't, I had more to worry about than a sad loser with a knicker fetish. Fuck it. Who was I trying to kid? I had more than that to worry about anyway.

"Well, normally I would say yes. But you have to admit it is strange that two reporters from the *Post* have been broken into in the last three days," he paused as our food arrived and waited for the waitress to walk off. "Was anything stolen?"

I looked down at my plate, suddenly I wasn't feeling so hungry. "I'm not sure. The TV and video are still there."

Llewelyn gave me a look. "Is there anything you're not telling me?" I shrugged and picked up a piece of toast, dipping it in my fried egg before filling my mouth. We ate in companionable silence for a few minutes and sat with coffee refills.

"So what happens now?" I asked.

"We're releasing Ian on police bail, but he has to find somewhere else to live as a condition of that bail." He paused and looked at his watch, "In fact he should have packed up his stuff by now."

"So this was all just a ruse to get me out of the way," I surmised.

"Not entirely," he said, mysteriously. I waited for him to elaborate, but that was obviously all I was getting. We stood up to leave as his mobile phone rang.

"Excuse me," he pulled out a mobile not much bigger than my lighter and walked out ahead of me so I couldn't hear his conversation. I stood waiting in the doorway of Franco's, wondering if he was going to come back.

Within a minute he was at my side. "Have to go. Work," he said. "Will you be alright?"

"Of course," I said, feeling suddenly defensive.

He ignored the tone. "I'll be in touch." He walked off towards the city centre without a backward glance.

I took an incredibly slow walk back to my flat, partly to make sure that Ian wouldn't be there when I arrived and also to avoid the inevitable tidy up for as long as possible. I arrived back at the flat to find an envelope pushed through my brand new front door. It was a card with a heart on the front of it and inside all it said was *'Sorry'*. I had never seen Ian's handwriting, but I assumed the other burglar, if there was one, wouldn't be sending me a greetings card. I shoved it straight in the bin and rolled up my sleeves, ready to get down to some serious tidying up.

It was only then that I discovered my Monday pants weren't the only thing missing. Ian had also made off with my maternity pants. With a shudder I considered reporting the theft to Llewelyn, but balked at the idea of describing them – large nylon pants the colour of a pub ceiling, slightly used. Hmmm. On second thoughts Ian was welcome to them. Better in his grubby hands than sealed in a bag with my name on it, marked as evidence in Leicester's police headquarters. I didn't think I would be needing them again in a hurry.

# CHAPTER 22

Barrelling through the front door, balancing four carrier bags, I ignored the flashing answerphone and dumped the bags before going back out to the car for the remaining shopping. It was already dark, but I'd spotted Llewelyn lurking beside my car.

"Are you going to help me or what?" I said.

He picked up the remaining three bags out of the boot and slammed it shut. He turned the key and pocketed it, before carrying the bags through to the kitchen.

"Better," he said, referring to the cleaning up I had done.

"Yeah, my mother would be really proud." I turned to switch on the coffee machine and bent over the bags.

He leaned against the kitchen door, watching me hurriedly unpack my shopping.

"Very healthy," he said, referring to the large amount of convenience food on display.

I rummaged in one bag and triumphantly pulled out a tub of cottage cheese, holding it up like a prize trophy. "I take it you don't want to stay for dinner?"

"That would be nice," he said.

I went into reverse. "What?"

"How about I go and get us some takeaway?" he asked, "Curry? Pizza? What would you like?"

"Erm, surprise me," I told him, watching him walk out of the still-open flat door.

By the time he had come back, I had unpacked the shopping and returned a call from my mother to turn down her offer of a three-piece suite, offending her despite my repeated assurance that it wouldn't fit into my flat. I listened patiently while she explained that my father was still obsessing about the next-door-neighbour's dogs and neglected to tell her that I had been burgled. It was only for her peace of mind – I didn't want her to worry. Plus, if I told her she'd turn up and camp out in my flat, or worse still, send my dad.

I had finished the call with the promise of a visit at the weekend and decided I was going to ask Llewelyn why he kept popping up in my life of late the second he came through the door.

The question evaporated, however, when I smelled the contents of the two brown paper bags he was carrying. He held them up for my inspection. Curry. I followed him through to the kitchen and watched him dish out pilau rice, sag aloo, pakora and chicken bhuna onto new crockery bought that afternoon. Another bag contained naan bread, pickles, and spinach and onion bhajis.

I opened the fridge and grabbed a bottle of Budweiser for him and a can of Diet Coke for me then followed him into my lounge. Belle and Sebastian were playing on my stereo and I curled up on one end of my hastily repaired futon, with my plate, and dug in without ceremony. Llewelyn took a sip of beer before breaking off a chunk of naan bread.

Over the meal we chatted about Asian cooking and debated the perfect curry. I wolfed down most of my plate, only sparing a few mounds of rice to be polite. I looked up to find Llewelyn staring at a corner of the room.

"Different," he said.

I followed his gaze. "Had to think on my feet," I told him, referring to the two leaning towers of books and CDs. The shelves they had been sitting on were lying in the back garden, unsalvageable.

Among my purchases that day had been a drill. At some point I was going to have to attempt some serious DIY, but until then it was lying fully charged by my bed, just in case.

I stood up and piled up our plates to take into the kitchen.

"Another beer?" I asked, automatically going to the fridge as he followed me in with empty foil containers.

"No thanks. I should get going."

I stopped with a bottle in my hand, feeling awkward. "Oh. Right. Okay." I put the beer down on the table and watched him shrug into his brown suede jacket over a chunky-knit jumper the colour of dark chocolate.

I saw him to the door and closed it firmly after him, his warning to make sure I locked up echoing in my ears. I raced into the lounge as I heard the front door to the house close and peered out of the window through a gap in the curtains. He got into a silver car parked across the street and got out his mobile phone as he got in – ringing a girlfriend, maybe? I was just struggling to make out the registration number when my phone rang. I let the machine pick it up.

"If you want to spy on someone through your window, turn out the light first, otherwise you cast a very big shadow," Llewelyn's voice came over the machine. I jumped away from the window as if I had been stung and heard him laugh before he disconnected.

I cleared the message and rang Jen. She picked up after three rings. "Help," I said without bothering to introduce myself. "He turned up in my bedroom this morning and he had breakfast and dinner with me today."

"Maybe he was hungry," was all she replied.

I sat on the floor and invited Henry to bounce onto my lap. "What do I do? What do I do?" I asked in panic.

Jen laughed. "Shag him, of course."

I ignored her and told her about the burglary, pausing every few sentences to allow her to practise her extensive range of expletives in response.

"Shit, Cat. Do you think it was Ian?" she asked when I had finally finished.

"I'm not sure. I can't help thinking that maybe it was someone else looking for that file."

Jen agreed. "I think you should hand it over to Llewelyn and come clean about everything."

"Will you visit me when I'm locked up and playing house in a ten by ten cell with a violent bull dyke?" I asked.

"Don't be ridiculous. He obviously fancies you and he could make sure that nothing happens to you."

"Yeah, right. I'm sure he would agree to forego arresting me in return for sexual favours." Jen's view of the police was even more skewed than mine. "Do you really think he fancies me?" I asked, changing the subject.

"Well he's spending an awful lot of time with you, and I think it's fair to say that police officers don't normally socialise with their suspects – or at least they don't on *The Bill*."

"But he might just think I know something and is trying to charm it out of me."

"Well, you do know something," Jen replied. "So at least you know he's good at his job. Anyway, is it working?"

"What?"

"The charming."

I ignored her. I didn't want to think about the answer. Of course it was working. "I'd better go," I said, to end the conversation.

"Right. But I think you should come clean. With him, I mean.

You have to tell someone. What am I going to do if you get bumped off?"

"Okay, okay, I'm just going to get a copy of it before I hand it over. I'll do it at work tomorrow."

# CHAPTER 23

Waking the next day, I decided that the best thing to do would be to stay in bed all morning and pretend the last few days hadn't happened. In fact, make that the last two weeks. My time was most definitely up as far as this story was concerned. I was going to have to hand it all over to the police on a promise that they would give me the exclusive when it all broke – or at the very least not arrest me.

I pulled the duvet over my head and groaned. The ink had hardly dried on my press card and I might be handing it in by this time tomorrow. Resisting the temptation to spend the next hour sitting in my pyjamas watching daytime television and feeling sorry for myself, I had a rare urge to return to the bosom of my family. I wanted to go home.

It took just over an hour to drive to Marswell and as I entered the village I saw yet again the entire place was caught up in the annual fever of the national Spring into Summer competition. Every village in the country seemed desperate to prove they had the greenest fingers in the land. Spring flowers were beginning to bloom as far as the eye could see and every patch of grass was alive with daffodils and bluebells. Walls, lamp-posts and even street signs were adorned with hanging baskets filled with ivy and green shoots which would blossom in time for the judging at the end of April.

My parents' home was no exception. The house where I had grown up was a Seventies semi-detached masquerading as a quaint country cottage. Wisteria and clematis grew up the front walls and were just beginning to show signs of life. In the summer they became a riot of white, purple and pink, covering the red brick walls and the blue latticed archway over the front door.

I pulled up in the drive and ignored the front door in favour of the back, which had been the children's and tradesmen's entrance for as long as I could remember. I walked into the kitchen, shouting hello, and carried on into the hall looking for my parents. Reaching the lounge door, I heard a squeal of pain from the top of the stairs and saw my mother come running down, flapping an orange duster at me in a panic. I instantly froze. Something was wrong. Had they found me here?

"What? What is it? Mum? *Mum?*" My voice reached a high pitch to match hers as she got to the bottom of the stairs, clearly distraught. "What's happened?" I demanded.

My mother jabbed violently towards the floor, pointing at my feet. I followed her eyes and the fear evaporated. I had broken her cardinal sin. I was wearing my shoes on the carpet.

All my life, my mother had insisted everyone take off their shoes at the kitchen door. As a child I would mumble apologetically to friends who came around and make faces behind her back, explaining to them in the safety of my bedroom that she was nuts. As I got older and those friends turned into boyfriends, I just stopped inviting them home out of sheer embarrassment. Now, as an adult, I accepted that my mother was a germ freak and avoided coming home too often. If she ever lost her marbles and needed to go to a nursing home, I had promised her that I would find one that was all white tile and stainless steel so she would be able to gibber nonsense to herself, safe in the knowledge it was clean.

I unzipped my boots and left them by the back door, rejecting her offer of a pair of slippers, and padded into the lounge. Against one wall stood a mahogany sideboard filled with her precious Royal Doulton china, which she had threatened to leave to me when she died. The room smelled of the synthetic outdoors, which can only come from spray air freshener, and matched the faux autumnal shades of the carpet, curtains, sofas and rugs which were patterned in clashing green-and-brown leaf designs.

"This is a nice surprise," my mother said, barely hiding her sarcasm. At least I knew where mine came from. "Are you staying for lunch?"

Looking over at the mantelpiece clock, I saw it was eleven o'clock. I could probably make it through another hour before the stress of being back home got to me and I ran screaming out of the house. For some reason visiting home had become like trying to get through an episode of *Last of the Summer Wine*. It wasn't just that it was boring and I had no interest in it, but that it somehow plunged me into the depths of despair within ten minutes of starting.

"That would be nice, Mum," I told her. "I have to be at work at two, though."

She bustled into the kitchen and I followed behind.

"Lunch will be served at twelve, as it always has been in this house on a Sunday," she stated firmly.

I sat at the pine kitchen table, which doubled as a dining table - unless my parents had company, when they opened up the dining room next door. My mother got to work, cutting up vegetables and putting them into a pressure cooker where they would stay until they were the consistency of baby food and any nutritional value had been removed. The only good vegetable in my mother's kitchen was a mushy one.

"You should get a steamer," I told her, watching her furious chopping. "It cooks them without taking any of the goodness out."

"Faddy," she said and went back to her chopping.

"I'm not sure the Far East would agree with you," I muttered and stared aimlessly out of the steamed-up kitchen windows. "Where's Dad?"

My mum tutted before pointing to the garden. I stood and wandered over to the window for a closer look. My father stood with his back to the house, gazing over his garden. Like many men his age, he saw gardening as the ultimate display of his masculine prowess. Beaten by an overbearing wife inside the house, the garden was his domain – a sanctuary where he spent most of his time.

Since I could remember, he had always been particularly proud of his lawn. The large green rectangle was flat and smooth, like the felt of a snooker table, and was painstakingly cut to a precise three centimetres in length at all times. Even in March, with a dull, overcast sky and everything wet from weeks of rain, the grass had a rich velvet green colour that looked out of place in a Midlands garden on a dank day. Throughout my childhood, as now, I could only admire it from afar. Sitting on it or - God forbid - playing on it was strictly prohibited.

My knees and elbows bore the scars of a childhood played out exclusively on concrete slabs and a tarmac driveway.

My mum tutted. "He's out there from the early hours keeping watch over his precious grass. These dogs are going to put him into an early grave."

I shrugged back a laugh. A lawn-related trauma was nothing new. Last year it had been threat of moles that kept my father up at night. Before that it had been a particularly virulent strain of moss. Now it was a pair of red setters.

Lunch was a hurried affair as my father rushed to return to his post, promising to come back for pudding. I helped my mother wash up and she repaid the favour by loading me up with a set of plastic food containers, assuring me they were freezer-friendly and microwave-safe despite my protestations that I didn't own either. I left at one o'clock, fed, fed up and secure in the knowledge I would rather have a homicidal maniac chasing me than return home to live.

I got into work a little early for my shift and parked my car in the company car park, ignoring the threats to clamp unauthorised vehicles. Unsurprisingly for a Sunday, it was empty. I felt underneath my passenger seat for the envelope containing Mr Scott's research papers, rolled it up, and stuffed it into my rucksack before getting out of the car. If whoever broke into my flat had been looking for it, I guess I had to congratulate myself for being clever enough to leave the file in my car, even if it had been totally accidental. I had decided to send copies out to *New Scientist* magazine, the *British Medical Journal*, and any other publication I could find on the internet that might understand its significance. Over a week of trying to find out had got me nowhere.

Tony was discussing ideas for content of the following day's paper with Max, the Picture Editor. Max had worked at the *Post* since his teens and looked like someone had left him in developing solution too long. His skin was the colour of aged sepia print and his hair a nicotine yellow. I stood behind them for a few minutes and tried to read the diary over Max's shoulder.

"Caitlin." Tony stopped talking to Max and turned around to me with a smile. "Everything sorted?" he asked, referring to my burglary.

"Thanks," I said.

"I didn't realise you had such good police contacts."

I blushed. That meant that Llewelyn had given his rank and title when he had rung in for me and it also meant that Nina had probably by now explained to the whole newsroom that I was sleeping with a cop.

Tony noted my blushes, but didn't pry. "There's not a lot happening tonight. Tomorrow's front page looks like it's going to be another health story – bed crisis sets back a thousand operations since Christmas. Check on your high-rise woman and keep an eye on the wires for something interesting for page four."

I nodded and wandered off back to my desk. I was just weighing up the pros and cons of getting an extra lock on my door with Nina when she stopped mid-sentence and began to study her computer screen intently. The hairs on the back of my neck stood up and I turned to see the Editor standing behind me.

"I understand you two women have been burgled," he said.

Nina and I both nodded.

"Any reason to think it has anything to do with a story you are working on?"

Nina and I shook our heads.

"You haven't upset any of our local criminal fraternities?"

Again we shook our heads.

"Mmm," he turned away, disappointed. "There's still time."

Within the hour, most of the skeleton shift of reporters who work on Sundays had left the office and Tony had finally hung up his clipboard and gone home. The building was pretty much empty, although the printing presses housed in the basement were usually on the go almost 24 hours a day. Tonight they were silent.

# CHAPTER 24

I made ten copies of the research paper and wrote up an anonymous letter to put in with them, explaining about the possible significance, the suspicious deaths and the link with Fifen Pharmaceuticals. Copies were going out to the country's top science and medicine journals and one to Leicester Police. I stuck them in the first post out-tray on the newsdesk and dumped the original back in my desk drawer. I felt better already. I might have failed to get the story, but it hadn't been for want of trying.

To celebrate, I put in a call to Mrs Bishop to check how she was doing.

"Fine, dear. Keeping myself busy," she said as I scribbled down a few quotes for her latest story. "I've got a lovely chocolate walnut cake in the oven at the moment, hope you can pop over tomorrow and share it with me over a nice cup of tea."

Noting it in my diary, I wrote up a story on her continuing protest and cake-baking activities.

The newsdesk phone rang as I finished the story.

"I want to return my copy of the *Post*," a shrill voice rang out. "It was rubbish."

I stifled a laugh and asked how I could help.

"Today's copy of the *Post*," she repeated, "I want my money back. I know my rights."

I hummed in agreement with her as she launched into a litany of why the paper wasn't worth the 40 pence she had paid for it, not least that the TV was rubbish. I told her to come down to the offices where the staff on the front desk would be happy to help her tomorrow morning. They wouldn't be but at least it got her off the phone.

I returned to my desk and took a call from the Fire Service control room, ringing to tell us they had been out to a car fire on the Bankborough Estate, bringing their total for the week up to fifteen, only a few off their record. I wrote up a quick story to fill up page four, adding a quote from a scrap metal dealer I found in the *Yellow Pages* who confirmed old cars were no longer worth anything in the scrap metal market. This meant owners abandoned their old cars instead of paying for them to be taken away.

I sent the lead across and wandered off to the library to dig out a file photograph of a burnt-out car that could be used. The library was down on the second floor, close to the telesales girls, who had long since packed up their lip-gloss and gone home. It was dark in the room and I felt along the wall by the door to find the light switches.

I froze at the unmistakable sound of a chair creaking.

"Is someone there?" I called out shakily. I paused in the hope my eyes would adjust to the darkness. The library was windowless as part of efforts to protect it from fire. Someone had once told me that when the fire alarms went off, the room sealed itself and the oxygen was sucked out so a fire wouldn't get in and burn the precious archives. With a shudder I realised that would mean no one could get out either. After a few seconds it was still too dark to see anything and I let my hand creep back along the wall to find the light switch.

"Don't turn the lights on." My hand shot back at the voice and I clutched my chest in fear.

The chair creaked again and I felt myself fall back against the wall, shaking. "Wh… who is it?" I stuttered eventually.

A lamp came on at the far side of the room, the sudden brightness momentarily blinding me. I blinked several times and looked. The silhouetted shape of a man turned into the more familiar sight of our librarian, Michael.

I breathed out heavily. "Fuck. You scared the shit out of me."

I turned and picked out the light switch on the wall, flooding the room with garish overhead strip lighting to burn his retinas in punishment.

He stretched and rubbed his eyes. "Sorry. Fast asleep. What time is it anyway?"

"After nine. I'm the late reporter."

"Nine?" He stood up and grabbed the coat slung on the back of his chair, wrapping a scarf around his neck. "I'm really late."

"What are you doing here?" Since starting work at the *Post* I had never seen the library staff in after about four.

"Research for a book." From time to time, Michael put his encyclopaedic knowledge of the Leicestershire area to good use, producing little books called things like *Leicestershire's Waterways* and *Our Proud Sporting Heritage* that proved very popular with homegrown pensioners who made up the bulk of our readership.

He pushed past me into the hall.

"Sorry again if I scared you," he said without turning around as he headed for the stairwell. I let out a stream of expletives in reply as I took a minute to collect myself.

Turning to the bank of filing cabinets, I picked out a picture of a burnt-out car, from a large collection hidden away under F, for Fire. After picking out a picture for the story, I turned to the opposite wall, where photographs of people were kept. The *Post* was in the process of turning everything digital, but the old picture archives were the last to be done. Finding the drawer marked L, I opened it up and flicked through faded photographs of once famous Leicestershire faces until I found what I was looking for.

A picture of Tom Llewelyn was stuck to a story written in August last year. The story was only a few paragraphs long and was about a missing person. He was the officer to contact. The picture was never used, presumably they used one of the missing person instead. He stared out at me from under his dark brows, managing to look faintly embarrassed at having his photograph taken while still looking serious. His dark hair was longer than the cropped version he now had, but otherwise he looked the same. I glared back at him, feeling faintly stupid, before I put it back and slammed the drawer shut.

By the time I got back to my desk it was time to make the regular calls to the Police, Fire and Ambulance Service control rooms to see if anything was happening. It apparently helped to ensure we didn't miss out if there was a plane crash, motorway smash or major blaze. At the moment, though, there was nothing.

The shift lasted until midnight, but as long as calls were made to the emergency services every hour or so, it didn't matter where I was. I headed for the deserted canteen for a drink and a cigarette to kill some time before sneaking off home early.

I wasn't really in the mood for food, the events over the past few days had left an uneasy feeling in my stomach, which was doing marvellous things for my waistline but nothing for my sanity. Pushing aside my sandwich, I worked my way through a coffee and the day's national newspapers instead. After twenty minutes, I took the lift down to the newsroom and stepped out, ready to finish off and call it a night.

A figure sitting reading at my desk in the dark stopped me in my tracks. The newsroom was fitted with lights that were motion-sensitive, so you had to keep moving, otherwise they went off.

"Checking up on me?" I started to say as I moved forwards,

assuming Tony had come back to the office. My movement triggered the lights to come on and the words died on my lips. It wasn't Tony.

"I think this is mine," the man said, holding up the file that Mr Scott had given me. "Is it the only copy you have?" He didn't wait for an answer, but bent down to search through the rest of my drawers, finding my emergency packet of cigarettes and a silver Zippo lighter which he threw on the desk. "Good, you smoke." He continued to search until he was satisfied that it was the only copy.

I finally found my voice. "What are you doing here, Mr van der Hoven?"

He looked up. "I think you know, Ms McCall. Or at least you would have eventually worked it out. Have you any idea of the trouble you have caused me? Not to mention him." He pointed at a photograph of Mr Scott looking out from the front page of a newspaper lying on my desk.

He held up the file. "Well, we certainly won't be needing this," he said and flipped open the lighter, setting light to one corner of the paper.

I rushed forward to stop him, but stopped as my eyes caught sight of a shotgun lying casually by his feet. van der Hoven followed my eyes and nodded.

"What does it mean, anyway?" I asked in a desperate attempt to employ the age-old technique of keeping the murderer talking. But either he wasn't in a talkative mood or he had seen the same movies as me and had no intention of giving me any time to formulate a plan of escape.

"Ever the journalist in hunt of an exclusive," he said contemptuously. "How about I let you star in your very own front page story?" The flames licked up around his hands and he dropped the fat envelope into my bin, where it continued to burn, setting light to its contents.

I sneaked a look up towards the roof. Not only had the offices been fitted with motion sensors but also top-of-the-range smoke alarms, which cut off most of the electricity when they went off, including the supply to the lights.

At last an idea began to form in my racing brain. I picked a cigarette from the packet I had been clenching in my hand. "Do you mind?" I asked.

He shook his head and I lit up.

"Cancer is a very nasty disease," he said, more to himself than me. He looked up. "Have you ever watched anyone die from it?"

I shook my head and took a long drag on my cigarette. Cancer was the least of my worries, but I was happy to let him keep talking while my cigarette smoke joined the larger plumes coming from the bin and made its way up towards the ceiling.

"I have. Breast cancer. My mother. It took her four years to die," he said, "Four years of hoping, four years of different treatments. Thinking it was over only for it to flare up again and for her to die in agony after all." He stopped abruptly and I tried to think of something to say. "You can't tell me that I don't know what it's like. Cancer."

"No," I muttered, encouraging him to go on, all the while my eyes fixed on the fire alarm on the wall above his head, willing it to go off. I looked briefly over to the newsdesk where the remaining copies of the file were still sitting safely in the post out-tray.

"People are always so ready to criticise my company," he began again. "But you people don't seem to realise that without us there would be no chemotherapy drugs, no insulin for diabetics, no steroids for asthmatics." He looked at me, "Not even any aspirin for hangovers."

I nodded again, still watching the smoke going over his head towards the fire alarm sensor. I was trying to guess when it would go off so I could make my move when the lights went out.

"The government hold back drugs because of the expense all the time. Think of all those people who would have been saved if the AIDS vaccine was available, or a million other drugs. But if a company holds back research like that - that's immoral." van der Hoven raised his voice, "Even though it will ruin the company. And there will be no more life-saving drugs. Cancer is the gravy train for pharmaceutical companies like Fifen today. There's so much money in it these days. We all think we are going to get it. We give millions, billions, of pounds to cancer charities in the hope of finding a cure in time to save ourselves. Yes, we like to think we are being philanthropic, but it's really just self-interest."

"That's a very cynical view," I said, picturing his words quoted in a newspaper story.

He shrugged. "True. That research, though, that would have finished us. No more chemotherapy and no more Fifen, no more billions of pounds to spend on research. Maybe even no more cancer."

A light went on in my mind. "Is that what this is about? Holding back cancer research?" I asked incredulously.

"What did you think?" he snapped. "Fifen wanted to specialise in cancer drugs – he thought we were so close. And when we got closer I realised it would have finished us."

"How did it work?" I asked.

"I'm not a fucking chemist," he suddenly snarled. "My job isn't to listen to the scientists, but protect the shareholders' interests. Make sure that they get a good return on their investment."

"And that drug wasn't going to do that." I motioned towards the bin, where the papers were blazing.

"I'm glad you seem to understand. Not everyone is as sensible. Take Mary Stanshaw, for example." My eyes widened at the mention of her name. He took in my reaction. "Very principled young lady. Not a good thing to be in our business."

"You killed her." It was a statement not a question. "But there was no murder inquiry or anything," I added, keen to continue to make conversation as smoke continued to drift upwards.

His smile had little humour in it. "There wasn't for Fifen, either."

"But how?" I was beginning to lose hope. Maybe the fire alarms were faulty. I couldn't believe the number of times I had panicked in the past that the tiny curls of smoke from my illicit cigarettes smoked at my desk on late shifts would set them off.

"I work in the pharmaceutical industry. There are chemicals and compounds everywhere. Many of them are unheard of and a few are undetectable."

So he had given her a drug to stop her heart. I remembered that Andrew Fifen had died of a cardiac arrest while out fishing. The same method. A near-perfect murder weapon.

van der Hoven continued. "Tell a chemist that you are looking for a painless drug to use if euthanasia ever becomes legal, and they set to work in their laboratories without question. The range is now quite extensive. Scientists understand. They are amoral creatures – set them a puzzle and they set out to solve it, they don't consider first what their answers will mean. Do you think Einstein meant to invent the atom bomb?"

I shuddered at the boredom in his voice. I suppose if you do it often enough, even murder can become a drag. My eyes slid away as van der Hoven picked up the shotgun. I noticed the battered state of the arm of the gun and remembered with a shudder that Mr Scott had died after a blunt blow to the back of his head before he had been burned. I struggled to find some words to say that would prevent him from taking aim at my head, knowing there was nothing.

Instead, I looked down at my feet and willed them to move. I dropped my cigarette on the floor and ran to the other side of the desk, hoping that keeping some distance between us would keep me alive. If he planned on shooting me, it was a wasted effort, but if that were the case my embarrassment, like me, would be short-lived.

"Don't make this any harder than it has to be," van der Hoven said flatly, "I'd rather not have to chase you around the desk." He pointed the shotgun at me and called my bluff.

As he took aim, the fire alarm finally sprang into life and shocked me out of my frozen state. I ducked under the desk and barged through the chaos of computer wires straight at his feet, deciding my only hope was to take him out before he did me. He wobbled over and landed with a thud on his back, the shotgun going off in his hand and taking out my computer screen before it fell sideways, knocking over the bin and scattering the burning contents across the carpet.

A chair started to smoulder and eventually caught light, carrying the fire up and across the desk to the computers, lighting all my paperwork as it went. I came from under the desk on my hands and knees and crawled crab-like away from van der Hoven. His hand shot out and grabbed my ankle, pulling me towards him. Within seconds he had flipped me onto my front and had crawled on top of me, his hands inching towards my throat. With one hand I reached behind to the front of his trousers, grabbed at the handful of soft flesh and squeezed hard. His sudden gasp told me I had got the right spot and he loosened his grip long enough for me to put a hand up to protect my throat. But he quickly recovered and he clasped his hands vice-like around my fingers until I was starting to strangle myself.

My vision went cloudy and I thought I was dying until I realised that van der Hoven was coughing and had removed one of his hands from my throat to wipe at his streaming eyes. The fire had spread rapidly along the bank of desks, carried by the amount of paper and the full-to-brimming recycling bins. I sent up a silent prayer of thanks that the *Post* had not made efforts to become a paperless office. Smoke was starting to fill the room but because my nose had been pushed into the floor, it hadn't reached me yet.

I pulled a hand out to grab at an object and felt a round, hot metal tube. Ignoring the searing heat melting through my skin, I pulled it up with a swift arc and, out of the corner of my eye, saw the shotgun arm crash into the side of van der Hoven's head. His hands came away from my throat and he pitched forward on top of me. Unconscious, he lay there as I struggled to push his inert form off me. He rolled off and landed on his side, revealing a gash from where I had hit him. I threw the shotgun away, feeling the scorching hot metal rip skin away from my hand as it flew through the air and landed close to the newsdesk.

I stood up, but was forced immediately back onto my hands and knees as smoke entered my lungs, burning my throat like acid. Looking around, I realised the fire was spreading across the newsroom rapidly and I had no choice but to get out – fast. Rolling up my polo neck jumper over my mouth, I crawled on two knees and my good hand across to the stairwell and pulled the door open with my injured hand. A swift glance over my shoulder confirmed that van der Hoven was now surrounded by fire and I couldn't have saved him, even if I had wanted to. I ran down the four flights of stairs in darkness, missing a step halfway down the last flight, and fell the rest of the way, passing out before I got to the bottom.

When I came to, I was lying in a crumpled heap at the bottom of the stairwell. I looked up to see the booted feet of four firefighters who, complete with full breathing gear, had smashed through the glass double doors which opened onto the foyer of the *Post*'s office.

"Fire," I rasped at them redundantly before passing out.

# CHAPTER 25

My first thought when I woke up was that I wasn't at home. The second was that I really needed to stop smoking, judging by the blistering fire raging in my throat and lungs. Pulling the covers off my head, I peeked out onto the hustle and bustle of a hospital ward. Thinking I must have been in an accident, I pulled up the hospital blankets in panic and looked down at myself to survey the damage, but could only find my left hand had been rather heavily bandaged. I looked under the sheets again and checked that I could wiggle my toes, just to be sure, and noticed a series of magenta and midnight blue bruises running up and down my legs.

A fire. It was all beginning to come back to me now. van der Hoven, attempted murder, falling down the stairs, the firefighters. Fuck. I pulled the covers back over my head and did some deep breathing, only to come up gasping for air as my lungs heaved painfully. Sitting up, eyes streaming and blinking heavily, I noticed a gaudy bunch of orange and pink gladioli lying on my bedside table alongside a bottle of Lucozade and a mask attached to a canister of compressed oxygen.

How long had I been in the hospital for? Looking across for the answer, I spied a copy of the *Gazette* sitting innocently among the belongings of my next-door neighbour who was absent from her bed. Getting out, I scuttled across, ignoring the pain which shot across my shoulder as I grabbed the paper.

A quick glance at the front page had me hyperventilating.

*'BLAZE CLOSES DOWN CITY NEWSPAPER*

*A blaze ripped through the offices of the Leicestershire Post last night.*

*More than 50 firefighters fought the blaze, which took over four hours to put out.*

*The fire is believed to have broken out on the newsroom floor at around 10pm and quickly spread to all six floors of the building, including its state-of-the-art printing presses, bought just last year for £1 million.*

*Fire chief John Robertson refused to speculate on the cause of the fire and said that one person who was on the premises at the time of the fire was taken to hospital with minor injuries.*

*He said: "At this time it is not clear if the casualty was in the building legitimately. As far as I am aware they have only suffered minor injuries and police will no doubt want to speak to them later on today after we have finished our investigation of the scene."*

*He said that the extent of the fire would mean the building would have to be demolished.*

*Harry Thomas, editor-in-chief of the Post confirmed the fire had closed down operation of the paper, but that he hoped to set up an alternative office within the next day or so.*

*He said: "Obviously now our main concern is that the Post, which is enjoyed by more than 400,000 readers every day, is up and running as quickly as possible. In its 105-year history the Post has always managed to come out, only missing one day – back in 1943 when the offices were bombed during World War II."*

*Mr Thomas refused to speculate on the cost of the damage and said only that he was confident they would find alternative printing premises quickly and that the disruption would be temporary.'*

The *Gazette* had given the story three pages filled with photographs of the fire and had even managed to sneak in an advertisement for people wanting to cancel their subscription to the *Post* and switch to the *Gazette* instead.

"You're awake, then," a voice said from behind the paper.

I looked up to see a nurse, not much older than me, leaning over with a thermometer, which she wasted no time sticking into my mouth.

"You had a couple of visitors while you were asleep. A young woman, called Nina?" I nodded. "She brought the flowers and Lucozade. And a policeman – very good looking – he wanted to speak to you about the fire. He said he would come back later."

I took some deep breaths and wondered if I bit hard enough on the thermometer I would overdose on mercury.

"Are you alright?" The nurse frowned at me and took out the thermometer. She looked at it, "Well that's normal, but you look awfully pale. Are you in pain?"

She gestured to my bandaged hand.

I shook my head, "No. It's just that I really need to get out of here, now." My voice came out in a whispered rasp I hardly recognised.

"I'm afraid that's not possible, Caitlin. No doubt your lungs are sore from the fire, but just use this mask when it gets bad. The oxygen will help. Not too much, though – it makes you a bit high," she told me in her Mother-knows-best voice.

I stared hard at her. "Why can't I leave?"

"We need to keep you in for observation, or at least until the doctor has seen you."

"And when will that be?"

"Any time now," she said, straightening her uniform and bustling off, throwing a smile back at me.

I looked at the flowers from Nina and the card attached that had been signed by most of the newsroom. Instead of the usual 'get well soon' it appeared to have *'thank you'* written on it. Peering a little closer – my glasses were nowhere to be seen - I realised that Nina had written *'for the holiday'* underneath it. It seemed they were enjoying the fact that it was most definitely not business as usual at the *Post* and were in no doubt where the blame lay.

That was another reason to get out of here as fast as I could. It was just a matter of time before I was sacked, but I preferred it to be later rather than sooner.

Looking under the bed covers again, I noticed that I was wearing a paper gown like the ones people wore as they were wheeled into the operating theatre on TV. Putting my good hand behind me, I realised it opened up at the back. For the third time that week I appeared to be knickerless.

Pondering my desperate situation, my eyes lighted on the chair by my bedside table. My still absent next-door-neighbour had a fluffy terry towelling robe hanging on the back of it. I slipped out of bed and into the robe, finding a pocketful of coins for the payphone at the end of the ward. I padded barefoot to the end of the ward and managed to get past the nurses station without anyone standing up and shouting "Stop! Thief!"

Outside the ward, I headed off to find the foyer where I could make a couple of calls and get the next edition of the *Gazette*.

It appeared I was worrying unnecessarily about my state of undress, as the tiny foyer shop was full of people in dressing gowns and even one patient in a paper theatre gown like mine – although she had matching paper knickers. Trying to ignore the *Post* stand, which lay ominously empty, I went straight over to the *Gazette* stand, which was bustling. The second edition of the paper was just being delivered and the delivery man was discussing the big story with the shop staff.

"I heard that one of them reporters was smoking fags in the

office and that's how the fire started," he was telling the woman behind the counter.

"Really?" she asked. "I knew that fags killed, but not that quickly," she chortled to herself.

I had heard enough. I pushed my way through the crowd and grabbed a copy of the paper. Throwing the money down on the counter I went off to find a quiet corner to read the latest instalment.

*'BODY FOUND: POLICE LAUNCH INVESTIGATION*

*A body has been found by firefighters after a blaze ripped through a former city newspaper office.*

*The Leicestershire Post has been forced to close down after a blaze ripped through its offices last night.*

*More than 50 firefighters fought the blaze for four hours before bringing it under control.*

*But it has been revealed that firefighters made the grisly discovery as they damped down the building in the early hours of this morning.*

*Fire chief John Robertson said: "My officers found the body as they were damping down. We informed police of the discovery and they have now launched their own investigation."*

*A police spokesman confirmed an investigation had been launched but refused to confirm whether they were treating the death as suspicious.*

*One casualty was taken to hospital with minor injuries and police are expected to question them later today.'*

The rest of the story repeated what had already been said. Although I noticed the editor's quotes had been cut out. Looking up, I saw a couple of police officers walking towards the lift lobby of the hospital and fought the urge to hide behind a display raising awareness about the anonymous Crimestoppers hotline. Searching the pocket of the dressing gown, I made my way towards a row of pay phones and thought briefly of ringing my mother. Nina wasn't home, so I called Jen at work.

"Cat, are you alright? What the fuck is going on?" Jen squealed down the phone at me.

"Jen, I haven't got time, I need you to come and pick me up and take me home."

"Are you running from the law?" she asked.

I laughed nervously, "Don't be ridiculous. I just don't have any clothes and they are letting me out of hospital."

"Hospital?" Her voice reached a pitch which only dogs could hear. "Hospital? What the fuck are you doing in hospital?"

"Jen, please, I haven't got time. Everything's fine, I promise. There was a fire and I hurt my hand and my leg, but now I am fine and they are letting me go home, only I need a ride."

"What's wrong with your voice?"

The smoke had turned me into a huskier version of Lauren Bacall.

"A throat infection," I rasped. I figured the lie would get her off the phone quicker than the truth.

Eventually she agreed to meet me outside the hospital's maternity unit in an hour. Suddenly desperate for a cigarette, I reached back into my pocket to see if I could scramble enough money for a packet of ten. Walking back to the shop, I looked behind the counter for the array of cigarettes normally found there, but was greeted by a blank wall.

"We don't sell cigarettes – hospital policy," the woman behind the counter said, dismissively turning to the customer behind me.

Great. I walked slowly outside and took a few gulps of fresh air instead. Looking up, I noticed the line of smokers huddled against the cold and rain, similarly clad in dressing gowns, one or two had even trailed down with drip stands. Deciding it was too cold to scrounge a cigarette and join them, I went back upstairs to see if I could grab my stuff off the ward before meeting Jen. I got back to my bed without incident and thankfully, my next-door-neighbour was still missing from her bed.

Replacing her dressing gown on the chair, I scribbled a note, using her pen and pad, explaining I had borrowed 50 pence for an emergency and left my name and number in case she wanted to collect the debt.

I noticed a white plastic bag full of rags had been stuffed under my bedside table. Pulling it out, I recognised my clothes from the night before. Hiding behind the curtain around my bed and ignoring the strong smell of smoke, I pulled on the trousers and polo neck jumper, wincing as it stretched to accommodate my heavily bandaged hand, and zipped up my boots. I gave myself a quick once-over. Not bad - only seven holes, a couple of rips and a few black scorch marks. My glasses weren't in there, but it suited me not to see too well. Using my good hand, I explored my face to find I was missing some eyebrow and sporting some very sore grazes around my cheeks and on my chin. I pulled the curtain back, ready to do a runner, and came face to face with a doctor surrounded by seven of his fresh-faced juniors.

"Ah," he said, looking down at his notes. "Here we have Caitlin McCall. 23. Came in last night with mild concussion, smoke inhalation, a rather nasty burn on her left hand and quite a collection of vicious cuts and bruises." He paused and looked around him expectantly.

One of his minions piped up and informed his peers that I'd had a chest x-ray, hand x-ray and CT scan on arrival. He pulled out films of my chest, skull and hand to prove it and they nodded to each other as though I wasn't there. I looked at the x-rays, they all looked pretty good to me.

The senior doctor gave them a quick look. "No permanent damage done, young lady, but I should take it easy for a few weeks. We'll be letting you out, but you'll need to pop back and get that dressing changed at the burns clinic once a day for a week or so. We'll give you some pills for the pain as well."

With a nod he walked off up the ward to his next patient with his juniors following behind him at a respectful distance.

Checking I had everything with me, I took off down the ward, and didn't stop running until I reached the lift, despite the pain in my burnt lungs. Pausing outside the main entrance long enough to relieve a smoker of a cigarette and a light, I ignored her strange looks and took a slow walk over to the maternity wing where I sat outside, waiting for Jen. A couple of drags from the cigarette sent a searing pain down my sore throat and into my blistered lungs. I hacked for ten minutes, receiving several disapproving stares from expectant mothers going in and out of the building until Jen screeched up in her ancient Fiat Uno.

Opening the door, I got in and ignored her look. "Take me home via an off licence. We'll talk then."

I must have looked bad; Jen obeyed without argument, not even questioning me when she had to pay for the large bottle of vodka and a packet of twenty cigarettes.

Jen still didn't speak when we got into my flat. I went into the bedroom, stripped out of the clothes and bit back a few cries of pain and fear at the cuts and bruises zig-zagging my legs, arms and back. I pulled on a pair of grey jogging bottoms and a matching hooded top. Adding thick woolly socks, I went into the bathroom in search of my emergency glasses and noticed for the first time the black-and-blue choker of bruises around my throat. I could see the shadow of van der Hoven's rage, his fingers had left their mark. Biting back tears, I zipped my top up over them and walked into the lounge, making sure the curtains were firmly drawn, and plugged in a lava lamp which cast a warm glow around the room, but prevented Jen from examining my wounds too closely.

Jen, meanwhile, had put out cat food for Henry and poured two large vodka and tonics, leaving a little room for ice.

"Right," she said, grabbing a cushion and joining me at my position by the warm radiator.

"Right." I repeated and, taking a large slug of vodka, I told her the whole story.

By the time I had finished, it was dark, the vodka bottle was half-empty, and my hand had started to throb.

"Shit. Cat."

"I know. I know. Do you think I still have a job?"

Jen choked on her drink. "A job? If I was you I would be more worried about whether I still had my freedom, not to mention all my mental faculties."

I shrugged. I suppose I had withheld information. But I didn't know there was any connection between the deaths and the file and besides, no one could prove it. The research was now lost forever and that was my fault. From what van der Hoven was saying, it could have saved lives. "Jen, you know you said you had got rid of your copy of the file? How did you actually get rid of it?" I asked, clinging to one small hope.

Jen wasted no time in putting it to rest, "I set fire to it in the kitchen sink and then washed the ashes down the plughole." She got up with her glass, "I'm going to give Steve a ring and let him know I'm staying with you for the night and then I'm going to cook us some dinner."

She wandered off into the hall. I heard her press Play on my answer machine.

"You have 47 messages," the automated voice said.

"Shit, Cat, do you want to listen to these now?"

"No." I got up, picked up a pair of trainers that were nestling under the futon and shoved my feet in. "I'm going out for a walk." I added a quilted jacket, wrapped a scarf around my neck and put a glove on my un-bandaged hand.

Jen frowned at me, but she let it go. "Okay, but let me give you my mobile phone, in case you get into trouble." She dug it out of her bag and I stuck it in my jacket pocket, along with my spare set of house keys and my wallet.

Outside, I found myself walking in the direction of the *Post's* office. Turning the corner of the street, I looked up at the building and took a sharp intake of cold air into my raw throat that left me hacking. From the pictures I had seen in the *Gazette* I knew it was bad but I wasn't prepared for the view I now had in front of me. The once imposing Victorian red brick building was now the colour and consistency of burnt toast. It was surrounded by a sparkling moat of smashed glass from all the windows that had been knocked out either by the fire, firefighters, or the millions of gallons of water that had been used to put the fire out.

A couple of fire engines were in the car park, alongside a police mobile incident room and, rather bizarrely, my car, which from this distance looked undamaged. Ignoring them, I walked up to where the main entrance should have been, stepped over the police cordon and into the foyer. Everything was blackened and dripping with water, but the stairs still looked structurally sound. Walking up them through the puddles of water, I headed straight for the fourth floor to the newsroom, ignoring my sore legs and blistering lungs which were struggling with the effort.

Going through the doors, I paused. Here the damage was the worst. You couldn't even tell that it had been an office, let alone the nerve centre of a newspaper. Walking up to my desk – or where my desk had been - I noticed paint markings and shuddered. This was where van der Hoven had died. I stood, thinking over the events in my mind, wondering for the 50th time that day if I could have pulled him out and saved him. Tears stung every cut and bruise as they ran down my face. I wondered if any copies of the files had survived the fire but, looking over to the newsdesk, I realised there was no chance. Everything was black and charred.

I was awakened from my musings by a torchlight behind me and the crunch of debris underfoot. I turned around, expecting to see Tom Llewelyn making ready with his handcuffs, and looked into the sad eyes of the Editor instead.

"Well," he said, looking around himself. "That's that."

I moved forward slightly and found myself muttering "Sorry." It seemed woefully inadequate.

He shook his head, dismissing my apology. "First came into this office 35 years ago, fifteen at the time. Started as a copy runner," he paused and looked at me. "Know what that is?"

I shook my head.

"Doesn't matter." He stopped. "Just came for a look around the old place before it's demolished."

"What's going to happen?" I whispered, half hoping he wouldn't hear me.

"We've set up a temporary office – printing from London for a few months until we get some permanent offices and a new printing press," he paused. "Missed this story, though."

I shook my head. "But there's a lot more to it. The dead man, he's from Fifen Pharmaceuticals and he killed his chairman and two of his staff because he was going to reveal that they had held drug research back for profit. He was going to do away with me the same way..." I broke off as he threw over a copy of the *Gazette*.

I failed to catch it with my left hand and picked it up off the floor, wiping some of the soot off it with my already grubby bandage. I looked at the front page. It was the final edition and it was all there.

*'DRUGS CHIEF DIES IN FIRE*

*Police have revealed that drug company boss Sebastian van der Hoven died in the fire which ripped through a city newspaper office last night.*

*The 43-year-old had been under investigation for some months after the death of former chairman of Fifen Pharmaceuticals, Sir Andrew Fifen, who was thought to have suffered a heart attack while out on a fishing trip in January.*

*Now police say they believe that bachelor van der Hoven may have been responsible for the deaths of two of his employees, as well as that of the internationally renowned scientist, Professor Vincent Johanson, killed in a hit-and-run several days ago.*

*A police spokesman said that a vehicle had been found in a search of van der Hoven's £1.5 million country home and forensic tests were expected to reveal it was the same vehicle used in the hit-and-run.*

*The spokesman said: "We will now be closing the file on Professor Johanson's death, as well as that of laboratory technician*

*James Scott who was found dead more than a week ago following an arson in a derelict building on the Broughton Industrial Estate."*

*A further death in January of pregnant laboratory assistant and mother-of-one Mary Stanshaw is also being looked into.*

*An inquest held last week recorded an open verdict on her death after a post mortem was unable to clarify why she had died. She had been eight months pregnant at the time.*

*van der Hoven is also believed to have been responsible for the attempted murder of an unnamed journalist who was investigating him.*

*The reporter was taken to hospital with minor injuries following the blaze which killed van der Hoven.'*

With some difficulty, I did some deep breathing and it was a few minutes before I realised that the Editor was talking to me.

"There's more to being a hack than bylines. Have to have a nose for a good story and investigate it. Not many of you college kids seem to realise that. Too many press releases these days. Just after the fame and glory that comes with having your name in print." He stopped and tapped his feet around in the pools of water that had collected on the floor. "I fancy something a bit more modern, myself, perhaps somewhere lakeside," he looked up. "What do you think?"

"Sounds good," I said, wondering why he was asking me.

"We'll want an exclusive interview with you – I'll send a reporter around in the morning. And pictures." He pulled a cigar out, lit it and walked towards his once plush office. Then he paused and turned back to me. "If you speak to the *Gazette* though, you're fired."

I made my way slowly out of the newsroom. So I was going to be a celebrity. Front  page news, just like van der Hoven had promised. At least this way I got to read all about it. I supposed I had to be grateful for that. I wondered if the Editor would be keeping my position open for me until I got out of jail - whenever that was.

# CHAPTER 26

Walking through my front door, I discovered Jen had been busy. She presented me with a list of the people who had rung me. As well as several messages from her, my mother had rung fourteen times, Nina five and Tony McFadden had rung twice to arrange the exclusive interview for the morning and give me the details of where to report for work. There were several from other work colleagues asking how I was. At the bottom of the list was the name I had unconsciously been looking out for. DC Tom Llewelyn had rung six times.

"They all just want you to ring them, when you get in. I rang your mum back and said that you were fine, just tired, that she didn't need to come and stay and that you would ring her tomorrow. She kept me on the phone with twenty minutes of hysterics, but eventually she calmed down. All the rest you can do yourself."

"Jen, you are a star." She beamed at me and reversed into the kitchen, coming back with a large plate of pasta.

Halfway through dinner, the doorbell went. We both paused and listened carefully. "Shall I get it?" Jen stage-whispered.

"No, leave it," I told her.

We both sat stock-still and listened – Jen with a forkful of pasta halfway to her mouth, worried the noise of her chewing would give us away. The bell rang again and then it went quiet. Then we heard something being shoved through the letterbox. Jen jumped up, fork still in hand, and moved towards the window.

"Jen, come back," I whispered at her furiously. "Who was it?"

Even as I asked, the churning in my stomach told me the answer. I stood up and carefully opened my flat door a crack. The hallway was empty but for a small package leaning against the wall opposite my door. I crept out, keeping against the wall so that my shadow wasn't cast against the front door, in case someone was watching.

"What is it?" Jen had followed me to the front door of my flat.

"Dunno, get back in," I whispered back at her. I picked up the large brown envelope, opened it and looked inside. There was a medicine bottle, but it was too dark to read the label. We crept back into the flat and went into the lounge. I took a slug of my drink as I read the bottle.

It was a prescription bottle with my name on it and today's date. "Codeine," I whispered to Jen.

"Painkillers," she whispered back, and then laughed. "Why are we whispering?"

I laughed back at her and looked inside the envelope again, there was a piece of paper. I pulled it out and unfolded it, and read it aloud to Jen. "Caitlin, you forgot to take these with you when you did a runner from hospital," my face flushed, "The docs say you should take two, four times a day, and avoid alcohol, if it's at all possible. You can't avoid me forever, Tom."

"Did he put any kisses after his name?" Jen asked and started to laugh.

I tried to look outraged, but failed and joined her in a giggling fit.

While Jen cleared up I went into the bathroom for a long bath. Before I got in, Jen helped me wrap a plastic bag around my bandaged hand and seal it with an elastic band to keep it dry. It took a while but I managed to wash the smoke and grime out of my hair one-handed.

Lounging on the sofa afterwards, Jen and I channel-surfed for a few hours and finished off the bottle of vodka. I would start taking the tablets and stay off the alcohol from the next day, I decided. The booze seemed to be doing a good enough job at keeping the pain down to a dull throb. Jen agreed to stay until the morning when she would drop me off at the hospital's burns clinic to get my dressing changed and then pick up my car for me, before it was buried in a pile of rubble forever.

I curled up on the bed with Henry for a few minutes while Jen rang Steve and explained what was going on. Helen had also dropped in while I was out and left me a mother-load of a spliff.

"For the pain, she said," Jen explained.

I smiled. "Purely medicinal, then."

van der Hoven was trying to put my hand into a food mixer and I was screaming for him to let go. I could feel the blades cutting into my flesh and see blood mixing in with whatever was already in the blender.

"I must have that file," he was saying to me as he stood over me. I screamed and begged for him to let me go and that I didn't have the file, but he wouldn't believe me and now his face had changed into Jen's. She was standing over me, shaking me gently.

"It's a bad dream, Cat, wake up, you're having a bad dream."

My eyes were sticky with tears, but I opened them and realised that my hand was still hurting. "Pills," I muttered.

Jen ran into the kitchen and came back with the prescription bottle and a glass of water.

"Is it really hurting? You poor thing," she said, watching me gulp down four of the pills. "It's time to go, anyway."

I looked up and realised for the first time that she was dressed - it felt like I had only just closed my eyes, but I had been asleep for ten hours.

"Time to get up and get down to the hospital," Jen said.

"Okay. Can we wait until the pain drops below my admittedly girly threshold please?" I asked, still feeling tearful.

She nodded and I lay back down on the pillow for a few minutes, breathing deeply.

By the time we got to the burns clinic, there were only a few people waiting. Some of them looked a lot worse off than me, but I've always been a bit of a baby when it comes to pain and it had taken all of Jen's patience to get me there in one snivelling piece. Once in, the doctor cut the bandage from the back of my hand and slowly unpeeled it, away from an enormous blister that had formed on my palm. Ignoring my pleas for stronger painkillers, the doctor examined the blister closely, before spraying some antiseptic solution on it and bandaging it back up. With his reassurances that once the blister popped it would hurt much less ringing in my ears, Jen drove me out to collect my car.

But when we got to the *Post*'s office, the *Post*'s office was gone. The demolition squad had been busy in the last 24 hours. The impressive six-storey building had been reduced to a rather pathetic one-and-a-half. More importantly, the missing four-and-a-half storeys had been relocated to the car park – last known residence of my car.

"Shit." Jen succinctly summed up the situation. She wasn't referring to my car, but the building. "You did all that?" she asked, sounding almost impressed.

"Jen, my car was there," I said, ignoring her and pointing my bandaged hand towards the pile of rubble.

"Oops," she replied.

She drove over to the demolition squad, stuck her head out of her window, and shouted at a group of builders.

One broke away from the pack and walked over to the car. "You can't park here," he said.

"No kidding," I muttered under my breath.

Jen ignored me. "What happened to the car that was parked in that car park?" she asked him, pointing to the pile of rubble.

"There weren't one. Not when we got here."

"There was one parked there last night," Jen told him patiently.

"Well it weren't here this morning. Maybe it's been towed away?"

"Thanks." Jen wound her window back up and I lit a cigarette.

"What now?" Jen said, turning to me, tutting as the smoke made me cough again.

"Home," I mumbled. I couldn't deal with it at the moment. I had been chased by a psychotic millionaire hell-bent on world domination and had been solely responsible for burning down a multi-million-pound newspaper office. The whereabouts of my £500 car, which I couldn't even drive at the moment, was the least of my worries.

We drove back to my flat in silence. Pausing only to give Jen a hug and thank her for all her help, I went into my flat, took two more codeine and slunk under the covers of my bed, fully dressed.

Despite the exhaustion, depression and pain, I couldn't sleep. After an hour of tossing and turning I got up and wandered into my lounge to see what Henry was up to. I was just considering what to do with my afternoon when the doorbell rang.

I hurried to my door, hoping it was Nina come to interview me and keep me company. I stopped dead when I realised the shape visible through the spy hole on my door was more masculine than Nina would ever be. It was Tom Llewelyn. And what's more, he had heard me.

Damn, he was right, I couldn't avoid him forever – especially if he was going to camp out on my doorstep. But I still wasn't sure if he was going to arrest me.

His voice interrupted my thoughts, "Caitlin, I know you are there."

"So?" I replied. Great. Very mature response. Well done Caitlin.

"You can't avoid me forever," he said.

"You already said that," I croaked through the door, referring to his note. "Go away."

"No. We need to talk."

I knew it. He was going to arrest me.

"I didn't do anything," I blurted out.

"I'm not here to arrest you." It was as if he had read my mind.

"Is that a promise?"

"For the moment, yes."

Hmmm, did I trust him? He didn't have any uniformed officers with him, which was surely usual practice when arresting a fugitive.

"Anyway, if you don't let me in, I can't tell you where your car is," he shouted through the door.

"Okay, okay." I opened the door, realising too late that I hadn't brushed my hair all day. He smiled at me as I opened the door and headed for the lounge.

"Well?" I said belligerently, standing by the door.

"Coffee, black, no sugar," he said, ignoring my tone.

I stomped through to the kitchen and fiddled with my coffee machine, single- handed. Tom stood in the kitchen doorway and watched me.

"How are you?" he asked.

I held up my injured hand. "In pain."

He tutted and moved forward to help me make coffee and I caught a waft of Givenchy.

"What about the rest of it?" he probed.

"Well I'm sure the nightmares will fade eventually," I replied with mock bravado. We walked into the lounge; he carried the coffee in front and I followed with a lit cigarette and an ashtray balanced on my bandaged hand. Out of pure stupidity I was continuing to smoke. Or at least I lit them and then left them to smoulder, unable to inhale into my bruised lungs.

He got straight down to business. "How long did you know what was going on?"

"What do you mean?" Even to my ears I sounded ridiculous.

"The only reason I can think of for van der Hoven coming after you was that you were connected in some way," he took a sip of his coffee. "Besides, the hospital said you were shouting in your sleep."

"Fuck."

He took out his pad. "Look, you would be better to give me a statement now. It would help us tie up the loose ends. Otherwise a couple of uniforms are going to camp out on your doorstep to take you down the station when you are recovered."

His first choice suddenly sounded more appealing and so I began to talk.

He took out a recording device. "I was supposed to do this at the hospital," he said, pressing the Record button, "but you gave me the slip."

I went through it all. The mysterious phone calls that had started a few weeks before, culminating in the meeting at the Branton Estate and the research paper. Professor Johanson. My visit to Fifen. I kept my eyes firmly on my cup of coffee as I related the story, pressing ahead and knowing that the further I got into the tale, the more ridiculous I sounded. I decided it would be wise to leave out my little trip to Mary Stanshaw's house.

When I had finished telling him what I knew, I gave him the details of what van der Hoven had told me when he came to kill me. The fight. The shotgun. The fire. "But you already seem to know all that," I said when I had finally finished, pointing to the copy of yesterday's *Gazette*, lying front-page-up on the floor.

He pressed Stop on his recording device. "This is all off the record, okay?"

I nodded.

"About the same time as your mystery caller came to you, we started to get some random calls, accusing van der Hoven of murdering three people. It didn't take long to work out that they were talking about Andrew Fifen and Mary Stanshaw, but we couldn't figure out who the third was."

I closed my eyes, remembering the framed scan of Mary's unborn child that had sat on her bedside table. "The baby – she was the third victim. Mary Stanshaw's unborn baby daughter."

Llewelyn leaned back, picked up my lit cigarette and took a heavy drag on it, exhaling the smoke in one big sigh. We sat in silence for a minute. "Scott must have known what was going on, but Mary Stanshaw was the one who went to van der Hoven and confronted him," he said.

"He said she was a very principled young woman, not a good thing in their line of work," I repeated van der Hoven's words with a shudder.

"He couldn't reason with her, so he killed her," Llewelyn added.

"And Scott couldn't prove what had happened, but he wanted to make sure that van der Hoven was investigated. And so he had to die too," I finished.

Llewelyn got up and went into my kitchen, coming back minutes later with two more cups of coffee. "I wish you had told me what was going on," he said, handing me a mug. "It really should be brandy for the shock, but I couldn't find any."

I sighed heavily, "I know, I know, if I hadn't been so hell-bent on getting the story, we might not have lost that research." My voice broke and I shut up.

"That's not what I meant, Caitlin." He spoke so gently I suddenly found pools of tears that had being building up behind my eyes for the last days brim up and spill soundlessly down my cheeks. Wiping my face on my sleeve, trying to hold it together, the pain of choking back the sob in my chest mingled with my raw lungs and made me cry harder.

"How are you sleeping?" Llewelyn asked after a minute.

"Badly," I admitted, relieved at the change in subject, wiping my eyes and nose again.

"Here," he reached into his pocket and pulled out a small prescription bottle of tablets. "The hospital gave me these for you as well."

He got up and took my untouched mug into the kitchen, returning with a glass of water. I took two tablets.

"Would you like me to stay until you fall asleep?" he asked.

"Would you?" I asked, trying not to sound whiny, my heart suddenly hammering and sleep the last thing on my mind.

He smiled down at me and I wondered for a brief second if he could read my thoughts. I stood up and walked through to my bedroom. Tom stood in the doorway, watching me pull back my duvet.

"We still didn't settle whether you were going to arrest me for all this," I said.

"Well there is a little matter of petty theft from a fellow patient. But I used my charm and she decided not to press charges."

I got into bed and pulled the duvet over my head. After a few seconds, I felt Tom sit on the bed. Slowly, I pulled the duvet down and tucked it under my chin.

He leaned in close. "As appealing as the image of you in handcuffs is at this moment, I think we can wait."

He lowered his face to mine.

The kiss started out gentle but as he pulled away, I snaked my undamaged hand around his neck and lifted my head up to his. As his tongue touched the tip of mine, I felt a rush of heat enter my pyjama bottoms and sent out a silent prayer that he would follow.

Unfortunately God wasn't listening and Tom pulled away, smoothed my hair out of my eyes, and left the room.

# CHAPTER 27

Henry would have to go on a diet. That was my first thought when I woke up and found my stomach pinned under a heavy weight. I put a hand out to try and push him off and realised it wasn't Henry – it was an arm. Looking across the pillow I saw a mop of curly red hair lying next to me. Jen.

I smiled to myself and pulled her arm off me and was considering drifting off back to sleep when my front doorbell went. Getting up, I winced as a muscle spasm ran down the inside of my thighs. I pulled on my dressing gown. A courier stood at my front door, holding a large, square box. Ignoring my scary reflection in his helmet, I took the box and signed with my good hand, closing the door with my foot. I used the bathroom and gave my hair a quick brush and my teeth a quick clean, while examining with wonder the new shades of blue and green covering my bruised body.

Standing there, despite the pain all over my battered body, I felt better. Better than I had in days. My confessions of the night before had been the proverbial weight off my shoulders. For the first time since the fire, I realised I was going to be alright.

With a smile, I went back into my hall, picked up the box and wandered into the kitchen to make tea. The label was addressed to me at the now non-existent *Post*'s office with *'Handle with Care'* stickers and *'For addressee only'* written in careful block capitals. I slid a knife under a flap as Jen walked barefoot into the kitchen in an old rugby shirt.

"Where did you come from?" I asked her. My last waking memory had been of an entirely different person in my bedroom.

"Relief shift. Came about ten, but you were fast asleep. Llewelyn was still here, though," she turned her questioning glance to the box. "What's that?" she asked sharply.

"Dunno. Package for me. Why?"

She took the knife out of my hand and slid the parcel to her end of the table. "Bit weird. Are you expecting something? Ordered anything through the mail?"

"No. My mum occasionally sends me things."

"Her handwriting?" she asked, pointing the blade of the knife at the address label.

"No," I frowned. "Actually, it isn't."

I suddenly cottoned on to what she was getting at. Two nights ago someone had tried to kill me. The end scenes of the film *Seven* flashed into my head.

"Where's Henry?" I asked as the panic rose.

Jen bent under the table and I sighed loudly as I heard a meow, seconds before Henry's ginger head appeared in her arms.

"What are we going to do?" I asked, waiting for Jen to decide.

She sat back. "Don't touch it," she instructed, going into the hall and picking up my phone. After a few minutes of mumbled talking, Jen came back in. "I rang the police. They say don't touch it, they're on their way. Get your coat on, and take Henry with you."

"Where am I going?" I asked.

"Out. It could be a bomb."

"A bombhhh?" I spluttered incredulously.

"Look, two nights ago someone was going to club you to death and set you on fire."

"Yes I know, but he's dead and it's all over." I stayed in my seat, staring over Jen's shoulder. I could see a blisteringly cold morning out of my kitchen window and wasn't too keen to step out into it.

"We don't know that for sure. There could have been someone else involved. And we are talking about someone who works with chemicals – more than capable of blowing this whole building up."

I put my head to the box. I couldn't hear any ticking, but I supposed this was the digital age.

"It's over," I said, still not keen to go out into the cold.

Jen threw my blue leather coat at me. "He could have sent it before he died."

I realised she wasn't going to let it go and padded off into my bedroom to pull on socks and trainers, before grabbing Henry and my bag. Jen pulled me out of the front door just as we heard the sirens. Two police cars skidded to a halt outside my front door as a police van opened and spilled out uniformed officers, who began knocking on doors and pulling residents out of their houses. The police van blocked the street off as a second team of police entered my building.

"Who are they? What are they doing?" I whispered to Jen.

"Scanning the package with that little machine to see if they need to call out the bomb disposal squad." Jen suddenly sounded like an expert. I raised my brow at her. She shrugged. "We've got a new combat section in at the bookshop."

At least she was off the crime and romance shelves.

Another police car arrived and I looked up from my place on the wall to see Llewelyn get out and walk into the house, without a backward glance at me. Remembering our kiss, I blushed and pulled Henry tighter towards me, trying to look none the wiser as my fellow neighbours, many in dressing gowns and slippers, whispered to each other about what was going on.

Suddenly remembering I was still a journalist, I borrowed a mobile phone from a student who, having been turfed out of his bed, was sitting on the wall, nonchalantly rolling a joint, blissfully unaware that he was surrounded by most of the city's police force. It took a while to get through to the newsroom, which had set up in a temporary office ironically close to Carson Park and Fifen Pharmaceuticals' plush headquarters. Eventually I got Nina and began whispering to her that the bomb squad could be about to arrive in my street.

"Did you get it?" she asked, not listening to me.

"Get what?" I asked.

"Mrs Bishop rang. She's come out at long last. Been offered a cosy little set up in a brand new estate for old dears."

"That's good, Nina. But I've got something to tell you," I said, trying to interrupt.

But Nina was on a roll. "Bless her. She said she wanted to say thank you to you for keeping her company, so I found it in the postroom and sent it over to you this morning by courier. Did you get it?"

A sense of dread grew in my stomach. "Get what?"

Nina sighed. "The cake. What did you think I was talking about?"

Pressing the End button on the mobile phone, I closed my eyes and exhaled heavily before handing it back to the student. I walked through the police cordon, ignoring the shout from a policeman to stand back.

"Cake," I croaked at the uniformed officer standing guard outside my open flat door.

He looked down at me with an expression of total incomprehension usually reserved for dopeheads and drunks.

"It's a cake," I croaked again.

But I was too late. I heard a snort of laughter from the direction of my kitchen and distinctly heard someone say, "Chocolate and walnut."

I walked away, went back to the wall and sat with my head in my one good hand, waiting for the police to inform my neighbours that they could go back into their homes. I wanted them to leave so I could die of embarrassment alone. Jen had conveniently vanished into her car.

Llewelyn was the first to come out of the house. He walked over and sat down on the wall next to me without comment. He put his arm around my shoulder, pulled me to him and planted a kiss in my hair.

He choked back a laugh as I tried to form a sentence that would sum up exactly how monumentally stupid I felt at that moment.

"Don't worry, Cat," he gave me a gentle squeeze. "I promised them all a slice for their trouble."